Evernight Teen ®

www.evernightteen.com

SASHA HIBBS & CHRISTINA HOOKER

DEDICATIONS

Christina

To the readers who pick up this book and find love and hope within its pages, thank you. Because of you, the journey was worthwhile.

Sasha:

For the Fool. Sometimes villains are the real victims.

THE HANGING NIGHT

The Threads of Fate, 1

Sasha Hibbs and Christina Hooker

Copyright © 2024

Preface
The Red String of Fate

He's more myself than I am. Whatever our souls are made of, his and mine are the same.
—Emily Bronte, Wuthering Heights

"Shh. Don't cry. I'm going to tell you a story," the young man, dirty and disheveled, said as he laid the girl, covered in the same dirt and filth as he, across his lap as though she were more precious than any gem. She couldn't have been more than sixteen-years-old, and he, maybe a year or two older.

She looked into his eyes, waiting.

"Once, there was a young boy who, given to his own devices, was a small-time thief for no particular reason other than he enjoyed the exhilaration that swiping a trinket from street vendors gave him. *'What does it matter to them, after all,'* the boy always thought. *'They have enough. What's a single trinket?'* But, as we know, a single trinket turns to two, which turns to three and four and five, a never-ending number of trinkets."

The girl in his arms listened with eager attention. Her ice blue eyes focused on him as if nothing else existed, and nothing else ever had, and nothing else ever would.

With his thumb, he wiped a tear on her cheek, streaking grime across her barely visible golden skin. "At one market, on a particularly hot summer day, just as the boy swiped a red apple from a vendor's table, an old man shouted at him, and fear, like lightning, shot through the boy. For surely he thought he'd been caught and was about to lose his hand for thievery. 'Boy!' shouted the old man. 'Hey, boy!' The boy tried to ignore the shouts of the old man and will himself to run, but the terror of a machete across his wrist, just at the joint, cleanly severing hand from arm, kept his feet glued to the ground.

'Come here, boy. I've got a story. Wouldn't you like to share an apple with an old man and hear a story? I've got a tale worth more than gold,' the old man taunted. Realizing the old man was nothing more than a hungry vagrant, the boy turned to him with a sigh of relief.

'Come, boy. Sit by me for a while. Have a rest. Share your treat.' The boy's head cocked as he considered the man's offer, and just as he'd decided no, the apple was his and his alone, something not entirely born of his own free will reeled him close to the old man.

"The old man stank of sour breath and stale body odor, and the boy could see sweat pooling in the cracks of the man's face. In stark contrast with his dark skin, his beard was white but stained by pipe smoke, and his words whistled through the empty spaces where teeth should have been. By the sight and smell of him, the boy reckoned he couldn't have been a day less than one hundred and ten years old. 'Sit,' said the man. And the boy sat. The man snatched the red apple, wiped it on his shirt, then cut it in half, handing one to the boy. 'Close your eyes, boy.' The boy did as instructed. 'Now imagine your body fading—first your clothes, then your color, then your skin. Let it all fade until your body is glass, and you can see your insides. Can you see the complex web of arteries and vessels, flowing blood like rivers, giving life to every part of you?' The boy furrowed his brow, receiving the image the old man was feeding into his brain. 'Now, boy, focus on your little finger. This one,' the old man said as he grabbed the boy's pinky and gave it a shake. The boy did as he was told, as the man kept hold of his finger. Behind closed eyes, the boy saw a light radiating where the man was touching him. The light glowed and flowed from his pinky finger straight to his heart. 'What you're seeing, boy, is a very special passageway. This channel I show you that glows makes your little finger a direct representative of your heart, and it doesn't stop there! From your little finger, it continues in the form of a red string, visible only to those who truly wish to see, and that red string connects you to the other half of your soul—your one true love."

Pausing a moment to attempt to wet his lips with a tongue that would not produce saliva, the dirty old man wiped his mouth with the back of his hand before he began talking again. Growing tired of the old man's words and ready to eat his half of the apple, the boy opened his eyes, yanked his hand from the old man, and spat at him. Stunned, the old man retaliated, 'Young, foolish, stupid boy, too narcissistic to want his soul whole and complete.' He wiped the spittle from his face. 'Your mate is there.' The man pointed a long finger, crooked and gnarled, toward a girl with light eyes and dark hair.

Angry at having been both insulted and tricked out of half his apple by a vile vagrant, the boy shouted, 'Shut up, you filthy old tramp!' And with that, the boy picked a rock up from the ground, threw it in the direction the old man had pointed, toward the girl, and took off running from the market. Behind him, he could hear the old man hurling hateful, vengeful words."

Already knowing the rest of the story, the tired and dirty girl began to cry harder, more freely. The young man placed his parched, cracked lips to her temple, "Be calm, love, for the story has a happy ending." Dehydrated lips pressed into her, and she closed her eyes, pushing tears from her lids. The young man kissed them as they spilled down her face, wetting his lips enough to continue. "When the boy grew into a man, he came upon a woman who fascinated him. She wore a veil covering her face and was a mystery to all who looked upon her, for she would not reveal her face to anyone. The young man, however, was persistent, and his persistence finally ended in reward, because one day, the woman conceded and allowed him to lift her veil. When he did, he saw she wore an adornment on her eyebrow, and lurking at the corner of the intricate golden hoop was a thin scar, lighter in color than the rest of her skin."

The young woman's body began to quiver and heave, for it was too dry to cry more, and she moved her face into the man holding her, dirty hair falling across her forehead. "When he asked her about her brow, she told him when she was young, a boy threw a rock, scarring her."

"Hush now, don't shake." The young man lifted the matted hair out and away from her temple, revealing an obscure, faded white line near the girl's eyebrow. He brushed his lips against the small scar, whispering, almost confessing, his story into it. "To this boy, now man, scar or no scar, there could never be a more beautiful woman in all the world, and he thanked the universe for forgiving him for his earlier sin against his soulmate." He kissed the scar and lifted his head.

She smiled in spite of herself. "I love you with something that is more than love." She pushed a hand into her pocket, and when her fist emerged, it was clenched, holding tightly to something not visible to the eye. "I have so little time left to touch you. The universe is cold and cruel," she whispered, reaching her other hand up to touch his beard, caressing the two areas at the corners of his chin that their time in a cell had specked with gray.

"No, no, my love," he whispered against her ear. "You are wrong. The red thread of fate may tangle, may stretch, but it will never break. Regardless of time, place, or circumstance, we will always be bound together. I will always find you."

Footsteps, heavy and foreboding, carrying with them the doom of two lovers crossed in fate, approached the cell and then stopped. Iron clinked as the door slid open, and the lovers knew their time for this story had ended. "I will always love you, even in death." This served as the end of the young man's story. The prison guard ordered him quiet as he yanked the young girl from his arms, forced them both to stand, and led them down a dank, moss cloaked hallway to a wide, wooden door with white light seeping through its cracks. Its hinges grated against each other as the guard heaved it open, and the lovers squinted against the first light they'd seen, in what felt to them like a lifetime, as they were pushed out onto a platform above a raucous, cheering crowd.

Silent seconds stretched infinitely between them

as a scarlet noose was cinched against both their necks, tying them together. The young woman looked to her love, eyes wild, searching, refusing to believe love could have led them to this horrible fate. In return, his eyes looked deeply into hers, and his gaze—a gaze meant only for her because nothing else could ever matter to him— conveyed strength, comfort, and encouragement that once their souls departed their current vessels, their essences would still be connected, through all time and all space, drifting apart only briefly before finding their way back to each other.

That was their curse.

And then it was over.

The lovers were thrown over the edge, necks snapping in sync, bodies limp, swaying ever so slightly right to left, left to right, right to left—together, a pendulum marking time as they dangled from the red rope connecting them—until they stilled. In death, the grip of the girl's hand loosened, slender fingers relaxing, revealing a small rock, and just as a stone skipped across water ripples, the rock falling against the ground created a wrinkle in the universe that stretched outward, outward, outward.

But it did not break.

Chapter One
Back to the Start

It is as if I had a string somewhere under my left ribs,
tightly and inextricably knotted to a similar string
situated in the corresponding quarter of your little frame.
—Jane Eyre, Charlotte Brontë

Josephine

You can attempt to mentally prepare yourself for something huge, something you know is coming, something you've spent your entire life trying to outrun, but when the day comes, there's a grave reminder you never asked for to begin with. I had spent the last two years of my life trying to stay ahead of sadness, and I could no more outrun sadness than I could keep my mother from dying.

At sixteen, only two days after honoring my mother with a celebration of her life, I was going to live with my maternal aunts—twins, Aunt Sophie and Aunt Lindsey, in West Virginia. My mother and I had lived in Connecticut for as long as I can remember. She said she moved us here after becoming pregnant with me, and when I asked her about her life back in West Virginia, she always gave some clever, vague answer. I sometimes felt as though she'd spent her whole life outrunning something too. Some nameless thing. It hung over her, and it continued to hang over me. But then one day, she didn't have to run anymore. After two years of battling breast cancer, the cancer won.

"Josephine," Aunt Sophie called out, waking me from my quiet reverie. "It's time to go. We don't want to miss our plane."

Aunt Sophie had a gaze that could pierce right through you and a face with equally strong angles and sharp lines. Everything about her looked rigid. Couple that with her not-a-hair-out-of-place tight bun and plain clothes, and she came across as unapproachable. In reality, Aunt Sophie was a kind woman whose heart did not match her looks. Her fraternal twin, on the other hand, Aunt Lindsey, had long, dark, fluffy hair that whipped around her haphazardly, and she wore long skirts and flowy tops embroidered with intricate designs. She had a carefree, bohemian vibe, listened to classic rock, smoked like a freight train, cussed like a sailor, and I loved her. I couldn't imagine Aunt Sophie ever letting loose enough to listen to music, let alone say a curse word.

"Your aunties are going to take care of you, Josie. We won't let any darkness get to you." Aunt Lindsey said, slightly pinching my chin between her finger and thumb while laying a kiss on the top of my head. She'd always had a quirky way of putting things.

My entire life was packed up in a bag. The aunts slid through the doorway as I held my bag in one hand and the doorknob in the other, pouring my eyes over the living room, which at one time seemed like the heart of the apartment, but now was very much lifeless. It had only been the two of us, but we were happy. As I scanned over each piece of furniture, trying to sear every nook, cranny, and tear into my brain, I could hear the echoes of the past life my mother and I led in that little apartment. If I looked hard enough, I could almost see a younger version of myself snuggled up to my mother on the couch as we watched some scary movie I'd insisted on. In the tiny kitchen, I could smell her cooking up my favorite dish—homemade macaroni and cheese with fried kielbasa—and see myself at the table for two, waiting patiently for it.

Like a veiled curtain sweeping away the past, I closed my eyes, and shut the door on all of it.

My chest constricted. There were so many things I would never get to do with her again. And it hurt more than words could ever describe. I couldn't fight off a tear that broke free and slid down my cheek as the apartment door slammed shut on life that was finished and turned toward a life that was unknown.

As though sensing my struggle, Aunt Sophie placed her warm hand in mine and gently guided me away. "Thank God we don't have to worry about getting you enrolled in school until the fall," Aunt Lindsey said as we made it to the bottom of the stairs. She didn't miss a beat—as soon as the door shut behind us and we were outside, she flipped open her cigarette case—this vintage leather pouch decorated with sewn-on beads she'd applied herself—and slid a menthol out. As she clamped the cigarette between her teeth and flicked her lighter to it, I watched the smoke snake around her face, wafting up, up, up, until it dissolved into nothing.

I groaned and grimaced at the burning, carcinogenic smell, and in response, Lindsey frantically waved the smoke away with her hand as she took a few more puffs.

"Yes. All summer with nothing to do will be just what you need. You need time to decompress." Aunt Sophie backed up what Aunt Lindsey said.

I knew they meant well, but all I could think in the moment as we trailed down the sidewalk to the taxi was that what I needed was for my mother to be alive, not a summer of leisure.

I gave a half-hearted smile.

Bridgeport, West Virginia was a small town situated in the central part of the state. My mother grew up there, and on occasion, we'd travel there to visit the aunts and stay with them for a week or two in the summer. They ran a convenience store downtown, *Blair's Lair*, selling all kinds of odds and ends—magazines, newspapers, cigarettes, beer, Aunt Lindsey's herbal remedies. Aunt Lindsey was a self-proclaimed witch, and in the back, she did tarot card readings and made various natural remedies for peoples' ailments. It was something my mother always played off as funny, but I thought it was cool. The biggest item sold at *Blair's Lair* was what Aunt Sophie always referred to as "the food of my people," that were her award-winning, homemade pepperoni rolls. They were a great source of pride not just for the aunts, but also for the state.

Pepperoni rolls were something native to North Central West Virginia, and had I not had family roots in the area, I wouldn't know about them. An Italian immigrant invented the dish in the 1920s. The man took the already popular lunch items of pepperoni and bread a step further by baking the pepperoni inside of the bread. The result was this savory little roll of crusty bread infused with the fats of the spicy meat. There are several slight variations, but it's rumored that my Aunt Sophie had the original recipe somehow, despite not being Italian herself. All I knew was that hers were delicious. When my mom and I would visit, Sophie would always send me home with a dozen to share with my friends, and they thought those foreign, little meat-stuffed rolls were the best treat. At that moment, I realized I'd never have that again, and another separate wave of sadness crashed over me—not only would I not have my mother, but I was also moving away from my friends. I was alone, save for the aunts I saw once, maybe twice, a year.

As I boarded the taxi headed for our plane, all I could think was this was my life now—two aunts, no mother, a convenience store with a three-bedroom apartment on top of it in West Virginia—a place I loved to vacation, but never in a million years thought I'd call home.

****

As we landed at Benedum Airport, the plane gave a slight jerk, rousing me from a restless sleep full of bizarre dreams, clips of visions about my mother leading me up winding paths and through tunnels and fields. I woke just as she was about to show me what was at the end.

"Come on, honey. We're almost there," Aunt Sophie said, giving me a gentle pat on the lap.

"Whew! This witch needs off this flying broom," Aunt Lindsey announced. "And about a hundred cigarettes," she whispered as she rustled around in the compartment above our heads for her bag.

"Maybe what you need to do is try quitting," I said. I adored Aunt Lindsey, but I despised her smoking. Mom hated it too.

"Well, good morning, sasspants," Aunt Lindsey said halfheartedly. Smoking causes cancer. And my mom had just died from cancer. It made me angry that she was so flippant about it.

"Whatever. But the least you could do is not light those gross cancer sticks while you're around me."

She rolled her eyes.

While I decided to let it drop, I had no plans of letting it go. Turning my head back to the moment, I thought about the many times Mom and I had come here, and, in the past, it was exciting. Mom would hang around the store with the aunts, and I would walk to the city pool, or grab an ice cream and check out the local shops. I never thought I would come here to live, especially without her. Bridgeport suddenly held less charm. I loved

17

my aunts and was grateful to them, but what choice was there in this? None. To date, I'd had no say in how my life had panned out.

We exited the plane, and Lindsey dug like a mad woman through her giant patchwork hobo bag. "Son of a bitch," she muttered, pulling another cigarette out of her pack with her teeth.

"Lind*sey*!" Aunt Sophie started, her voice getting intense and stern on the second syllable of Lindsey. "Don't tell me you lost the keys! When we left the parking lot, I told you to let me have them, but, no, you insisted like a petulant child…"

"Oh, calm down, Soapie," Lindsey retorted. Aunt Sophie hated when she called her "Soapie". "Don't get your old lady bloomers all up in a wad. I've got them!" She was smiling with her unlit cigarette still between her teeth, and, like a prize, whipped the keys out of her purse, the many keychains she had on them clanking and jangling.

Aunt Sophie rolled her eyes. "Well, let's go then and get our girl home."

Home. I sighed. It wasn't home. Absentmindedly, I looked around before Aunt Lindsey got my attention by softly putting her arm around me. "Come on, honey." She kept her arm around me the whole way to the car, still never lighting her smoke. She smiled sweetly at me, sadly, as I opened the back door. "When we have more time, I'll run you up to the mall, and you can pick out stuff for your bedroom, so you can make it just how you want it." She so desperately wanted to make me feel better.

I returned her smile but let my mind wander. *More time.* I guess that was something we all thought we had, and that thought haunted me as I looked at my aunts from the backseat. What if I lost them, too? My head ached, and everything felt empty and meaningless. Trying to make my mind go blank, I closed my eyes.

It was a short ride to the store/apartment combo, and the town passed in Monet images, hazy and out of focus. I was too worn out to actually process the images of the town, and by the time we pulled into the parking lot, I wasn't even sure I had looked. Aunt Lindsey put the car in park, and Aunt Sophie said, "Here's the key, Josie, honey. Grab your bag and go get settled. We are going to go pick up a few things for dinner, and we'll be back. We thought you'd like to rest instead of going out. Okay?"

I wasn't sure if that was a question or an order, but I nodded, key in one hand, bag in the other, and turned to go into the store while they pulled out of the parking lot. I stopped short, looking up at the long set of steps leading to the apartment. It looked like all the times before, but it felt wrong for me to walk up the steps, alone, to an empty apartment. In a different, more preferable reality, my mom could be away at the store, and I could be happy knowing, in the back of my mind, she was coming back, and we were going to have a fun West Virginia vacation. But, with each step my feet took, my new reality slapped me in the face.

Unlocking the sliding glass door, I stepped in and sighed. I knew the aunts had been in Connecticut with me, but it still smelled like pepperoni rolls had just been baked. Another knot formed in my throat. It was like my mom could be there, smiling, telling stories with the aunts, and getting ready to pull out another batch from the oven. Suddenly, the kitchen was like a vacuum, and my baggy t-shirt felt like a medieval corset, stiff, unyielding, suffocating. The immeasurable emptiness and silence of the apartment were shrill as a scream. How was I ever going to make it without her?

I threw my bag to the floor and ran to the hallway,

navigating my way toward the door that led down to the store from the apartment, breathing heavily as I descended. I was desperate to get out of that space and thought that, downstairs, I could grab a cold Dr. Pepper—my mom's favorite, though as she got older, she'd switched to Diet Dr. Pepper—and let the crisp cherry, vanilla taste make her feel a little closer to me, like she was on this side of heaven. I stood at the bottom of the steps for a few moments, mindfully breathing, trying to calm myself down, before I rounded the corner into the actual store.

The coolers and the aisles were exactly the same as they had always been—coolers against the wall: water, soda, beer. Facing them, aisle one: chips, candy, and snacks. Aisle two: magazines, books, and newspapers. Aisle three: Lindsey's potions and household items, like candles and incense. Nothing had really changed in the store, except for the creak on the last step—the one that had always been there. It had somehow disappeared between last summer and now. When I was little and would sneak down into the store for a treat, that step would always bust me. The thought of it made me smile, so I took off in the direction of the coolers, deep in a memory of being caught nicking candy in the night.

It's odd the things you notice in silence. As I held the door to the cooler open, reaching in for a can, I sensed someone behind me. My first instinct was to freeze and hold my breath, so I stood stock still, arm outstretched, my heart hitting my chest so loudly I was pretty sure it could be heard in the next county. The hair on the back of my neck stood up, and my skin prickled. Warmth flooded my stomach, my veins dilating from heat shooting up my body. My pupils expanded. Was this adrenaline? Fear? A cocktail blend of them both? What choice did I have but to turn around? Run? I couldn't. I wanted to face my fate.

Drawing courage from an unknown source, I slammed the cooler door and spun around. And there was a boy with his back to me, standing completely still behind the magazine racks in aisle two.

"What are you doing here?" I demanded in a voice that somehow had more moxie than I did. I'd slammed the cooler door to make my courage seem more authentic, and now, I didn't know what to do.

He turned to face me, and for a split second, I was stunned, not out of fear but in total fascination. This boy had the most intense, piercing green eyes I'd ever seen. From what I could tell in the semi-dark conditions, he was roughly my age, somewhat taller than me, with shaggy, sandy blond hair that framed his face in a way that softened him and made his green eyes seem kind, even through their intensity.

With some combination of anger and curiosity propelling me, I stormed over to him and looked down at the contents in his arms. He held a bag of pepperoni rolls, a large bottle of beer, a bright blue pack of American Spirit cigarettes, and a Rolling Stone magazine. His mouth bobbed open, and his eyes widened, but he didn't look embarrassed or surprised like I would have had the situation been reversed. He looked interested and … concerned?

"Uh, I'm checking the weight of these things." He moved them in his hands up and down like an unbalanced scale, smiling with the corner of his mouth, until finally, he settled them evenly like they weighed the same.

"You're stealing! You're a thief!"

"Well, I'm not really into labels."

Chapter Two
A Simple Twist of Fate

...for my mind misgives
Some consequence, yet hanging in the stars,
Shall bitterly begin his fearful date
With this night's revels, and expire...
—Romeo Montague

Caius
Journal

For as long as humans have gathered together in the public's various arenas, they've coexisted without understanding how important their encounters with each other are. Could a simple "hello" from a stranger have provided the extra few seconds necessary to miss the bus that took us to the school where whatever honky cowboy with the backwoods blues decided he wanted to play Klebold or Harris for the day? Or was that stranger meant to be there? Was it fate?

There could have been a thousand reasons you weren't in that place at that time—the power went out, and your phone died in the middle of the night, causing your alarm clock to not wake you. Or, you burned your Pop-Tart, setting off the smoke alarm, which woke your mother from last night's bender, causing all holy hell to rain down on you, so you left early, empty stomach, headed to school for whatever the vending machine had to offer.

Or was it a simple coincidence that you said hello to the stranger? The morning argument with your mom over the burned strawberry Pop-Tart caused you to need a soft hello from the middle aged woman on the corner, waiting to cross the street as she balanced three cups of *coffee, a bag, and a phone call ... because just maybe she reminded you of how your mom used to look, and you wanted to help her carry her load, get a smile from her, not feel like such a piece of shit? Or has that particular stranger saved your ass multiple times throughout multiple lifetimes with just being in the right place at the right time, and nothing could have ever prevented or changed that moment?*

There are so many moments in a lifetime where we're completely surrounded by strangers, sharing nothing more than a space and, say, a love for comedy. We're all laughing in unison as whatever stoned, white comic actor rolls around on the floor in fake agony, grabbing his nuts for the fifth time while we all stuff our faces with popcorn covered in salt and chemical yellow sludge. But we don't know shit about each other, even what we look like. We couldn't even pick each other out of a lineup if we had to, if one of us ended up coming unhinged and committing murder after the movie. But we just don't know, you know, if at any moment our lives will cross with one of these strangers, and we will become integral parts of each other's lives. The moment of hands touching while reaching for the same novel across opposite sides of the library shelf or lips meeting after sucking the same strand of spaghetti or whatever stupid horse shit brings you together. Was it always meant to be? Was it a contract written between two souls as their essences trickled down with the dust of the stars? Or is the spaghetti too long?

I don't know. But what I do know is that it's like this—we all live our own reality, and every motherfucker out there acts according to that reality, but no other motherfucker understands anything about that reality. They may know facts about it. They may know lies about it. They might not know fuck about shit, but they see you, and they judge you anyway. And this is exactly what I deal with every morning as I walk my broke ass to school on the Converse Express. Converses, I might add, that needed pitched 3 years ago but somehow still managed to keep my feet dry despite their ragged appearance. And that's the kind of thing I respect, you know? And at the end of the day, what does it matter what the people of this town think? I'll fall on the blade of whatever truth they want me to. Who really gives a fuck?

Because regardless of the reasons or outcomes, we all just keep on going. Because that's just what you do. Because nothing ever changes. Because it's all the same in the end. Isn't it?

From the time I could remember, I'd loved the rush of stealing. The first time I did it, I was eight years old. My mom was in a pharmacy that doubled as a liquor store—which, now that I think of it, is ironic—getting legitimately medicated and self-medicated all in one convenient location. Anyway, my mother was buying bottles of wine for her evening party of one, and I was hungry and had asked for a Baby Ruth. She was intensely counting change, sliding coins around the counter, and when I asked, she told me she didn't have enough money to buy both her "mommy juice" and a candy bar, but not to worry because we had food at home.

Bologna. We had bologna at home, and she'd picked the mold off the bread for the morning's toast, so did we really have what could be defined as food? So, as she stood, fumbling with coins and stammering at the guy behind the counter to give her a second, I stared at that Baby Ruth, stomach hollow and grumbly. I could taste the sweet chocolate dissolving over my tongue, and the salt of the peanuts combining with the richness of the caramel and whatever that delicious chewy stuff was in the middle. I later found out it was called nougat, and when I did, I laughed. It's still one of the funnier words I have ever heard. What the hell is a nougat, anyway? I digress. So, there I am, eight years old, desperate for this candy I wasn't allowed to have, and not being able to have it was simply unbearable to me. I imagined the crinkle of the wrapper in my hands as I opened it and the little bit of chocolate melting on my fingers as I held it, the weird but not wholly unpleasant skin taste as I licked it off each of them, and right then, I could not endure another second without that Baby Ruth. So, I didn't.

While my mom was busy flirting with the cashier over being short a quarter—I can remember her words. *"It's just a silly old quarter. C'mon, what's one, little quarter?"*—I snatched the candy off the shelf and shoved it in the pocket of my sweatpants. My heart was pounding so hard I was sure they could hear it, and at any moment, they'd turn around and see the candy bar glowing like a neon sign in my pocket, flashing: THIEF, THIEF, THIEF. When they didn't and kept right on about their business, this rush of fulfillment and pride came over me. I'd just made myself dinner. For free.

That night in bed, I began to get concerned about my mortal soul. My mom had this framed picture of the Lord's Prayer on my wall, and I'd stared at it, paralyzed, absolutely certain Jesus himself was going to pop out of the frame, handcuff me, and take me straight to Hell without passing GO. Each night that week, though, it got a little easier to look at that photo, and I eventually convinced myself that Jesus was too busy watching out for the *real* criminals to notice me. And plus, what evidence would he have had? That candy was long gone, and the wrapper was out with the trash. By the end of the week, I'd forgotten all about the moral and spiritual implications, and I was ready to do it again. So, I did. And then again after that. And again. And the rush felt so good I never stopped.

So, all this being said, I'm not evil, ya know? I'm not this great malevolent mind who plans my next covert mission in excruciating detail. It's more a spur-of-the-moment decision. I'll see some trinket or bauble on a store shelf, or maybe we need something at the house, and this wave of excitement burns through me, then temptation creeps up behind it, so I wait for an opportunity, and I take it. It's, like, I'll be standing in the back of a store, minding my business, leafing through a bible I've picked up off the shelf, but at the same time, I'm slipping a pack of hair ties into my pocket, because my last one finally broke. Getting caught doesn't even occur to me.

****

You know you can't see the air, and you don't have to see it to know it's there—it just fills the space, and you're grateful (whether you realize it or not) because if it didn't fill the space, you'd suffocate.

That's how I knew she was in the room.

I had my head down, searching through magazines, when what I can only describe as a heat chill rippled in me, causing me to shiver and the skin on the back of my neck to tingle. When I heard the cooler door pop open, I stopped breathing and stayed perfectly still, hoping this wasn't the day I got arrested for shoplifting … for stealing stale food and one lousy, domestic beer, no less. If I had to go to jail, I wanted it to at least be for something worth it—money, jewelry, a car. FYI: I've never stolen any of those things or anything like that—only necessary or completely useless items, which I know is paradoxical. Let me explain: I'd take a plastic bobble-head of an off-brand, generic Batman or a sandwich before I'd take something sentimental or valuable to an individual—it's just how I roll, ya know? And only from stores. Like, I don't want *your* shit, but if it's some dumbass thing on a shelf in a Dollar General, it's fair game, and of course, like I said, I learned to be my own chef at a very young age. And can I really be held responsible for what I do when I am hungry? Isn't that a famous candy commercial these days?

I wasn't startled when she spoke, but expectant, and resigning myself to the fact that I was busted, I turned to face the girl. When I looked at her, all I saw was sadness. There wasn't a stitch of makeup on her face, but she didn't need any because even in sadness, she was striking. The circles under her eyes were so dark and deep, they almost echoed, but her brown irises were flat, like something was missing in them—a spark, maybe, and at the very end of her left eyebrow, there was a tiny, pink crystal. I immediately loved it—it gave her an edge no girl I'd seen in this boring ass town had. Her espresso-colored hair was knotted up in a bun with frizzy strands sticking out everywhere, which, though messy, was somehow endearing. Overall, she looked defeated, though, like all the air had been let out of her balloon. So, despite the circumstances, despite me being caught, red-handed, stealing my dinner, I immediately wanted to make her smile. So, I made jokes, trying to be cool. *I'm not really into labels.*

"Put those back!"

"C'mon. They're five-day old pepperoni rolls. You're going to pitch them anyway. I'm hungry."

She seemed to contemplate for a moment, tilting her head and looking at me, taking me all in, trying to figure me out. Her shoulders relaxed a little, and she let out a quick breath, seeming to judge that I wasn't a threat. "And *cigarettes*? I know old people do, but what teenager smokes these days? News flash. They're bad for you. And if you're only hungry, what about the beer and the magazine?"

"Uh … after dinner entertainment?" I asked, trying to justify myself.

She reached out and grabbed for the 40oz beer I had, and as her hand brushed mine, my brain short-circuited. Ice formed around each of my ribs, cracking then melting, and in that moment, I felt the color red splash through me. She paused, momentarily looking dead into my eyes, and somehow, I knew she felt it too. Our hands had to have only touched for a nanosecond, but it passed in an eternity. The intensity—our brains somehow sharing the same image, as if connected by some weird fiber optic cable—was overwhelming, and I gasped, but the rest of my body was paralyzed as I got stuck in this strange moment with her. But for as quickly as it came and as long as it lingered, the cable snapped, and the moment broke, and the world spun in real time again. My body jerked at the sharp snap back to reality, causing me to yank my hand back, and when I did, the beer exploded in foam and glass shards at our feet, a kind of drunken mosaic.

SASHA HIBBS & CHRISTINA HOOKER

Chapter Three
Déjà vu

I am afraid that cord of communion will be snapped; and then I've a nervous notion I should take to bleeding inwardly.
—Jane Eyre, Charlotte Brontë

Josephine

Déjà vu, from what I've read, is an experience described as the feeling of having lived through the present situation before or a common intuitive experience shared between people. According to Wikipedia, the expression is derived from the French language, meaning "already seen". When it occurs, it seems to spark our memory of a place we have already been, a person we have already seen, or an act we have already done.

Attempting to disarm a thief in my aunts' store was never something I had done before. I had never laid eyes on this mischievous boy—and while cute with the bad boy vibes that seem to attract a certain type of girl—he was a thief, nonetheless. But there *were* these strange intuitive feelings that he wouldn't hurt me, and that faint sensation that led me to attempt grabbing the beer from him.

As our hands met, my eyes closed, and it was like the curtain to this life fell, and the curtain to some other spiritual realm was lifted. I felt myself suck in a sharp breath, and I was lost in a sea of red. I could hear red. I could see red. I could taste red. I could feel red. The only thing breaking through the shattering sensation of red seeping everywhere—around us, through us, as though it was us—was this boy's hand. It's as though we were tethered together, and the awareness of his skin against

31

mine was the only thing that could reach me, and just as it was he who had sent me there, into the red pool, it was only he who could reach me and pull me out before I drowned.

And then it was over. I was back, my eyes popped open, and my chest was heaving from the exertion of this otherworldly experience. As if through clouds, I could hear his voice coming from somewhere out in the real world, but I just wasn't quite there yet.

"Hey. You okay? Breathe."

Listening to his words, I focused on him and him alone. Each syllable he uttered brought me closer and closer back to reality. I locked eyes with him, taking a couple deep breaths. Around my feet, I could feel the cold, foaming beer spreading around my toes and squishing into my sandals, as though I were standing on a beach, the frothy remnants of a dying wave sloshing up far enough to touch me then recede back to its watery home.

I don't know how much time was lost between us, what universe we slipped into and then back from, but his eyes told a story, one of recognition. We shared a moment that felt like a thousand moments in one. I didn't understand it, and I couldn't shake it. But he felt what I did. His expression said as much, and I couldn't move. I was suspended in place, grounded in front of this boy with his long messy blond hair and startlingly comforting green eyes. Oddly enough, he wore a red checkered flannel. *Red*.

I blinked, and in that fraction of a second, the magnetic connection was severed. I flicked my eyes down, momentarily looking at the puddle of beer we were both standing in before catching the faintest lines of red circulating in the frothy mess. My mind didn't register right away, remnants of the red induced fog, I supposed, but finally, I was able to focus enough to figure out the origin of the red marbling through the yellowish liquid. The shock of everything had dulled out what otherwise should have hurt, but both of us had cuts on our pinky fingers. Shards of glass from the broken bottle. Had to be.

I opened my mouth to speak, but the store lights came on, and instead of my voice, it was Aunt Sophie's voice that burst through the store. "Good Lord in Heaven! Josephine, what are you doing!" It wasn't a question.

I jerked toward her, startled, and I could see from my periphery that the boy's gaze lingered on me before he turned it toward my aunt. I watched as she looked between us, down to the floor where the magazine he attempted to steal was serving as a mop for the beer he'd dropped, the pages now soggy and misshapen. Clues to what was happening were scattered dots at our feet, glass fragments floating in spreading liquid, and Aunt Sophie was finding them one by one, connecting them to solve the crime. From the floor, she snapped her irate eyes back to us then focused them solely on him. To his credit, whoever he was, he did not try to run. He could've, but he stayed, facing the music.

"*You*," she said venomously, raising her eyebrow and curling her lip. I had never seen her this angry. It seemed as though she knew him. "I have no tolerance for thieves! Who do you think you are, waltzing in here and stealing from hardworking people? I'll show you!"

"Well, technically, I haven't stolen anything. I'm still inside the store with the items."

"Don't you smart mouth me! Do you think that makes the fact that you broke in so much better? I know what you were up to here, and I'll not let you get away with it." She whipped out her cell phone, punching her finger into the glass screen so hard I was surprised it didn't shatter.

I stood, somewhat bewildered with the entire situation, watching her lips moving and listening to sounds coming out of them, but the words weren't making sense to me—it was as though things suddenly turned into The Tower of Babel.

My eyes traveled away from her, wandering instead back to the boy standing inches in front of me. My right hand was shaky and streaked with blood. I looked at his—it was the same. Then I looked up and down, taking him in more fully. I had never seen him before, of that, I was certain. And yet, I couldn't shake the uncanny feeling, a feeling I couldn't put a name to. I clawed back through my memories, and then it occurred to me that against all odds, I had to be experiencing déjà vu. But why?

While Aunt Sophie was talking into the phone, Aunt Lindsey came into view. Her eyebrows shot up, and her gaze went back and forth between us. I could see her take in the same scene Aunt Sophie did, but her reaction was quite different. She left momentarily, coming back with a towel that she dropped at our feet to soak up the beer.

"Be careful not to step on the glass. You two come with me," she said, turning her back to us as though she had no concern this boy might run or lash out. The three of us turned the corner leading to the small kitchen in the back behind the coolers. Aunt Lindsey put on a pair of latex gloves, the snapping sound against her wrist bringing me to.

"We need to wash your hands," she said, grabbing mine first. She looked down at my open palm, turning my hand over in hers and then submerging it in lukewarm water until all the blood from my cut was no longer visible. She handed me a paper towel. "Dry off, and I'll put some calendula ointment on that cut."

She turned toward thief-boy and never said a word. She grabbed his hand before he had time to react and did the same to him. She turned his palm up to face her, scrunching her nose and furrowing her brow in deep contemplation before submerging his hand under the water spigot. She turned off the faucet and dried her hands, then gave him a paper towel, instructing him to do the same.

He did as he was told.

She turned, reached above the sink, pulled down an intricately carved wooden box that looked ancient, and opened the latch, pulling out a tin of her homemade calendula ointment as promised. "Calendula is your average garden marigold," she said, slathering generous amounts on both my pinky and his. "It has anti-inflammatory and antibacterial properties and has been used for ages to heal wounds. I make a batch each year to keep on hand. It's way better than that nasty Neosporin stuff. Anyway, go on, you two. You're all cleaned up. Now, get out there and take the heat."

He and I stood in silence, his lips parted but no words coming out. I gazed into his green eyes, and what at first appeared to me as a comforting look soon turned hard and heavy at approaching footsteps. He huffed, rolling them as far as he could back into his skull.

The steps stopped at two thick black boots, and their noise was replaced by a loud, exasperated sigh. The officer's uniform was dark blue, crisp, and somehow matched his menacing looking shades, shades that slowly lowered to show a glaring gaze of disgust. He was intimidating, and I found myself relieved not to be the subject of his glare and, for some strange reason, worried that thief-boy was. "Jesus H. Christ—" the officer started.

"No, it's Caius R. Duke! But that's high praise coming from you," he said, lips curling into a smug grin.

My insides lit up, and little flutters spread under my skin at discovering his name was Caius.

The officer's face turned hard and twitched with anger, but Caius didn't flinch. "What the hell is wrong with you, Cai?"

"Nothing. In fact, I'm pretty great. Your concern doesn't go unappreciated, though. Thanks."

Shock washed over my face. Great? How was that even possible—he was about to go to jail! I watched as Caius and the cop rapidly fired words, like bullets, at each other.

"Oh, yeah. You're real great, kid." I could see fire flash across Caius's face at being called a kid. "Does being Bridgeport's token teenage hoodlum not bother you at all?"

"Why would it?"

"It's a distinction for my nephew that, quite frankly, I could live without."

Nephew. *That's* why the boy was being such a smart-ass.

"Noted. Why don't you go pick an old lady up off the floor or pull a cat out of a tree? Your help would be more appreciated there. Because quite frankly," he mocked, "I don't need it."

The officer's face twitched with repressed anger. "Oh, really? One day, Cai, you're going to get tired of these pathetic attempts for attention. I just hope it's before you end up a bad joke that no one is laughing at."

"The only joke I see here–"

Aunt Sophie interrupted their volatile uncle-nephew moment before Caius could hurl any hate back at his uncle. "I get back from dealing with a death in our family, and this is what I come home to, Kurt—your nephew stealing beer and cigarettes—"

"I'm sorry, Sophie. I heard about Janet," the police officer said to my aunt, cutting her off. My heart paused between beats at the mention of her name—this cop knew my mom. "I'll pay for the damages Caius caused today."

"Absolutely not!" Aunt Sophie interjected, hands on her hips, anger rising. "That is not how you learn anything. Why do you think he continues to do the things he does? You constantly save him. Do you think I had anyone to buy my way out of my mistakes? My mother would've taken it out of my hide, and since we all know his won't, I'd like to press charges."

At the mention of Caius's mother, the officer winced and sighed. "Now, Sophie, just calm down a little. What do you expect? He was only trying to get himself some dinner. He didn't walk out of the store with it. What would you have me do other than pay for it—cut out a pound of his flesh?"

"What I expect is—" Aunt Sophie was getting ready to launch another verbal attack, but Aunt Lindsey cut her off.

"I have a better idea!"

Kurt turned to look at Aunt Lindsey, slightly blushing at the sight of her, then moved his eyes to the tile floor. "Oh, y-yeah? What do you suggest, Linds?"

Caius and I were still mere inches from each other. I wanted to look over at him, see his face, gauge his reactions, but instead, I rubbed my pinky finger and looked at my beer-soaked feet.

Aunt Lindsey continued, "Well, Kurt, we could use some repairs around this place, some help, and your nephew seems young and *able-bodied*." She nudged me with her elbow, and I could just feel her grinning as my face flushed.

I caught the officer looking at her with something akin to awe in his eyes. "Really?"

She reached out and touched his arm. "Yes, really. We were all young once, Kurt. I remember well those things we just couldn't resist, don't you?"

Before he could respond, Aunt Sophie shouted, "Are you out of your mind? The boy just stole from us, and you want to willingly let him in? That's like opening the henhouse door for the fox," she spat out, uncharacteristically harsh. I was not used to seeing her like this. She was always so composed, but apparently, stealing rubbed her very wrong.

"I'm absolutely in my right mind, and I am perfectly sure. You weren't born forty, and you might do well to remember being young, too, Sophie," Aunt Lindsey retorted. Her tone held something, some urgency she was trying to convey to Aunt Sophie, and I don't know if it was a twin thing or what, but Aunt Sophie must have understood.

Her features relaxed. "So be it," Aunt Sophie said to her. "If you ask me, this is too easy a punishment, Kurt, so you better accept this deal before I change my mind."

Although I still had this pull, this desire to look at Caius, I fought against it, keeping my attention on the aunts.

Aunt Lindsey seemed lost in thought while Aunt Sophie was laser focused on Kurt, her stare demanding a prompt answer.

"We'll take it, Soap … er, uh, Soph." He corrected himself.

Aunt Lindsey smiled at him calling Sophie "Soap." Sophie blushed, then they all burst into laughter, sparking a "remember when" conversation. It seemed as though they'd all known each other quite well at some point in time, even my mom. As they all talked, I let the sounds of their voices drift away because all I could think, see, hear, and feel was the boy—Caius—standing beside me and red.

SASHA HIBBS & CHRISTINA HOOKER

Chapter Four
The Great Pinball Wizard in the Sky

If I told you I've worked hard to get where I'm at, I'd be lying, because I have no idea where I am right now.
—Jarod Kintz

Caius
Journal

  Red swirls and echoes from the past resound in my head, bouncing around my skull like a pinball wizard is using my eyes as ball launchers to play a furious game. Vague, unclear memories slap at me like flipper paddles, brutal and unforgiving. Occasionally, I feel a short reprieve, like it's all going to slip through the crack, and I will be granted rest—the player is done, game over— but just in the nick of time, he jams his finger into the button, and the feelings beat through my head all over again. They're like reflections against scratched and scraped playfield glass—I see only vaguely reflective, distorted images that even the sharpest eye could not bring into focus. Am I the game somebody else is playing, or am I the controller? Visually, the images do not make sense, but they evoke feelings of deep-reaching grief— grief that you're built with; grief that is dense and tangible; grief that is solid as bone. Can I make peace with despair I cannot identify? Will I find myself in it? Will I learn the answers? Do I have a choice? Will I care? The role of Cai will now be played by ... who gives a fuck?

  Because do we really need to know who we are and where we're going? Why can't we just go where the paddle throws us and assume it is taking us down the exact path we need with the exact momentum we need to travel it? Because maybe The Who was on to something, and God is the deaf, dumb, blind kid who plays a mean pinball.

Ordinarily, I would have resisted this type of corporal punishment. A whole summer's work for one measly bag of stale pepperoni rolls and a busted Schlitz? Hardly warrants hard labor, if you ask me, but there was something about that girl—*Josephine*—and that crazy experience we shared, and I had to know what it was, so if sweeping floors and pounding nails was how I was going to get the answer, that was what I was going to do.

The bell over the door chimed as I *legally* crossed the threshold into *Blair's Lair* to begin the first day of my sentence. The flickering lights caused me to squint as I came in from the morning sun. The savory-sweet, yeasty scent of baking bread immediately enveloped me, and it somehow made the whole place feel warm, like a hug, and, if I hadn't been there to do manual labor, I'd say it was an embrace I welcomed.

Lindsey, the hippy of the two sisters, was at the cash register, hair twisted up with a pen stuck through it, cigarette clamped between her teeth, grumbling as she sorted out receipts and plucked away on a calculator, seemingly oblivious to my entrance.

"Morning, dear," floated from her mouth like smoke would have, if her cigarette had actually been lit. "I'll be with you in a moment."

While I waited, I scanned the store, thinking back to the day I invited myself into the closed establishment. It was easy enough—their lock was an old, metal twist lock and nothing a credit card slid into the gap between the door and the frame couldn't handle. If they'd really wanted to keep intruders out, they'd have at least upgraded their basic security. I mean, aren't locks the first line of defense? How was it my fault they made it so easy? I saw it, and it was like, well, you know those old cartoon comedy skits with the frog—the one that wears a top hat and tap dances while he's getting dragged off the stage by the hook of a cane? That was just about the best way I could describe what happened to me the moment I decided to come in here. My stomach grumbled as I approached the joint, and an overwhelming desire for a beer came over me. I noticed the "Closed for Family Emergency" sign in the window, then I noticed the dinky lock and thanked the universe for the serendipity bestowed upon me. Happy hour awaited. The rest is history.

Sighing to remind Lindsey I was still waiting, I shifted my weight and glanced over to the cooler. Immediately, my heart rose to my throat and began thumping in rounds of three against my trachea—*Jo-seph-ine, Jo-seph-ine*. What was it with this girl? I'd never been all twitterpated over a girl before—they just came and went. And mostly, they went. I swallowed thick and hard, hoping to shove my overactive heart back down where it belonged and calm it into its normal beat.

"Earth to Caius," Lindsey's voice sang out as she snapped her fingers in my face. "*Hello.*"

I came to and looked at her. She was a pretty woman—long and wavy dark hair, smile lines that made her face interesting, and a whisper about her that made her curious, like a mystery you wanted to solve. I could see why Uncle Kurt stuttered and turned red when he looked at her. She smelled of Nag Champa and tobacco, which somehow complimented the smell of the baking bread and sizzling pepperoni inside it.

"Yeah. I'm here … on Earth … in this exact location … just to pay for my crime." I was sarcastic. I shouldn't have been, but I couldn't stand when someone snapped at me.

"Oh, you don't know how right you are," she said, smiling.

I looked at her dubiously, thinking how strange she was, when she held up a plastic bag from the local hardware store with a new doorknob, lock system, and screwdriver in it. The screwdriver had poked through the plastic. As she plopped the bag into my arms, I caught myself just in time to stop my eyes from rolling into my skull. Of course this was my first task. I thought about telling her that the screwdriver jutting out of the bag was a safety hazard but thought better of it since I'd already been a bit brass with the Earth comment.

"Since you thought the shitty lock on this place was your personal invitation to come in, this is the first thing you'll be doing."

Had I told anyone that? I was pretty sure I'd kept it to myself, but I guess it wasn't that important anyway. Anyone could have guessed a piece of shit lock was a good enough reason to do what I did. "Great." I smiled. "I'll get right on it, ma'am."

She seemed to sense the underlying attitude I thought I could hide. "Don't give me any *ma'ams,* kid. I'll be right here at the counter, keeping an eye on you."

"Sure. I'll do my time with no complaints. Could be worse, right? You could have put me in a pillory and thrown rotten tomatoes."

"Yeah, or we could have had you publicly hanged or something. Hard work never hurt anyone, Caius. Maybe you'll actually learn something."

At that, I chuckled. "Well, if the choice is to either learn something or be hanged, I guess there really isn't much of a choice, is there?"

She smiled. "See? You're *already* learning."

"Yeah, yeah." I paused, surveying the room, looking for *her.*

"She's still sleeping," Lindsey said, reading my mind.

"I wasn't—"

"*Right*, right." She grinned. "You want to impress her? Get to work fixing your mistake, mister."

I flashed her my best patronizing smile. "Sure thing," I said, turned, and headed for the door. How did she know the things she seemed to implicitly know? The lock, Josephine. These were things I'd never expressed out loud. I had always heard she was a witch, and though I never bought into it, maybe there was something to the talk of the town. Or maybe there wasn't, and I was more of an open book than I thought. I quit dwelling on it and set to work on the lock. The sooner I started, the sooner I would be finished.

"Shit," I mumbled as I jammed my cut pinky into the door frame for the third time.

"Watch your language! This is a business, young man," I heard the other aunt—the one who didn't want me there—say. I had been so focused I hadn't realized she'd come into the store.

I looked up, did another quick scan for Josephine, then apologized. When I focused back on turning the last screw, I saw blood pooling under my Band-Aid. "I'm done, but, hey, uh, Lindsey..." I held my hand up. "I think I need to go take care of this before we need to call in Hazmat."

"Oh! The blood again," she said as though she were expecting it. "It's a reminder."

"What?" I had no idea what she was talking about.

"Never mind. There are clean bandages in the back room and a private bathroom. Go ahead. You'll be working in there next, anyway." She pointed at a doorway with glass beads strung down it, color melting from clear to gold. They clacked as I parted them with both hands and ducked through.

Lindsey's gypsy room smelled of incense as thickly as the store smelled like pepperoni rolls. This room was dark, and as my eyes adjusted again from the harsh fluorescents, things took on ominous shapes. I clicked on a single lamp, and it cast an orange candlelit glow, illuminating mostly shadows. I could see peeling flowered wallpaper behind purple velvet drapes that hung on every wall. A small square table covered with an ornate tapestry sat in the center of the space, and cards with strange pictures were laid out in the shape of a cross with a stacked deck sitting at the foot of that cross. At the back of the room, there was an open door, and I could barely make out the male/female symbols on a plaque at the center of it.

It took a while for me to get the blood to stop oozing from my pinky, but after I had taken care of business, I crept around the room, looking behind all the drapes, opening drawers, smelling the herbs that were stored in them. I saved the card table for last. I ran my hands over the topography of the tapestry, feeling every texture of the fabric, then touching the smoothness of the cards and studying them. I was simultaneously intrigued and repelled. What were these things? I grabbed the top card off the deck, flipped it over, and gasped.

What stared back at me was a skeleton in black armor, holding a black flag bearing a white symbol and sitting atop a white horse with a blood red eye. Scattered on the ground were bloody bodies, dead, dying, and pleading with the skeletal figure to spare them. The bottom of the card read DEATH in capital letters. Goosebumps prickled up the back of my neck. "What the…" I whispered but trailed off.

"You know, the Death card is probably the most

feared of all the cards in the tarot deck."

I jumped when Josephine spoke and turned, staring at her in shock.

"It's completely misunderstood, though. *Kind of* like someone else in this room," she continued, wryly grinning.

"Tarot?" I'd heard of tarot cards, cards used for divination, but I'd never fooled with them. "How do you know about this stuff?"

"Aunt Lindsey taught me a little. That Death card that you pulled, for instance? It actually isn't bad. It symbolizes the end of a part of your life that is no longer serving you, opening up the possibility for something new. You know, like the whole one door must close for another to open kind of deal. It's telling you that you need to part ways with a past that no longer serves you and be ready to welcome and even embrace new possibilities. Like, stealing, maybe? Maybe that's no longer serving you. That's just a guess, though." She winked, and when she did, the pink jewel in her eyebrow caught the light and sparked for a split second. A wink? Who winks? Under any other circumstance, I would have made fun of a winker, but for her, it was kind of endearing.

"Oh, yeah? Do you read palms, too, Miss Josephine?"

"It's Josie. And, yeah, actually, I can." She flipped her dark hair over one shoulder, grabbed my free hand, and pulled it toward her, then suddenly, her face flushed as if she was embarrassed over her brazenness. She let out a slight school-girl giggle and finished, "Well, a little, anyway."

Electricity sizzled behind the lines as she traced her index finger across my palm, brows furrowed, studying. I wanted her to both never stop touching my hand and throw it away from her in shock because it was burning her, too. But if it was, she didn't seem to mind.

"Um, well, I have never seen anything like this, not even in a book. Your heart line intersects with your lifeline, and that cuts into your fate line. See here…" She flipped my palm up to show me and continued to explain the various wrinkles, but her voice faded out into my own thoughts, and just like the day when I was eight years old and decided I couldn't live another moment without that Baby Ruth, I decided I couldn't live another moment without Josie's heart.

I interrupted her. "So, does it say anywhere in those skin lines that you're going to go out with me this evening?"

Without letting go of my hand, she stopped talking and looked me square in the eyes.

Chapter Five
The Empress, the Emperor, and Death

All my heart is yours, sir: it belongs to you; and with you it would remain, were fate to exile the rest of me from your presence forever.
—Jane Eyre, Charlotte Brontë

Josephine

My life had been turned upside down, inside out, and then put back together in this strange, disjointed way that I'd had no time to acclimate to, and then Caius... Caius, this thief-boy, with shameless petulance and a smartass attitude, had stolen his way into my life. Literally. The universe had an interesting way of timing life events. I was still trying to digest my mother's death and the slew of grief that comes with that, but right in the middle of it, Caius careened into me, trying to steal from my aunts, and pulled me toward him with this strange and unnatural feeling of a color—red—and it had overtaken all other senses, all at once.

I didn't know what to make of it all, but I knew whatever *it* was, was undeniable. It was something I couldn't ignore. I was astonished that Aunt Lindsey suggested he work in their store and even more astonished that my level-headed, thief-hating Aunt Sophie agreed. I had a mix of feelings about the deal—he was someone I wanted to run away from, and I knew I should want that, but there was also something inside me that didn't want to run away at all. Not even a little bit.

For as long as I could remember, I'd get "gut feelings." Aunt Lindsey called it claircognizance. She'd handed me a crystal on the end of a chain one time while I was visiting and told me to use it to develop my skill.

She told me to pay attention to the answers that popped into my mind, that what I was experiencing was different than regular thoughts. Regular thinking is busy and self-centered, but claircognizance is your higher-self guiding you, so it is insistent and not usually what you'd want to hear. And that's why you have to listen.

I didn't call it that or always pay attention to it, and I never used the crystal. I just let it be and accepted that I had little intuitions about things that had not happened before they actually happened, and I'd *just know* when I was right. Generally, they were just things concerning me, which, I assumed, was what separated it from any kind of psychic ability—I'd know exactly what to study for a test, or I'd know a friend was about to call before the phone rang. It wasn't some kind of superpower or anything that I could use at will—sometimes it was there, and sometimes it wasn't, but it never seemed to be about anything major. Then again, I'd never really had anything major to worry about before my mom got sick.

When my mom was diagnosed, I started ignoring my intuitions. If I *just knew* all this random stuff, why didn't I know to tell my mom to get checked sooner, before it was too late? Now, I was starting to get those gut feelings about Caius, and they were loud and intrusive. Like, when I first saw him stealing from my aunts, I somehow knew he wasn't dangerous. At all. There was also something else about him, something familiar, something I couldn't quite put my finger on, but it was there, nagging at the back of my mind for me to pay attention to it, but I wasn't going to. The boy was stealing from my aunts, and I didn't need to have anything to do with him. But I wanted to. I shook my head and said aloud to myself, "Stop it, Josie." But I still didn't want to stop it.

I was able to push most of my intuitions away,

mostly forget about them, and operate with my regular thoughts alone, if I distracted myself—that was when I started walking to clear my head. When my thoughts were chaotic, and intuitions were zooming around in my head, walking outside usually did the trick to organize my mind. I snuck out the back door, and from my aunts' store on the corner of Virginia and Main, I crossed the town's railroad tracks, and as I passed all the buildings on Main Street—My Little Cupcake, smelling of sweet vanilla, Winnie's Cafe & Coffee, bustling with all the morning caffeine addicts—I tried sorting my thoughts from my feelings. I ran over and over every emotion in my mind, calculating why I was feeling each of them, but walking was not working this time.

Secretly, as I walked, what kept popping through my logical thoughts was a fantasy I didn't quite want to admit I was having—this vision that Caius would see me walking, and he'd pull over in a cherry-colored Jeep Cherokee and offer me a ride. When I got in, he'd grab my hand, and we'd have that whirlwind feeling all over again. Then maybe it would make sense, but even if it didn't, at least I'd get to feel it again … but no such luck. One red Jeep passed me, and I looked in so expectantly that the old guy with a long, gray goatee who was actually driving it waved to me. Embarrassed, I smiled but quickly looked at my feet and hurried on. *No thanks.*

I couldn't make any sense of any of it, so I decided right then that since I couldn't use my rational thoughts, I was going to have to rely on my senseless gut for answers, which I didn't like to do, and wait to see where it led me, but my gut wasn't making much sense either. The answer that kept popping up was Caius. More specifically, the words "it's him" kept repeating, but I didn't understand. Part of me wanted to believe it was the little crush I had because I thought he was so cute, but most of me thought it was deeper than that.

Once I decided that my little fantasy wasn't going to happen, I turned to head back to *Blair's Lair*. The aunts didn't realize I was out, so I entered the store through the back and into Lindsey's tarot room, or the "Witch's Hut" as she jokingly referred to it, just as quietly as I had left it earlier. Immediately, I could tell Caius was there, somewhere in the store. I don't know why exactly. There wasn't a smell or a noise. I just knew. But did I want to *just know* about him? I still wasn't certain.

Instead of going in search of him, I sat in Aunt Lindsey's room where I was somewhat trying to find the solitude walking denied me before seeing my aunts, who, out of kindness and concern, were being a bit smothering. I was also trying to concoct some crazy situation I could get into where Caius would touch my hand again.

And as I waited, he came to me.

I was in the dark, in a corner, when I caught sight of him, holding his pinky finger between his thumb and index finger on his opposite hand, and I watched as he ducked into the bathroom. I was frozen, not with fear, but with exhilaration. How was I going to talk to him? Should I even talk to this thief? I wanted to, desperately, but now that I had the actual opportunity, I felt like I shouldn't. It felt like talking to him would disappoint my aunts, and they were all I had left. But, no, I had decided on my walk to follow my intuition, and that was what I was going to do. My aunts had to know that if they had him here, eventually, he and I would have to talk.

Caius came out of the bathroom, both hands at his sides, and began wandering around, snooping in the room. I couldn't blame his curiosity. My Aunt Lindsey was interesting, to say the least. Her room was full of lavish tapestries and had an overall charming aesthetic about it, like it called to the wandering soul to come in and discover its purpose before finding its final resting place—like the place held all the answers.

I watched him give her tarot cards a slight caress as though deliberating on whether to pick one up or not. His hesitation lasted mere seconds, and then his curiosity overpowered whatever was holding him back. He pulled the top card off the deck, flipping it over quickly, like it burned him a little. He murmured something under his breath, his eyes widened, and his mouth slightly dropped in a gasp.

Because he was spooked, I thought it was a good time to make my presence known. He jumped when I did. Flicking my eyes down, I saw what had him so disturbed—the Death card. I tried setting him at ease with some small talk of what the card meant or could potentially mean. It seemed fate took over and followed through on my hand touching fantasy because he made a joke about palmistry, and I instantly grabbed his hand to check out his palm. And while I felt the smallest charge sizzle up my arm, disappointedly, I wasn't thrown into the red haze that happened when we first touched.

The lines on his palm were interesting. Very interesting. I was intently trying to interpret them when Caius asked me if any of the lines on his hand indicated I was going to go on a date with him.

I locked gazes with him, taking an eternity to look into his eyes. I squeezed his hand as though I could convey to him this pull I felt for him because I believed he felt it too. I didn't know what it meant, and I didn't know what he meant, but the undeniable truth was I *knew* I didn't have a choice in the matter, that fate was with us on the road we were both walking on, maybe it was guiding us, because now that our paths crossed, I felt like they had always meant to. Or was that wrong to feel about some boy you'd only met for thirty minutes as he was about to get arrested in your family's store? Against my better judgment, I wanted to know more about this boy. No, I needed to know. I needed to know who he was and the origin of this nameless pull we had when together.

Very seriously, I began, "Well, I'm not sure." I literally felt disappointment roll off him when I said it. "But," I continued, pointing to the center of his palm, then tracing a light circle around it, "I think that's what it says right here." I smiled and closed his palm up, holding it between both my hands momentarily before releasing it gently, like how you open your hand to let a lightning bug go. "Yes, Caius. I will go out with you this evening," I said, directly. My seriousness didn't seem to intimidate or scare him but rather seemed to relieve him. I watched his shoulders relax and a smile slowly curve his lips upward.

"You know your aunts are never gonna let me just take you out, so how do you feel about breaking rules?" he asked, the smile never leaving his lips.

"If they are the right ones, I feel pretty good," I answered, unsure where this honesty was coming from. I had just met this boy, yet my guard was lowered farther than it should be.

He seemed amused by my answer. "Good. How familiar are you with Bridgeport?"

"A little. Enough, I think, to find my way around."

"Do you know where the Circle-K is, right down the road?"

"Yes."

"Meet me there at 10:00 P.M. I'll be waiting for you."

"Caius," Aunt Lindsey yelled, blowing into the

room. We jumped apart quickly, hoping we hadn't been busted, but if we had, she made no indication of it. I kept my eyes on him, and he kept his on me, throwing me that crooked smile. "You still have some work to do before leaving for the day."

Caius never spoke, just kept looking at me, then turned to go back out into the storefront to finish whatever chore the aunts had assigned him.

I turned my gaze to Aunt Lindsey, anticipating being scolded for talking to a criminal, but her attention was fully focused on the tarot cards on her table. I watched as her fingers lightly grazed the Death card Caius had turned over. She, too, pulled her hand back as though the card were hot. Her brows furrowed as though she were struggling to interpret something. She slowly turned over another card, and then another, but kept them to herself. I was used to her odd behavior, but given my own weird experience with Caius, I wanted to know what cards she'd pulled and why she was keeping them to herself.

I opened my lips to speak, but no words came out.

Aunt Lindsey cut me off before I had the chance to ask what she apparently already knew I was going to. "I don't know, Josie. I just don't know yet," she said, turning, visibly troubled, to me.

"What do you mean?" I asked. The last twenty-four hours had me questioning a lot about the physical and metaphysical world.

She tucked whatever two cards she had in her hand into the pocket of her patchwork skirt. "Josie, can you go tell Sophie I went out to smoke, and I'll be back in five?"

"Sure." I barely got the words out before she turned and left. She was acting strange. Very strange.

****

I didn't want it to come off like I'd dressed up for him, but I thought I would put a little more effort into my hair, like brushing it, for starters. I applied a thin layer of mascara, and as I watched the reflection of myself doing it, eyes wide, lips parted, I saw my mother staring back at me. I looked so much like my mother had when she was young, most notably my dark brown eyes. How I missed her. Swallowing the lump in my throat that thinking of her usually produced, I foraged through my meager wardrobe. I had no idea what Caius had in mind or where we were going, but I thought it wise to wear loose fitting jeans and an old, comfy Led Zeppelin t-shirt.

My mom had loved Led Zeppelin. I remember us dancing around the living room of our apartment when I was very young as "Dancing Days" blasted through her stereo's speakers—her laughing as I bounced with no coordination. I so loved her smile, and I missed it. She taught me how to slow dance for my first formal dance to their song "Thank You," looking wistful and telling me that she'd always wanted that to be the first dance song at her wedding, if she'd ever had one. But she'd had me instead, and that was "better than any dumb wedding" she'd always said. "It's our song now, Josie, because I will always love you. Even if the sun stops shining and we are left in the dark, and all the mountains crumble, and we have nothing but rocks to walk over. It will always be us, Josie. Always." She'd kissed my forehead then.

The memory brought tears to my eyes, and their sting snapped me back to the present. I didn't want my grief to ruin my first date, and she wouldn't have wanted that either. It seemed like she was in everything, though, and she was everywhere I looked. Everything was a constant reminder of what I'd lost.

I hadn't thought too much about how I was going

to sneak out until time to do so. I slipped on my shoes and tried to make my feet as light as possible, cursing underneath my breath at the slight sounds I still managed to create. If I could just make it down the stairs, I felt confident I could pull off slipping out unnoticed.

The store lights were off, and I almost went out that door but remembered Caius had changed the lock and thought better of it. I glanced up at the clock on the wall.

9:45 P.M.

I quietly turned, glancing down the aisles toward Aunt Lindsey's Witch Hut. There were no lights on. Really my only option was to go out the back door from her room like I did earlier that morning when I went walking. I tiptoed back there, and, looking around, I made my way toward the door without a sound. I was almost there when a corner lamp came on.

I nearly jumped out of my skin as I turned to see who had caught me.

Aunt Lindsey sat with her legs crossed, dark hair framing her ominous looking face, one hand turning stones over and over while the other she let rest on her knee.

"Uh, Aunt Lindsey—" I began to explain.

She cut me off. "Be careful, Josie. Just be careful. Please." Her voice was low and hushed, and it bothered me.

"What do you mean?" I hoped I wasn't going to get the birth control speech.

She uncrossed her legs, leaned forward, and pulled the two cards from earlier out of her pocket. She gently laid one out before me.

"The Empress…" I said, trailing off. My gaze was fixed on the woman sitting on a throne wearing a crown with twelve stars situated evenly about her. She held a scepter in one hand and an orb in the other. I knew that card, too. The Empress was, essentially, the mother figure of the tarot deck and was generally all about feminine energy: love, abundance, nurturing, and pleasure. The Empress card was a clear indication that someone is on the right path and should be encouraged to participate in activities that reinforce love in our hearts, which was exactly what *my mother* would have wanted.

I looked back up at Lindsey. She turned over the other tarot card in her hand and placed it atop the Empress card. "And the Emperor," she said, my eyes leaving her solemn face to look at the Emperor, the father figure of the deck, staring back at me. My body erupted in a cold chill as a shiver ran down my spine and turned my stomach over. I had seen that card a million times, I was sure, but at that very moment, his stern eyes stared back at me with malice as he sat atop a throne in front of a barren world. The card was epitome of authority, dominance, abuse of power.

The man pictured had a long white beard, suggestive of the number of lifecycles he had covered and the wisdom he possessed, and the gold crown on his head indicated him as the superior authority. It was obvious that he demanded respect. He held an ankh, a symbol that represented life, and an orb—he was literally holding life and the world in the palm of each of his hands, controlling them.

But who did this card represent? I didn't know my own father, and it certainly wasn't Caius. The aunts were not paired with uncles. What man would have this kind of power around me? Did it represent me? Was it telling me I was in control of my own world and fate? Truly, the Emperor and Empress cards together could have many interpretations—marriage, even pregnancies—but I didn't get a good feel from this card, and one thing Aunt

Lindsey always said is that a lot of tarot divination relies on intuition and feelings.

If Lindsey noticed my distress, she kept it to herself, and as she threw the last card down with the flick of her wrist, the eyes of Death looked up at me, but it set me completely at ease, erasing the dread of the Emperor. Death, *Caius's card*, but it was also the end of something. Perhaps the end of whatever the dread was I got from the Emperor. I went over them in my head:

The Empress: me, my mother, love, indication of the right path.

The Emperor: stern authority, old man, power, abuse of power? Or man and wife? Father? Something that needed my total and immediate attention? Am I the master of my own fate?

Death: the end of something no longer suited to you, new beginnings. Put the past

behind you. Focus on the future.

I'd have to take time and think about it later.

Aunt Lindsey was concerned, but she didn't seem as fearful of the Emperor as I was. Maybe she was better at hiding it. Or maybe I was wrong altogether.

"I know where you're going, and I don't know if I like it, but I feel compelled to allow it. The universe is always bringing seemingly unrelated events and unimportant people together, but if you could look at the big picture, you'd see that it isn't unrelated or insignificant at all. Bad things happen, and good things happen, but there is a reason for all of it. Caius is here for a reason. You two collided for a reason. Let's let the universe's plan play out … for a while, anyway. Unless you or I get a bad feeling, then we may have to revisit your permission to see him. Until then, be careful and be on the lookout."

"For what?"

"That's what's missing," Aunt Lindsey said absently, almost to herself as if in deep thought. "I don't know. Maybe nothing."

I left Aunt Lindsey in her room and set off on foot to Circle-K. My mind was racing. In one week, I had lost my mother, moved in with twin aunts far from home, and was sneaking out to meet a thief who, against all odds, had some kind of magnetic pull that clouded my better judgment. I glanced up at the neon lights spelling out Circle-K in one single red thread, then looked at the full moon to clear my head. Taking a deep breath, I searched the parking lot for Caius.

And I didn't see him. I looked at my watch. My tarot reading with Aunt Lindsey had made me late—it was 10:07 PM. Did he leave? Fear and disappointment drove through me like nails. Was this some grand joke at my expense? A way to get back at my aunts for making him work? *This* is what I got for wanting to go out with a thief. How could I be so dumb? Tears sprang up in my eyes. I didn't want to care as much as I did. That's what that Emperor card must have been telling me—that Caius was an asshole! I turned on my heels to leave and go home, embarrassed and rejected, but as I did, something caught my eye at the edge of the light.

And there he was, hitched up against the brick building, staring at me with a lopsided smile, and seeing him seemed to bring everything back into focus. He made everything make sense.

Chapter Six
Two Halves

Two souls are sometimes created together and in love before they're born.
—F. Scott Fitzgerald

Caius
> *Journal*
> *Magnetism. A force caused by electric charges that is exerted when magnets attract or repel each other. It's all invisible, and so many things instinctively use it to find their way—honey bees, fish, birds. But humans? No. Humans need a guide, a compass, an external magnet free to move on its own. We don't listen to our hearts, our blood, or our souls (our own magnets looping through and beating in our own bodies). We need an actual thing made out of what's already inside us, compelling and repelling and circling and pointing, to tell us what we should already know. Go there ... now. But, unlike innate animal instinct, external magnets leave room for error or mistake. Due north may be due north, but is that where we should be going? Makes you wonder if any of us upright apes will ever find our way?*
> *Magnets. You think of them sticking to things like your refrigerator after you vacationed somewhere and stopped at the cheesy corner gift shop, but all magnets have two sides or poles—one side pulls, draws inward, while the other side pushes, rejecting. It all depends on what you put near the magnet. Poles that are alike push away from each other. Poles that are not alike pull toward each other.*
> *Surely, cavemen thought magnetism was magic. Rub two sticks together, and you get fire ... duh. Friction*

is tangible. But line up invisible, spinning electrons the right way, and shit sticks together, or it floats ... like, woah, right? It's the difference between cooking the rabbit and pulling the thing out of your hat. I guess cavemen didn't have top hats, but you get the picture. What was more beneficial to them? Friction. But they had to be fascinated with magic, didn't they? Now, we know it's science-y shit—electricity and minerals and movement—but maybe there is a little magic about it all, too.

Because I know what I felt with her.

And it wasn't science.

When our hands first brushed, there was a spark and an instinctual, compelling impulse—a deep and vaguely familiar pull. But at the same time, I could feel this ... I don't know, like, resistance or repulsion from her. She wanted to be near me, but she didn't all at the same time. It's like when you cut a single magnet. You don't end up with just a singular pole, like one north or one south. You end up with four poles—two north and two south, and two individual magnets that were once one whole, singular magnet. Two halves totally independent of each other but made from the same whole.

Are she and I the same magnet? Is that weird?

I couldn't believe she'd said yes. I hadn't really expected her to, but then again, I had. It's weird, this push/pull thing we had going on. Today, I felt her pulling toward me, wanting to touch me so badly. She was eager to grab my hand and survey the features of my palm, and I was eager to let her. But the day we first touched, entirely by accident, both of us were taken off guard at the synchronous explosion of compulsion and revulsion, swirling around in flashes of crimson and cherry and ruby and scarlet. Fever red. Blood red. The color of life and love. I'd never known you could *feel* color before that. Why red? Why now? It immediately made me curious, so I followed the compulsion, but her? I wasn't so sure she would. She had caught me stealing from her family, red-handed (pun intended). Revulsion would have been the more likely choice. But, somehow, it wasn't. It was there, though, that little part of her that wanted nothing to do with me, so I had to make sure I impressed her tonight. I needed her to want to be as near me as much as I wanted to be near her.

I'd never really been on a date. I generally just had girls come over to my house. Yeah, I know it sounds forward and bad, but it isn't what you think. Nothing ever really happened. Most girls just wanted to hang with me because they knew I had liquor and a place to be alone to drink it. Often times, they'd bring their friends, and they'd all end up giggling about girly shit and watching stupid TikTok videos I had no interest in, which was fine. They knew I was safe and nothing would happen to them at my house. Sometimes, a girl would come alone, flirt, leaf through my journals, get curious, and call me "dark" or "mysterious". And I liked that. They'd usually want to kiss me then, and sometimes, they wanted to make out. It's not like I said no, but I never let it go further than that because that seemed, I don't know, mean or something— I was never really into them the way they were into me. After it happened, I would always try to let them think they were the ones who lost interest first. I'd intentionally try to be extra dull until they quit trying to figure me out altogether.

Guy friends of mine kind of came in spurts—we never really shared any interests for long. I didn't like video games, and I didn't like sports. I'd taken some guitar lessons, but I wasn't garage band material, and I never took any of them on a stealing adventure. A couple dudes would come and smoke some weed or have some beers for a while, then stop. Sometimes, they'd start again when football would end or whatever. I liked observing them more than I liked interacting with them, so I never much cared if they came around or if they didn't. I didn't miss them when they were gone.

All I really had an interest in was writing, mostly journal entries, observations, and thoughts. I was gathering it all together to become the next Gonzo Journalist the world loves to hate like Hunter S. Thompson. I'd always kind of had a dream of taking off after graduation in a van and just exploring, catching a job here or there, staying a while in one place or another, and just living life where no one ever knew me, adrift and by my own rules, landing wherever the Pinball Wizard launched me. Total anonymity. Caius Duke, an enigma. Catch him if you can. *You can't*, but watch out—you might end up in his next book. That was the dream, anyway, so it just didn't matter who came to my house and who didn't. I could take any of them or leave them. It was all the same to me.

Honestly, I don't know how my mother managed to keep the house we've lived in for friends to come over at all—it was left to us by her parents, so it was not like she had a mortgage or anything, but she was just such a general mess that it was hard to believe our home hadn't been sold on the courthouse steps to the highest bidder. The house is a big, one-level house with a basement. The basement is like its own house, so basically, it's like two houses in one. My mom and I lived in the basement together until my grandparents died—together in a car crash, tragically poetic—then we moved into the whole house. Now, though, she lives upstairs, and the basement is my domain. Bedroom, bathroom, small kitchen, living room, and most importantly, a bar. Like an actual bar with stools. It's a total 1960s vibe—the furniture is the same from when my grandparents first decorated, down to the old ashtray stands, and I love it. Apparently, they were quite the entertainers back in the day, and I think that's why people still liked to come over. They could feel the old party atmosphere seeping through the walls when they were here, like you'd open the door to the bathroom and walk in on a girl in a mini skirt and go-go boots freshening her lipstick after she'd snorted a line of coke off the back of the avocado green toilet.

I was pacing around the room, jittery, flipping through notebooks, organizing pencils to one side of my desk, then the other, picking up empty water bottles I hadn't bothered with for a few days. Finally, when I'd had enough of my anxious self, I flung the fridge open and downed a cold beer to calm down. Burping, I crushed the can, turned to throw it into the trash, and banged my knee on a cabinet door that was slightly ajar.

"Son of a...." I sucked in breath through my teeth. "Ouch!" That door had always been wonky—sometimes it would shut, and sometimes it wouldn't. Sometimes, I'd slam it shut, only to find it open again later. When I was younger, I used to pretend it was my grandfather sending me messages from the great beyond, or wherever people go, and I would set up booby traps to catch his ghost in the act, you know, like when you are done believing but you still try and catch Santa Claus because ... *just maybe* there is magic in the world. And *just maybe* it is for you.

When I was thirteen, I was snooping around one day, and I found an unopened bottle of Old Crow shoved way back in that cabinet. It was my grandfather's favorite drink, and he was known to have stashed bottles all over the house. Thrilled, I opened it, gagging when I gave it a sniff, but I tried it anyway, taking two deep swallows from the long neck. As it rushed down my throat, I had this vision of myself being exactly like him when he was a young man, drinking his Old Crow on the rocks, being the gracious host of the party. But I didn't like it. And not only did I not like it, I didn't know how anyone could like it. It burned every inch of my esophagus and crackled like fire in my belly, leaving the taste of rotten caramel vomit in my mouth. Feeling guilty I hated it, I screwed the cap back on and put it back where he'd left it like maybe he'd come back for it. Five years later, the whole bottle was still waiting, all but two swallows of it, anyway. As I rubbed the stinging pain out of my knee, I thanked my grandpa, as though me whacking my knee against an old pine door was a ghostly replacement for him clapping his hand on my shoulder and giving me the manly advice to get out of my own head, have a good time, and to go and get the girl.

Having no experience with one, I didn't know what to wear on a date. I rummaged through my closet for a t-shirt and decided on my Led Zeppelin shirt with the Hermit on it, wondering if she'd ever heard of the band and kind of excited to share them with her if she hadn't. I tore through my dirty clothes hamper, tossing things out, searching for my cleanest dirty flannel, sniffing each one I pulled out, then tying the right one around my waist. June nights could get pretty chilly. Luckily, I had one clean pair of shorts left, but I couldn't find a belt, so I used a random shoestring to cinch the front two belt loops together and make them fit better, flopped down with my back on the bed, and sighed. How was I going to make this girl like me, trust me?

I grabbed my phone, checking the time for the forty-ninth time—9:45 PM. I hurried to the door and jammed my feet into my scuzzy Chucks, puffing my cheeks, then blowing air out of them. I was still a little nervous. I gave my armpit a quick sniff, again, just for good measure, and headed out the door into the night. It wasn't until I was almost to the Circle K that I came up with what we were going to do, and as I did, my mouth twisted upward, involuntarily. It was perfect. I'd show her around town, telling her stories about the place, getting to know her, her getting to know me, and we'd end up at the park behind the high school, watching the stars.

I was in the dark at the corner of the building, waiting for her. I wanted to be the one to see her first, and as she approached, I couldn't help but grin. She was so pretty, and she absolutely had no idea she was, which made her even prettier. As she got closer and closer, I realized we were both in Led Zeppelin shirts. Hers was also a Zoso one, but it was a different print. How funny—I had never known any girls into Led Zeppelin, but I didn't know any girls with an eyebrow piercing, either.

She stopped at the front of the parking lot, planting her feet so firmly into the ground it was almost like she stomped. Whipping her head up and down the asphalt, she scanned every square inch looking for me, getting noticeably flustered. I realized she must have thought I wasn't there, so I scooted into the light and leaned against the wall.

She lit up when she saw me. It made my heart flutter a little bit, and wiping my palms against my shorts, I headed toward her as she waited under the neon Circle K sign.

"Hey," I said. The sign cast her skin a vibrant, artificial color of red, like I was looking at her through a glass of Kool-Aid.

"Hey." She put both hands in her back pockets and rolled her feet outward to stand on the edges of her shoes.

We spoke at the same time, nervously. Me, "I

got—"

Her, "I didn't—"

We both stopped, started again, and talked over each other a second time. This time, I laughed, a blank, nervous sound that was closer to a grunt. "I'm sorry. I was just trying to tell you I got the memo about the shirts." I pointed to them.

She gave a small smile. "Yeah, they're one of my favorite bands. I was, um, just saying that I thought you'd stood me up."

"I would never."

"Sure."

"Why, Josie! Just what kind of boy do you think I am?" I awkwardly paused. "Wait. Don't answer that."

She giggled out, "So, what do you want to do?"

"Well, I thought I'd give you a flashlight tour of Bridgeport, ending at the park behind the high school."

"Yeah. Okay. Cool."

I turned on my phone's flashlight, grabbed her hand, and tugged slightly, moving forward into the dark. "C'mon, this way."

I led her back the way she came, past the closed coffee shop, beyond Music on Main, the new concert venue, and as we trudged on toward Dairy Queen, she asked where we were going.

"You'll see." I smiled, pulling her forward. We crossed the railroad tracks, and I turned to face her, still guiding her as I walked backward toward our destination. "Not much farther, now." I grinned at the look she had on her face—confused, yet intrigued. "I couldn't *not* start our evening here. Close your eyes."

"*Okay…*" She was starting to crack a smile. I desperately hoped this wouldn't piss her off.

"Surprise," I said so softly that the night carried my word away as we walked to the front door of *Blair's*

Lair.

"What?" The word fell out of her mouth with all the enthusiasm of a dial tone.

I let all the air out of my lungs.

"Are you taking me home?" Her voice went up an octave, apprehensive.

"No, not exactly. I'm starting here because I want to apologize." I clicked off my flashlight because I didn't want her to see my face. I wasn't accustomed to saying I was sorry—generally, I wasn't. "See, obviously, I never meant to get caught—"

"Wow. This is *some* apology you have started," she interjected sarcastically.

"Now, wait. Let me finish." I explained to her why I did what I do, something I'd never told anyone. Everyone kind of knew I did it, but no one really knew how it started or why. "So, I'm sorry I was stealing from your aunts. I am. But I'm not sorry it happened. I'm not even sorry I got caught. Because if I hadn't gotten caught, I wouldn't have met *you* ... and there's just something about *you*..." I let my words die in the dark, hoping for a response.

SASHA HIBBS & CHRISTINA HOOKER

Chapter Seven
Magnets

A kiss is a lovely trick designed by nature to stop speech when words become superfluous.
—Ingrid Bergman

Josephine

When he said it, all the fear melted out of me. Twice, I'd thought he dragged me out in the dark just to make a fool of me, to punish me for my aunts punishing him. But he wasn't like that. Something in me knew he wasn't, but there were still faint warnings scratching at the back of my brain. My mom always told me never to ignore red flags. "Don't confuse a red flag with a red rose, Josephine." Was that exactly what I was doing? He was cute and kind of charming, but stealing is a pretty big deal, and while he had explained his reasoning, did that really justify his actions? As I pondered, silence fell between us, and I let my eyes run over Caius.

He really was a picture—smooth and grungy all at the same time, a combination that was really working to kickstart my heart. I knew he was waiting for me to respond, to say anything to reciprocate his feelings, and I wanted to, but I also didn't want to upset my aunts or disappoint my mother. What would she have said? Red rose; red flag; red rose; red flag. Seemed to me as though either one could have thorns.

"Josie?" he finally said, unable to wait any longer.

I looked him square in the eyes … his beautiful green eyes. "I know there is."

"You know you're special, huh?" He covered himself in a veil of sarcasm after hanging himself on a line for me.

"No," I replied, shaking my head. "That's not what I mean. I *know* because there is *just something* about you, too. I am not sure if I want there to be, but there is." I thought about Aunt Lindsey, her tarot cards, and the chill I got from the Emperor card. "It's like everything in my brain is telling me you're a bad idea, but a magnet is buried somewhere deep inside me, pulling me to you anyway, and I can't help but want to figure out why."

He smiled that lopsided smile that was growing on me more each time I saw it and put his arm around me, hugging me into him. He was warm, and I fit into him perfectly, like we were two pieces to a puzzle. It was just that we just couldn't see the bigger picture. "Welcome to Bridgeport, Josie. Allow me to be your tour guide."

A silence settled around us as we walked, but not an awkward one. It was the kind of silence old friends fell into—quiet comfort, easy peace. He and I just fell into sync, and as we walked in stride together, I couldn't help but think to myself that we were meant to be doing this exact thing in this exact moment. It felt right, like I was in the right place at the right time. But that made me feel guilty, too, because the only reason I was in this place at this time was because my mom had died.

Every so often, I could see Caius stealing glances at me, and it pushed me to make conversation. He listened seriously and intently, honestly interested, not just waiting for a turn to speak. He actually wanted to hear about me.

"So, tell me about the eyebrow ring," he said.

"It actually happened down here when me and my mom came in to visit the aunts. There used to be a skate park somewhere around here."

"Yeah. I remember. I used to go there all the

time."

"No way! Maybe you were there when all this happened! So, when I was thirteen, I went through this huge Avril Lavigne skater-boy phase. The baggy pants, the chain wallets, the skate shoes, the whole nine yards. Even though the one time I was actually on the skateboard I insisted my mother buy me, I rolled two feet, freaked, and crashed to the ground. And when I hit the ground, I hit my head, and I'm not really sure what happened next, except when I stood up, I got hit in the face with a rock from somewhere. Someone had to have thrown it, but there was so much blood, and I was so shaken up, I couldn't tell where it had come from."

Caius gasped slightly, holding his breath.

"You okay?"

"I'm okay," he replied. But he didn't seem quite okay.

"So, that flying rock gave me a deep gash right by my eyebrow, and the doctor who stitched it did a really shitty job, and it left a scar. I was devastated to have this ugly scar on my face. It was all I could focus on. I kept swearing that I looked like Quasi Modo, begging my mom for plastic surgery, and even though she assured me it was hardly noticeable, I didn't believe her.

"And, long story short, I told her that summer about all the teasing and that I didn't want to start high school with classmates calling me ugly, and I begged her to homeschool me, which, honestly, was a bit of on the dramatic side, but I really felt terrible about having a mark on my face. 'Now, bullshit,' she said, 'we'll fix that.' She took me to get my eyebrow pierced, and now, you can't see the scar unless you really search for it. Looking back, it probably wasn't as bad as I thought it was, but just like that, I went from Scarface to the cool kid with a piercing. No other kids in my class had anything like that ... not yet, anyway."

"Wow. They teased you for that? You went to school with a bunch of dicks."

"Kinda, yeah. But there were a few good ones. I do miss my friends."

"Tell me about them."

Talking about them only made me remember the distance between us, but I continued, "Well, there's Jamal. He and I have been best friends since first grade because we carried the same Hannah Montana lunch box. He's the one who taught me how to match my clothes and do my make-up, reminding me constantly that his name meant beautiful *and* handsome, so obviously, he knew best. When I was so hung up about my scar, he always used to tell me he could never have ugly friends— you know, because it went against the very core of his nature. He would absolutely disapprove of you." I smiled, thinking about the two of them meeting. "And he would be appalled at my outfit choice for this date."

Caius chuckled, a short, breathy sound, not much more than an exhale. "I'm too ugly for Jamal, huh?"

I blushed. "That's not what I meant. He would have told me that just because there are red flags, it doesn't mean there's a carnival. My mom used to say something like that, too."

"Red flags, huh?" He smiled. "Yeah, I wouldn't want my friend to date me, either. Scary shoplifter and all." He waved monster hands in the air and gave an evil laugh.

"And then there's Maeve. Maeve's the very definition of extra, but we love her anyway. After about sixth grade, she only hung out with us between boyfriends, and even then, all she'd want to talk about was them. Sometimes the juicy details were fun, and sometimes they were entirely too much. What about you?"

"Nah, I don't really have juicy details to divulge. Nice boys don't kiss and tell, Josie." He joked.

"No! Your friends."

"Don't really have any of those, either. Not close ones, anyway. My mom is kind of a hot mess, so I never really made any friends when I was younger. Sometimes, people come over and chill, but none of us are tight. I like hearing about yours, though."

As I blabbed on about my school and friends, we walked past the pool and basketball courts, places I was already familiar with. I was comfortable talking to Caius. I didn't usually open up like this, but with him, the words came easy. "And, well, that about sums up my social life in Connecticut." I hadn't realized how far we'd walked, but when I finally took a breath from all my talking, I took in my surroundings and realized we were at the city park. It was as black as spilled ink, except for one street light at the corner, shining down a hazy blue flicker on its surroundings, illuminating pieces of trees and playground equipment. There was something peaceful and hopeful about the emptiness of it, like a stage just before a play. And that stage was for us. And we were the actors.

"Let me push you?" Caius asked.

I followed the line of his gaze to a swing-set lightly touched by the edge of light, a tall rusted frame holding swings that, as we got closer, revealed they had held many children over the years.

"I'd like that." For a fleeting moment, as the rubber seat bent and hugged my hips, I felt the same thrill a child would, excitement rising in me at the thought of going higher and higher as I cut through the air, and the wind rushed against me. As high as the sky. I gripped my hands around the cool chains of the swing, and a blend of ice and fire flooded me as I felt his hands slide over mine.

I didn't see any flashes of color, but there was something I didn't quite have a name for between us—like if home were a person, it would be him. He squeezed gently, then let go, sliding his hands down until they were close to the small of my back, and I could feel the heat of them radiating at my sides.

Every hair on my body stood at attention, pulling toward him. I could feel his breath against my hair as he dragged the swing back, then it disappeared, and I was flying. I'd close my eyes on the down swings, then look up, wide-eyed, as I got closer and closer to the sky. I pretended I was soaring to the stars and that reality was tiny and falling so far below me. I was an angel, the sky was my home, and I could sail to the moon. The sky was a beauty that never failed me, and it never failed to amaze me. And somewhere in all of the ups and downs, the stars began to move, perform almost, for me. Or maybe it was for us? Were those burning balls of light writing our script, or was this a scene they'd seen many times before? Aunt Lindsey always said that the stars knew everything.

"Push me higher!" Joy rushed through me, escaping my throat as a giggle, and this time when I swung back, he caught me, and the swing stopped. His hands wrapped around me from behind and rested against my stomach. I leaned into him and looked up to see his face.

His eyes seemed to glow like stars all their own, burning in swirling patterns of energy, almost flickering different shades of green. They were as deep and hypnotic now as they had been intense on the day I met him, and I wanted to swim inside them.

He bent toward me, and his hair brushed over my face, and the scent of cedar it left behind was intoxicating. The longer we touched, the more I could feel our connection, not just body touching body, but almost like we were the same body. Promise hung in the air, sweet and delicate, gossamer strings of sugar webbed and woven around us, and I wanted it to dissolve. I wanted to put my mouth to his and taste cotton candy, taste the future, taste the past, taste the present. I wanted to taste it all on his lips, and he seemed to sense it.

My entire body screamed in anticipation. My heart was a banshee in my chest, waiting, wailing, grieving, wanting, until finally, our lips connected. And it was right. And it always had been. And it always would be.

He pulled away first, lips lingering close to mine, his carbon dioxide, my oxygen, my exhale, his inhale. And like actors at the end of a scene, frozen in the dark and waiting for the curtain to fall, he remained there, sharing my breath, for what could have been seconds, minutes, or days. I had no concept of time or space as we were touching. It was the most intimate thing I had ever experienced. Then it broke, and he smiled against my mouth, rocked his head back and forth, lightly rubbing his nose against mine, and stood up to take a seat in the swing next to mine. "So," he said, "tell me more about what makes you *you*, Josie Blair."

It seemed like a fair question. "Well," I began, "you know the twins are my aunts. My mother, Janet, was their sister." I swallowed the small knot forming in my throat at the mention of her. "She and I lived in Connecticut for the majority of my life, at least what I can remember. I don't know my dad. I don't have any siblings, and after my mom died, my aunts came to get me so I could live with them."

When I said it all out loud, my life seemed so small. I didn't have family beyond my mother and aunts, and now with my mother gone, it was just them. And, I thought to myself as I summed up my family tree in one paragraph to a boy I'd only just met, if I hadn't had those crazy aunts of mine, I don't know what would have become of me after losing my mother. "My family tree is pretty much just a stick. If my aunts hadn't taken me in, I would have had no one. No one would love me, and I would be completely alone…" I trailed off in that thought. How insignificant my life would be without them.

"Hey, where'd you go," Caius said, bringing his swing closer to mine, placing himself in my line of view.

I smiled weakly at him. "I was just thinking how lucky I am to have my aunts."

"I'm sorry about your mom. Do you want to tell me what happened?"

I'm not sure why it didn't feel awkward to talk to Caius, but without much resistance on my part, I just started talking about her. "She was diagnosed with a rare form of breast cancer. It's one of those asshole brands of cancer that have virtually no warning signs, and once you are aware, it's usually too late," I said, looking him fully in the eyes. This would be the point where the tears generally welled up, but something in his eyes kept me grounded and gave me the courage to keep going in spite of the hurt talking about her caused. "It was always just me and her. She was the best mom I could've ever wished for."

"What was she like?" he asked, softly kicking his feet into the ground so his swing would stay beside mine.

"She was kind and patient. She made the best peanut butter fudge, the kind that wasn't too marshmallowy but not too crumbly either. It was just simple peanut butter perfection cut into equally perfect squares. She always went overboard for Christmas, like it wasn't enough to just have one tree for me and her, nope. She had to have the big tree and then three other small ones littered throughout our apartment. And lights," I said as I gave a light chuckle. "There were always crazy amounts of Christmas lights. Strand after strand, you'd have to start wrapping them around the branch from the inside and work your way out. She loved classic rock and old country music, like Loretta Lynn and Conway Twitty era music." I saw him playfully raise his eyebrows at this, but I kept going, thankful to have an ear that wanted to hear about the beauty of my mother. "She'd wear these hot rollers in her hair way too long, sometimes going out in public with them in. Like, no one does that anymore, you know? She loved watching old black and white romances. Loved finding anything on clearance—as long as it was marked down, in her eyes, it was worth having– it didn't even matter if it was junk. And above and beyond all her quirks, she loved me. '*To the moon and back*,' she'd say. And now she's gone. And I hope she's gone to the moon, and she just hasn't made her way back yet."

Seeming to sense I was on the verge of tears, he looked at me, his eyes shimmering flecks of emerald, and all the hardness I had ever seen in them faded away like the fog with the sun. He held out his hand to me as he stood up. "Come on, let me show you something."

I slid my hand into his, thankful that in such a moment of vulnerability, there was no judgment, just silent and kind acceptance. I stood up and walked beside him. It was dark, but like magic, the moon and stars seemed to light our path through the park, kind of like the Christmas lights my mother loved so much—the sky seemed to be decorated with them tonight, and Caius and I were walking hand in hand under the glowing canopy of them, and I couldn't help but imagine my mom, sitting on the moon, smiling and lighting strands of stars just for us.

Chapter Eight
The Witch Who Wouldn't Stay Buried

Terror made me cruel . . .
— Emily Bronte, Wuthering Heights

Josephine

I'd never kissed a boy before. Except for Jamal, I'd never even so much as held a boy's hand before. There was nothing that had ever been more perfect than this, though. All of it—the walk, the hand holding, the talking, the way he listened, the kiss ... especially the kiss. While it was all new to me, it didn't feel new—it was easy, like what we were doing, we'd already done, and not just once, but a scene we'd played out a hundred times before. We weren't strangers; we were friends, but not new friends. We were the kind of friends whose connection went deeper than friendship—our souls recognized each other. I'd never been more comfortable with another human being in my life, except for my mom.

Caius led me down train tracks that followed a line of thick woods as we headed back toward town. While still holding my hand, he balanced, easily and quickly walking along the beams. It was a struggle for me to keep up, stumbling across the big rocks on the ground. "Ouch!" I cringed as one the size of a boulder stabbed into the sole of my shoe and caused me to turn my ankle a bit. I bent to cater to my injury as he hopped down.

"Josie, are you all right?" he said in mild panic.

"I'm okay. It just stung a little, that's all."

"Okay, good. I didn't want to have to carry you all the way back," he said, a smile playing about his lips. "Try walking on the tracks, Miss Graceful."

I stole a sideways glance at him and hiked myself

up on the track. "Sure, tell me the thing that makes sense to do now."

We continued a while in silence, me with my arms outstretched precariously balancing on the beam, him below me, bouncing foot to foot between the larger rocks. As we approached a small break in the trees, the wind picked up, and he wove his fingers back through mine. "Have you ever heard of the witch who wouldn't stay buried?"

A gust of wind blew through the tops of the trees, and they groaned, as though answering on my behalf. "No," I said, looking up through the swaying branches, a chill running the length of my spine.

"I think you'll appreciate this story—it's local folklore, at least," he said, squeezing my hand gently. "You know, something to get you acquainted with the area a little more."

Smiling, I squeezed his back in reassurance I was interested in his story.

"There are different versions of the story, but the most common ones say the witch was a scorned woman." He used the hand that wasn't holding mine to mock quotation marks when he said the word "witch", then continued. "A scorned woman who died young—in legends, they always die young. Of course, locals have romanticized and dramatized the hell out of it as to reasons why she died—at this point, I'm surprised the cause of death hasn't come to be a primordial version of Covid19—but there must be some truth to the woman herself having existed."

"What makes you say that?" The trees creaked and wailed against the wind like they were trying to get my attention again.

He smiled slyly from the corner of his mouth. "Because I'm taking you to her grave." He steered us off the tracks, through the groaning trees, and onto a narrow dirt path that went into the dark forest.

I gripped his hand tightly, a little nervous about heading toward a witch in the dark. "Her *grave*?"

"Yeah! It's right up here, over this hill," he said, and as we crested the dirt path, it was like a fairytale from the pages of a children's book had come alive. The largest willow tree I'd ever seen cast a long shadow against the light of the moon, turning the blades of grass a radiant silver. The brilliant stars I dreamed of my mother lighting for us had kept my attention as we had walked the tracks, but they paled in comparison to the clusters of fireflies surrounding us as the dirt path slowly faded into the grass.

"I've never seen so many fireflies," I said, reaching out, allowing one to land on my fingertip. It stayed there, blinking yellow against my skin for mere moments, and just as gently as it had landed, spread its wings, fluttered, and took off, rejoining the pack. I smiled, awestruck and enchanted. Between the stars, the moon, and the fireflies, we needed no other light. It was as though they were individual compasses, working together, guiding us where we needed to be.

"Honestly, I've never seen this many before either," he said with the same wonderment I felt, "and I have been here a lot. Maybe the witch is expecting us." He shrugged and smiled.

"Who was she?" I asked, making an effort to tear my eyes away from the beauty of the night and look at Caius ... not that looking at him was difficult.

"The witch doesn't have a name, at least there isn't one on the tomb, and no person alive today has ever known it," he said, and as we continued down the path, under the twinkling glow of the night, the leaves of the willow tree danced in the breeze, rustling a harmony in tune with the hollow sound of the wind. "But legend has it that she was wronged in some way and swore vengeance."

I should've been completely spooked. A vengeful witch. A tomb. The dark. But I wasn't. I guess there was just enough light to make his story a little less ominous, and for some reason, I still felt as though I belonged in this exact place, in this exact moment in time. It was a feeling like every moment of the night had been written amongst the stars. That tonight, I should be walking this path with Caius, the night's lights and creatures guiding us somewhere, someplace we were supposed to be.

The closer we got, the more I could make out the outline of a barn behind the willow tree and a large concrete box with a lid hiding amongst the drooping branches. "The tomb isn't in the ground," I said, somewhat surprised.

"Well, the witch wouldn't stay buried," he chuckled. "Where did you expect her to be?"

Ignoring his sarcasm, I walked faster, pulling him to the grave with a feeling akin to concern racing through me, taking over me. The closer we got, the more the moon, stars, and yellow flicker of light from the fireflies shone a gentle spotlight on the old tomb. Cracks, splintering the cement like veins, ran from the ground to the top—dark chasms in hard stone that had once been whole, bringing the spirit of the earth to the witch and the witch to the earth. Vines of ivy grew, wrapped around the edges of the tomb as though in response to her energy, the earth had sprouted arms to hold her, keep her rooted where she was. The top was slightly askew like someone had tried to open the box to spy on her but failed. Littered across it were crumpled pieces of half burned paper, smears and mounds of colored candle wax, a broken Ouija board planchette, a pentagram in red, bleeding spray paint, and an overturned bottle of Jack Daniels filled with what looked like urine.

I was appalled. "Why would someone do this to her?" I shouted, trying to clear off the top of her tomb.

"I don't know. People have always come to party here, talk to her, try to gain answers to life's mysteries, her mysteries. At the high school, it's always been a running dare to come here and have sex on her grave."

"That is awful! Why? Her life isn't a joke! Whoever she was, somebody loved her." Images of my mother ran through my mind. I couldn't imagine if this was her grave and people had desecrated it like this. Furious at the state of this unknown woman's grave, furious that people treated her like a joke, furious that my mother was gone, and she'd left me, and especially furious that I was helpless in all those matters, I picked up the liquor bottle and hurled it in the direction of the barn and away from her, the witch who wouldn't stay buried. I followed the launched bottle with the planchet, the scraps of paper, then began chipping away at the old candle wax until I scraped my fingers raw against the concrete of the tomb. When I couldn't take the pain anymore, I picked up a stick and threw it, then frantically searched the ground for something else and didn't settle until I was sure there was nothing left I could throw.

Caius let me get out my anger without saying a word, and he stayed quiet until I stopped, breathless, ears ringing, heart pounding.

"I'm sorry," I wheezed. "I don't really know why I did that."

"Hey, it's okay. Sometimes, it feels good to break shit."

"Yeah…" I trailed off. It felt like more than that, though. This all felt personal.

"I wonder if your aunts know the story?"

"I don't know." I was surprised I had not heard the legend of the witch that wouldn't stay buried until now—my mother had grown up in Bridgeport, and my aunts had never left it. "Why do they say she wouldn't stay buried," I asked, leaning against the tomb.

"Revenge," he answered. "I've heard different versions of the story. I've heard the witch was hanged in this willow tree, and when she wouldn't die by hanging, they buried her alive in this tomb, and on the inside of it, you can see her claw marks on the concrete." He patted the top of it before continuing. "The spooky part that follows that version of the story is that on her hanging night, you can hear her screams, and those that hear them without helping her will die within a year. I don't know. That story seems a little too Halloweenie to me.

"Some say she wasn't a witch at all but cursed by an actual witch. Jealous that the young woman had the affections of the man she loved, the witch gave her a potion that appeared to cause death, put her in this tomb alive, and cursed her to the box. That way, the young woman's spirit would never rise again, and her soul would never find the soul of the man the real witch had wanted. Revenge for unrequited love seems a little trite and a little extra to me, but who knows? I guess there was nothing else for a witch to do back then but be a jealous, obsessive bitch." He laughed. "The most common story, though, is that this woman was pregnant by a married man, and when he wanted nothing to do with her or the unborn baby, she hanged herself in that barn back there." He pointed. "But before she did, she created a curse for all the descendants of the man who scorned her, that they'd never know true love or true happiness," Caius said.

I could hear in his voice that he believed that none of those were the true story, just simple, local gossip that snowballed because it happened to be accompanied by a pretty cool backdrop.

"Spooky, huh?" He smiled his lopsided smile and nudged me with his elbow.

"Yeah ... spooky. I'll have to ask the aunts about it. I'm sure they are familiar with the story," I said, running my raw fingertips along the rough concrete just to feel the sting as I traced the cracks and to think about all the things those lines could connect to when my brain flashed red. Immediately, I looked at Caius, but when my eyes met his, my hand splayed, frozen against the tomb.

Gasping, I felt my knees buckle and my body go cold. I couldn't believe what I was seeing—Caius was Caius, but not. In the air around him, red blood vessels erupted, wrapping him in strange, alchemic patterns that twisted and extended, fiery ribbons stretching out like demon fingers, reaching for him, for me. The fireflies were stunned, suspended in air, not moving, and their emanating light morphed from yellow to pink—pale red—creating an ethereal silhouette of Caius, and his face started to change and blur, take on the look of someone else ... or something else.

A laugh broke through the night, and an old man, or rather, the image of an old man, a holograph, stood over top of Caius with a maniacal grin. It was an ancient face, sinister, pitted and gnarled by the hand of time. Malice carved around yellow eyes in deep set lines, like crow's feet, and they bore into me with hatred I'd never seen, not in this lifetime—but somehow, I knew it.

My mouth opened to scream, but no sound came out of me. I watched as the red lines around Caius began to thin and come closer and closer toward me until they were inches from my face, wrapping around me like the ivy on the tomb—and, like a film strip running on a reel, I saw the faces of everyone I'd ever loved in those red veins—faces I recognized and faces I didn't, but I knew I loved them all. I wasn't afraid of the red river of faces playing before my eyes, just of the old man behind them, superimposing himself over Caius and curling his lips up at me.

Time had stopped, frozen with the fireflies, then it broke, and all the seconds that hadn't ticked by rushed forward at the same time. I had been screaming silently, horrified by the image of an old man with hate so deep in his eyes I couldn't fathom it.

And then the night was back, and Caius—the Caius whose face I recognized—had his arms wrapped around me, supporting me completely because my legs had given way. I felt like I was out of air, heaving breath like I'd run across entire lifetimes to get back to this moment. When I finally found my bearings enough to look up at Caius, I didn't think it was my imagination that he looked just as spooked as I felt. "What was that?" I asked, my voice a hoarse, shaky whisper.

"I don't know. You, like, fainted or something. You okay?"

"I think so," I answered, my voice still barely above a whisper. "Caius?" I buried my face in his chest. "Did you … did you see all that?"

"See all what? I saw your eyes widen, and then you went down. I had to dive to catch you, so you didn't hit your head on the witch."

"Am I crazy?" I couldn't have been more unsettled.

"I don't know, maybe you are, and maybe you aren't, but I think I need to get you home either way," he said in a vague, flat tone.

Surprised to hear no sympathy or concern in his voice, I turned to look at him. There was no comfort in his green eyes, and his arms around me just felt like arms, not like where I belonged.

I peeled myself off him, leaning back so I could fully look at him. "Caius, I don't know what's going on. I don't know what just happened." Whatever it was, it was more significant than the day we'd first touched. He had to have felt it, too.

"And?"

"And, I'm scared."

His eyes were hard, and his stare icy. "I don't know what you're talking about. Nothing happened, Josie. I shouldn't have told you a scary story in the dark. C'mon, stand up. Let's get you home."

It felt like he'd slammed a door in my face. Why was he acting like he didn't understand? Why was he being so cold?

Chapter Nine
Finding the Light

Happiness can be found, even in the darkest of times, if one only remembers to turn on the light.
—Albus Dumbledore

Caius

I'd always felt drawn to the witch, and I'd never understood why. I didn't particularly buy into any of the "devil woman" lore that had woven its way through the town, but I did dig it. Her story died a long, long time ago, and I liked that there was a truth about her that no one would ever be able to discover—you just believed what you wanted to believe because even if you did know the truth, that's what you'd do, anyway.

Tonight, on our way back to town, I felt compelled to bring Josie to the witch. She had to meet her, and I wanted her to know the story, or rather, make one of her own. And she did, kind of. Josie was so moved by the fact that this woman had lived and loved that she couldn't believe that people had made her into a story at all. Josie's anger at the violation of this woman's memory was astounding. Though I'd never tell her, I couldn't say *I'd* never put a candle on her tomb and made a wish ... but it never came true.

Or did it?

The last time I did that, I was thirteen, and I'd wished desperately for a purpose. I was lost without my grandparents, and I didn't want to end up like my mother, but I could feel it inside me. You see, I'd always felt like I had a phantom limb, which is weird because I don't know what not having an appendage feels like, but it always felt like something was missing from me, and there was this itch in its place that I couldn't scratch. There was this hollowness in me I couldn't name, and I was afraid I'd fill it with alcohol like my mom. Or worse. Mostly, I filled it with stealing because if I was a thief, at least I had some purpose, and Uncle Kurt tended to save my ass before the trouble ever got real. The strangest thing was that the day I'd met Josie, I felt that void a little less, and the day after that, less still. Tonight, I didn't feel it at all. In fact, whatever it was overflowed when I kissed her, and all my senses woke up at once.

And then at the grave, an even stranger thing happened. Right before Josie fainted, I saw myself through her eyes, and I could feel our connection—heart to heart and soul to soul. It radiated from her, through me, and back again. And all I wanted to do was snap it.

From somewhere deep within me, a laugh came— a terrible, sickening laugh, and as it echoed through me, I hated all of the moments I'd spent with Josie, and the red we'd seen when we first touched was nothing but anger. It was all I could do to not leave her there and run home. The goodness in me, though, what little there was, wouldn't let me, and I made sure to get her to the door of her aunts' store before I ran.

I felt her disappointment and hurt as we walked, and, like a vacuum, it sucked everything out of me. I heard the slight sniffles of her trying to cry in silence, and, out of the corner of my eye, I could see her watching me, trying to figure out what had happened, but I didn't have an answer for her. Nothing happened, but everything happened. All at once.

I didn't look at her when we reached the parking lot of *Blair's Lair*.

"Bye," she whispered expectantly, hopeful I'd change my mind and be the guy I had been an hour ago. I knew it, but I couldn't be. I just wanted it all to be over. I wanted to be alone.

And in the dark of my basement, I could be.

I didn't say anything as I walked away.

****

I downed a six pack almost as soon as I walked through the door, pounding one after another, crushing the cans, and tossing them as I went. Each beer got me closer to where I wanted to be, which was nowhere, until finally, I stumbled to my bed, evil laughter still rolling through me in waves of sickness, and passed out.

In the throes of alcohol induced sleep, something within me shifted, and I woke. Sour breath and the taste of stale alcohol made me queasy, and I fumbled my hand across my nightstand, looking for water. Instead, I felt a crinkled soft pack of Marlboros and lit one. Who knew how long they'd been there, but I was taught years ago that one of the building blocks of a man was a cigarette to clear his thoughts. The stale smoke did nothing but parch my tongue to the point it felt wrinkled, but with the inhale of chemicals, the night came crashing into me, immediately causing me to smash the cigarette out. What had I done to Josie? What was that wicked feeling that had overcome me?

I sat bolt upright in my bed and half expected to look down at my legs and see the legs of a beetle. The whole night had been Kafkaesque—so terrible you'd almost think it had been a nightmare, except it wasn't a nightmare because you'd been awake, and it had all happened, and it was all still happening. "What the actual fuck, Caius," I whispered into my empty room, feeling the weight of oppression I'd doled out to myself.

Raw emotions buzzed and moved through me like neon flashes of electricity in a plasma ball, and I knew I needed her. I grabbed my phone—the battery bar was on red, warning five percent remaining. I called anyway. As I waited for the call to connect, I scanned my room and watched as the familiar corners twisted and bent, becoming strange and foreign. I shook my head to try to clear it, erase the alcohol haze and make things normal again, but nothing changed. In my peripheral, I could almost make out the shape of a man sitting at my desk. He appeared to be weaving thread in his fingers, like a game of Cat's Cradle. It felt like every nerve in my body was moving, stretching, and tangling with the thread. All the hair on my body stood on end. I shook my head again, slowly blinking my eyes. When I focused, the image was nothing more than my backpack and the fraying fringe and zipper moving with the oscillation of the fan. I was beginning to regret the six beers I'd polished off in a hurry.

As I heard the ringing on the line, something within me shifted again, and I was unsure of what I wanted, why I was calling her. *This is just a girl*, I thought. *This is not just a girl and you know it. This is just a chemical reaction, dopamine flooding my hypothalamus, a total hormonal eclipse of my brain, a teenage need to feel erotic, alive and virile. No, this is something more. This is Josie.* The thought of her was making my body feel both hollow, like the wind could blow through me and overstuffed, like my organs were too big to fit in my human-shaped meat sack. My heart began boiling, more intense with each ring, until she answered, and it turned to ice.

"Uh. H-hey," I stuttered.

She said nothing, and all this bitterness flashed through me. I wanted to hang up. I wanted to throw the phone, smash it against the wall. I wanted to forget her. I wanted to have never met her.

"Hey," she finally replied.

My mind was blank. I was speechless. *Stop it, Cai. This is Josie. This isn't some random girl.* Love and hate wrestled inside my throat, and I wasn't sure which was going to come spewing out of my mouth.

"Hello?" she said again with impatience.

I still couldn't speak.

"What the hell do you want, Caius?" Anger. Anger bred by hurt … hurt I'd caused.

It felt like I had been stuck for lifetimes, and I couldn't tell her what I wanted. Nervously, I grabbed my lighter and flicked on the flame, and that's all it took. A light against the dark. "I was, uh, having a dream about you … and, uh, I wanted to tell you—"

The phone beeped twice, and then it was dead.

"I wanted to tell you I was sorry."

Chapter Ten
The Tick-Tock of a Crumbling Clock

We all have the choice to stay mired in our own pain and mess, or we can try mending the broken pieces inside ourselves.
—Gabriel Maddox

Caius

Journal

My mother always preaches about happy endings. "Search for your happily ever after, Caius." She is probably so adamant because she is still expecting hers to happen, and she drinks until she believes it. She still expects my sperm donor, the tenured Literature professor, to leave his wife, the Dean of the English department, and come to us on a white horse with sixteen years worth of red apology roses. When she's sober, and reality hits her, she chases the dream all over again, glass by glass. But, telling yourself lies only leaves you punch-drunk and wanting. "Wish in one hand, shit in the other," Granny always said. "See which one gets full first."

Because the truth is this: real life ain't pretty, and it doesn't give a flying fuck about your story because you aren't a hero, and you're never going to be. It especially doesn't give a shit about your happy ending because, in this tango, only one of you is gettin' off, and guess what? It ain't you. And when you're lying there, covered in sticky disappointment and feeling used, life puts its pants back on, slaps you on the ass, and thanks you for the ride. Then you gotta clean yourself up and do it all over again, expecting a different outcome. It's a deliberately cruel cycle, and we're nothing but hamsters chasing something we're never going to get.

After my phone died on the line with Josie, I left it dead for the better part of a week. I couldn't stand the thought that Josie wouldn't call and that she probably wanted nothing to do with me, so leaving it off was the best way to not get my hopes up. I didn't want to feel the sting of disappointment every time the thing buzzed and it wasn't her. Beer was the other way to keep my hope squashed. As much as I did not want to end up a ridiculous quasi-idealistic drunk like my mother, it was kind of my family heritage. Happy? Drink. Sad? Drink. Any subset of those two emotions? Drink. Happily ever after? Make it a double! It wasn't my fault I defaulted to alcohol—it was just bred into me. I didn't know how else to deal and I hated myself for it.

My room reeked of stale beer and cigarette smoke, and I added the subtle undertones of raw onions and sour breath to the aroma. Crumpled cans were littered across my bed, above and below the black comforter. As I stirred, repositioning myself and stretching, the cans rattled and clanked against each other, and with a quick scan, I counted a dozen of them … and that wasn't counting what was under the covers.

Sighing, I reached for the final smoke out of my crinkled pack, and as I propped myself up, my arm crunched into a half-eaten bag of pretzels, spilling pretzel dust and hard salt onto the covers. Cigarette between my lips, I moaned out a bleak sound that got angrier at the thought of cleaning up the mess I'd made over the last several days—both the literal mess and the metaphorical one.

I didn't understand what had happened at the witch's grave with Josie. She'd freaked, and as that happened, I suddenly couldn't stand the sight of her, and it wasn't until I was home, away from her, that I could control it. I knew I didn't hate her, but at the same time, a streak of anger and revulsion writhed inside me. It slithered like a snake through my rib cage, wrapped itself around my heart, and choked out every ounce of warmth and love I'd ever had. And I did love her that night, at least, I think I did. I'd never felt more alive than I did at the park with her, and that's what love is, right—something that wakes up inside you that you can't ignore?

Hungover and rhythmically smoking, I played the night over and over in my head. I hacked each part of the hateful way I'd acted to pieces with a mental machete, but I couldn't kill it. I didn't know how to undo what I'd done, and the worst part was, I couldn't understand why I'd done it. Every molecule of my body knew being with her was what I was born to do, but I destroyed it. All of the sorry wanted to explode out of me. And just a few minutes out of the entire incredible evening had the potential to destroy my whole world. And that was what it felt like—she was my world. Or at least she could be.

I needed to write. It was the only way to collect my thoughts and clear my head. As I threw off the covers, cans clattered between the sheets and onto the floor. A partially full one hit my bare feet, spilling flat warm beer across them … almost like the day Josie and I had met, except instead of artful foamy swirls, this just soaked into the crummy carpet and became more for me to clean. I rushed to my desk and, grabbing a pen, furiously began writing.

Certain experiences, over time—maybe lifetimes—seem to grind down the soul, and love becomes the casualty. As your soul wears down, you become harder and harder, and then you become so hard that you're brittle, so brittle that you begin to crumble. And as you crumble, there is so little left in you that indifference replaces hope. And indifference means love is no comfort, that love will never be a comfort ... because love is an invisible force that still lets bad things happen. And how can you believe in the good when you've only got the bad? What's left to hope for?

But without love, what is life? Why do you have a heart? Without something to beat for, the heart is nothing more than the second hand on a watch, ticking away time until there is no time left to keep.

It was then that my mother burst into my room, startling me, causing me to drop my pen. "Jesus!" I shouted. "Haven't you ever heard of knocking?"

"You're my kid! What's the big deal?" The force of her words caused her to lose her balance, and she braced herself against the door frame. Mascara tangled in her lashes and pooled under her eyes, branching out and settling in the fine lines around them. Cherry blossom lipstick feathered around her lips, not quite smeared, but not quite where it needed to be, either. Cherry blossom was what she liked to call her "signature shade."

I didn't necessarily appreciate knowing the story, but her signature shade came to be during the romantic getaway where I was conceived. Since he couldn't take her anywhere in town but a cheap by-the-hour motel, my mother's first "date" with my father was him taking her to a teaching conference in Washington, D.C. The conference took place during the time the Japanese Cherry trees were blooming. She loved to tell the story of how magical it was, how she felt like the blooming flowers were symbols of their blossoming love. And how they walked through the night as fallen petals danced with the wind around their feet, and the elegant aroma of the flowers made the night sweeter. She'd always told me that she'd known my father was "*the one*" and that something special was going to happen when, as they walked, he recited Lord Byron to her. "She walks in beauty, like the night / Of cloudless climes and starry skies; / And all that's best of dark and bright / Meet in her aspect and her eyes." Except he'd added, "and the blossom pink of her beautiful lips is sure to be my demise." I didn't personally feel like that cheesy ending did Lord Byron any justice, but my mom had worn that color of lipstick ever since. It's weird to think she wasn't much older than me and Josie then.

My mother is the kind of woman who used to be pretty, when she cared, but her life stalled somewhere around the time my father started ignoring her, which, at this point, is going on sixteen years. Hell, I don't even remember the guy. His wife found out, he chose her, then left us in the dust. Now, every night, she drowned herself in wine, popping off cork after cork until her papers were graded, her vision was blurry, and she'd fall asleep on the couch. During summer break, she didn't have the papers to distract her, so she'd just drink until she couldn't see straight, sometimes at home—alone and sad—sometimes, at Exciting Irene's, the local watering hole, dancing alone with the jukebox, until some man would offer his half-assed pseudo-chivalry and drive her home. Misery seeking company.

"Privacy, Mom. The big deal is privacy."

She wrinkled her nose. "It reeks in here, Cai. When was the last time you took a shower?"

"I dunno…"

"Then it's been too long. My phone's been blowing up. Lindsey Blair and your Uncle Kurt have been calling over and over and over. With the way the phone calls have been timed, if I didn't know any better, I'd think those two were back messin' together, and that never ends well. What the hell do the two of them want with you, anyway?"

Apparently, Kurt hadn't bothered to tell her about the trouble I'd created or the restitution. Either that, or she'd forgotten. Because I couldn't face Josie, I'd no-showed my penance job at *Blair's Lair* for the entirety of the time I'd wallowed and thrashed in my bed. "Um, it's a long story."

"Well, I've got time," she said, walking over to my bed, plopping herself down, and picking up the bag of pretzels. As she started crunching one, her phone rang, and she groaned. "It's Kurt again. You answer."

She leaned forward and shoved the phone into my palm. Grumbling, I swiped "accept" and grunted into the speaker.

Immediately, he started. "God damn it, Cai! These sisters are serious. What are you doing? If you don't get your ass to that store today, Sophie is going to pursue charges. She was already furious that you broke in, and now I hear that you took their niece out and acted like an ass. There's only so much I can do for you here, kid. Lindsey's kindness will only go so far. If you don't take initiative to help yourself, you're going to catch charges, and there will be nothing I can do to stop it."

He was right. I knew he was right. But did I care? If I'd messed things up with Josie, I couldn't go to that store and rub salt in the wound. Her seeing me would remind her of that night, and me seeing her would remind me of what I could have had if I hadn't acted like a jerk. Or had I not messed anything up at all … yet?

"Caius! Are you listening to me?"

"Yeah. I know," I said with a little more attitude than I should have.

"Apparently, you don't know! The girl doesn't like you, so what? Put your ego aside and get back down to that store, or get your ass put in juvie. The choice is yours, but I suggest you get your shit together."

"She doesn't like me?" It was all I could say.

"Right now, what's there to like, Cai? You're a wannabe criminal who treated her like shit on a date."

I pulled the phone away from my ear in a daze. *She doesn't like me* echoing through my body the way a ghost echoes the rhythms of its old life. I looked at the screen, the timer for the call increasing second by second. I could hear Kurt still bitching at me in the background, but it was almost like I didn't know what to do with the phone—which end was up, what buttons did I push, where did I talk? It slid out of my hand and hit the floor with a thud, Kurt's voice still booming through it.

I could feel my heart in my chest, beating, and I could hear it ticking away time. The sound grew louder and louder until Kurt's thundering voice was nothing, and the sound of passing time was all I could hear.

Tick-tock. You're going to lose her.

Tick-tock.

Tick-tock. Without her, your life has no meaning.

Tick-tock.

Tick-tock. Fix it before the clock stops.

At that moment, I had the most epic realization I'd ever had in my life. I needed to get to Josie and explain. I couldn't wait until it was too late. I wouldn't let the experiences I'd allowed myself to have grind my soul to bits of nothing.

Out of all the crumbling pieces, I decided to choose love.

Maybe I couldn't be everyone's hero, but I could damn sure be my own. Because even I, Caius Duke, wanted a happily ever after. And I was going to break the cycle, and I was going to get it.

****

To get to the shower, I had to walk past the bar, and as I did, a wave of memory hit so hard it almost knocked me over, and I let it sweep me into its undertow.

The first time I had a drink was on my tenth birthday.

"Ahh, double digits," my grandfather said as we sat on our respective stools at the basement bar, him with an Old Crow, me with a Coke. We had all our good conversations this way.

"Yeah!" I exclaimed. "I'm ten! In ten more years, I'll be twenty!" Twenty had seemed like such a big number then, such a long way away.

He laughed the way he always did, pulling up the left corner of his mouth and breathing out a series of quiet hiccups while his eyes focused on something no one else could see. "That means I need to teach you the ways of being a man, son." I loved when he called me *son*—it made me feel important to him.

"Did you teach Uncle Kurt?" I said, bumping my dangling feet in rapid succession against the base of the bar.

"I did," he said soundly, wisely. "He was a little older than you, but I might not be around that long."

"Grandpa!" I was always appalled when he talked like that. Looking back, though, it was like he'd always known I'd end up raising myself.

"I'll tell you everything I know," he said, grabbing an ice cube from the bar bucket and plunking it down into a glass. "It isn't much, but it'll get you where you need to be," he continued, pouring a tiny bit of Old Crow from his glass slowly over the ice cube. "Now, look," he went on, sliding the glass down to me.

I caught it without much thought. "Look at what?" I asked petulantly.

"Men don't kick their feet against the damn bar," he said with his "I've had enough" tone.

Immediately, I stopped. "Sorry."

"Nothing to be sorry for, son. You're just learning the ropes." He winked at me. "Being a good man is a form of art. Now," he said, lighting a Lucky Strike and walking over to me. "You drink your bourbon straight and your coffee black, but it's going to take you a while to appreciate those two things in their natural state. So, we're going to start you off slow. The ice," he said, taking a long drag on his cigarette, "lets the flavors of the bourbon blossom and calms the kick of it down a little." He exhaled the smoke over my head and swallowed what was left in his glass as a single shot, slapping the empty glass against the counter. "Now, first thing's first. You keep your drink here" —he shoved my glass to my left— "and you keep your smokes here," he said, shoving them into my shirt's breast pocket. "And you've gotta get yourself a thing, a trademark, you know, your signature style. Something that defines you."

"But, Grandpa, how do I know what that is?"

He lifted his hat off his head and ran his hand over this thinning hair, before fitting it back down onto his skull. "It'll come to ya, kid." As much as I loved when he called me *son*, I hated when he called me *kid*. "And it will help you grow up. If you ask me, with the way you always have your nose in a book, it looks to me like you're going to be a writer. And being a writer is good—it's all about opening up and giving the world a glimpse of yourself."

I smiled at the thought of myself as an adult. I had always pictured myself much like him—with a drink and a book always in my hand. And now a laptop at my side.

Clearing his throat, he continued. "You're going to need to know how to change a tire and your oil. You're also going to need to know how to use a set of tools. You make sure you fix your own shit—don't rely on anyone else."

"What shit?"

"Everything. You need to know how to fix your toilet and your mistakes."

At that age, I couldn't understand how the two correlated, but as I got older, his implication became clearer.

"Never stop reading books. Travel the world. Hold doors for strangers. Find the right woman, and always treat your woman like a lady—"

"How do I do that?"

"You respect her." He pointed his finger at me. "And men don't interrupt. They listen."

I zipped an imaginary zipper across my lips.

"When you find the right one, you'll know. You don't come across many people in life who give you butterflies, and if you don't listen to those butterflies, if you don't open their cage inside you and set them free, your whole life will feel like a prison. When you find your person, you love her like there will be no tomorrow. You love her like you can't live a day without her because the truth is, son, that you can't."

"Is that how you love Granny?"

"I wouldn't live a day on this earth without her." His eyes went to that far-off place for a moment before he spoke again. "Anyway, back to business. Don't pick your nose, and don't be a bad speller. Whatever you're doing, make sure you commit to it—writing, loving, tightening a damn screw—it's all, or it's nothing. Don't be wishy-washy, and don't do things half-assed."

I giggled. "You said ass."

"Interrupting, Cai."

My eyes widened, and I nodded.

He went on with his list. "Don't drift through life oblivious. Life will teach you a lot, if you let it." His eyes wandered back to that place no one else could see.

"What will it teach me?"

He stubbed out his cigarette, blowing out the last of the smoke in his lungs. "It'll teach you everything I'm not teaching you. Life and love are their own kind of magic. But that doesn't mean they won't break you. They break all of us, and don't you forget that. We all break."

"Even you?"

"Yes, even me. The trick is that you've got to learn how to put yourself back together. Always put yourself back together. *Always fix your shit.* Sometimes, you'll want to stay broken, but you can't, Caius. You've got to live, and you've got to love, and don't ever turn your back on the magic." He rumpled my hair. "Now, cheers!" He held his glass up and nodded, telling me to do the same. "To all the magic you'll pull out of your hat, son. May your life be nothing short of spectacular."

And that's about where my memory of that day ends, courtesy of that one diesel fuel shot of Old Crow, which I didn't try again until three years later. I hadn't thought of that day in ages, but as I boarded the Converse Express to get to Josie, it seemed so very important to remember the magic.

Chapter Eleven
The Lovers

Be with me always - take any form - drive me mad! only
do not leave me in this abyss, where I cannot find you!
Oh, God! it is unutterable! I can not live without my life!
I can not live without my soul!
—Emily Brontë, Wuthering Heights

Josephine

The door squeaked on its hinges as I pulled it open to walk into the store. Home. But not home. The tears that had started on the way back from the grave poured down my face. Shutting the door as quietly as I could, I put my back against it and slunk down, heaving in a breath that sounded like wind blowing over empty glass bottles. I put my hand over my mouth and bit my fingers, trying to quiet myself so that I wouldn't wake up my aunts, but the more I fought against my body's visceral reactions, the more noise I made and the emptier I sounded. It was late enough that I knew Aunt Sophie would be in bed, but Aunt Lindsey was a wildcard, and since she'd known I was going out, I had a feeling she'd be waiting up, and I desperately did not want to draw attention to myself in the state I was in.

I'd had moments like this before, these hollowed out explosions born of a Molotov cocktail of emotions. The first time it happened was when my mother told me her prognosis. The next time was when, while holding my hand, she shut her eyes for the final time. That moment was like a wrecking ball crashing into my guts, tearing through me and collapsing all my bones. It was a hollowness I'd never experienced before. It was lonely. It was final in a way nothing else had ever been. Nothing bad or sad I'd ever experienced before explained what happened to me right then, and I expected nothing ever would. The finite loss of my mother was something to which no other atrocity could compare, but Caius turning cold during a moment of fear and vulnerability came in at a close second, and not only did it devastate me in a way I couldn't yet fathom, it really pissed me off. However, the response to my anger always fell short of where it should've been—it was never immediate rage. It wasn't shouting or throwing or breaking things, even though I wished I'd done all those things to him. I never got mad *in* the moment I should have, but after. When whatever bad thing would happen to me, I'd be shocked, a deer in headlights, simply unable to process the event or information at hand. *"I shouldn't have told you a scary story in the dark,"* and *"I have stage four cancer. There is no stage five,"* processed much in the same way as, *"Would you like to supersize that?"* Like, who cares? Bad news or traumatic events triggered an immediate void in me, a denial of sorts, and it usually wouldn't be until later—sometimes moments, sometimes weeks—that the gravity or the terror would hit me. It had always been that way—like all these emotions swelled up until something inside me broke and unleashed an unholy flood of grief and anger. That's when I'd cry.

It's not that I'm the type that is embarrassed about tears. Honestly, my mother is worth every single one I'd shed over her illness and loss. However, the tears I was crying from Caius making me feel comfortable enough to share my pain to only then be met with cold indifference … not cool. At all. I was sad to lose the affection of a boy I'd only just met, but I was also furious at him and furious with myself for even caring at all. I kept trying to reason with myself. Who was he? No one but a thief. And I wished I believed that, but the depth of my own heart was telling me there was more. I don't know why Caius was jerking me around, acting like he had no idea what had happened. I wasn't crazy. I wasn't crazy when we first touched and the both of us had a shared experience of cosmic electricity. I felt it, and he did too. Since then, we'd felt a pull toward each other that neither one of us could explain. While I might have been the only one to actually see and experience the terror of the ghostly, evil man at the witch's tomb, I know in the pit of my soul that Caius, at a minimum, *felt* something.

As I stayed against the door for support, I focused on the motor of the Coke machine as it hummed, trying to breathe along with it in rhythm to calm myself down. The more I calmed down, the more I thought something chocolate might make me feel even better, so, with puffy eyes, I padded through the store, but a light, warm glow spilling through the beads in the doorway of Aunt Lindsey's tarot room caught my attention, and I decided to go to her.

So much was churning inside me. The beginning of what felt like a perfect date had turned into a late-night horror flick, but with all the maudlin tragedy of a doomed romance novel. I wanted to make sense of it. I wanted answers. Maybe Aunt Lindsey's cards held them.

The beads clinked and clacked as I walked through, and Aunt Lindsey was there to greet me as though she had been waiting. She held my gaze momentarily before turning from me and going back to where she had been sitting at the reading table.

Protection crystals—smoky quartz, amethyst, labradorite, obsidian, and red jasper—were littered across the table, along with several decks of tarot cards. This was bizarre even by Aunt Lindsey's standards. The table on which she performed readings was nearly sacred to her, and she was meticulous in the placement of her deck, but tonight, it looked like someone had ransacked the table, and I was looking down at the scene of a crime. Each deck was scattered like she'd shuffled them a million times, unsatisfied with the results. But most peculiar was the fact that from each deck, she'd pulled the Emperor, the Empress, and Death. All in that order. Three sets of eyes, all of them were looking at me, and the energy coming from the table was thick and hot. What was worse was that she held The Devil card in her hand but turned it away when she saw my eyes graze over it.

"Have a seat, honey," Aunt Lindsey said, glancing strangely back and forth between me and the table. She didn't mention me looking distraught or having heard me crying.

Lowering myself in front of her, I tried obscuring the fact that her table and the look in her eyes had me a little concerned. This night was full of unsettling things.

"Tell me how your night was," Aunt Lindsey asked, raising her eyebrow as she crossed her legs underneath her long patchwork skirt, shoved the Devil in her pocket, and leaned back in her chair.

"Can you tell me anything about the witch who wouldn't stay buried?" I asked, ignoring her precise question.

Her eyes glazed, and there was a flash of worry with a hint of something else I couldn't quite identify. She started speaking, stopped, furrowed her brow, then sighed. Why she was so bothered by this was what I couldn't understand. She interrupted me just as I was about to ask. "So he took you there, eh?"

"Yes," I answered. "He did."

"Interesting choice. I'll give him points for creativity," she said, the corners of her lips turning upward in a stiff smile. She was trying to play cool, but her energy was as hard as a brick wall.

"I'm surprised tonight is the first time I've ever heard anything about it, especially since it's a local legend, and you're the local witch."

She laughed tersely.

"What do you know about it?" I asked again.

"Oh, I know just as much as anybody," she said quietly, leaning in toward me like she was telling me a secret. Who did she think was going to hear her?

"Yeah?" I was getting impatient. "What's that?"

She was acting strange, and I guess if strange was going to occur, I assumed it needed to happen all in one night. "Stories vary," she said, shifting, looking left, right, then back to me.

"That's what Caius said, but I'm surprised you, of all people, don't know anything at all about it."

"I'm not omniscient, Josie."

"Whatever," I said. "You really know *nothing* about her?"

"I don't know anything that nobody else doesn't know."

I rolled my eyes.

Aunt Lindsey pulled a cigarette out of her case and lit it.

I scowled at her, and she waved the smoke around, trying to fan it away from me while she took a long drag. "Oh, give me a break, sassy pants. You just asked me about a ghost," she said, stubbing the cigarette out in an overcrowded ashtray.

I coughed and crinkled my nose just to make my point of how much I hated smoking.

"Did anything else happen tonight, Josie? Is there anything you want to tell me? I wasn't going to mention it, but you look like you've had a rough night."

I allowed her to change the subject a bit because I

thought that if I opened up, she might be more inclined to also. "Well, Caius turned into a bit of a dickhead while we were there, and then he brought me back here and walked off." I left out what I had a hard time explaining since Aunt Lindsey was also being secretive.

"What do you mean, exactly?"

"It's just, like, he got all weird." I began to get angry again, because I knew I should be having this conversation with Caius, not my aunt—who was as cool as they came and understood a lot of crazy stuff—but how could I ever explain everything that had happened in a rational way? As open minded as she was, I thought the night's events would even evoke some skepticism in her. And if not skepticism, she would probably ban me from ever seeing Caius again, and I wasn't sure I wanted that.

"Oh, boys will be boys. He didn't … *try anything* with you on that tombstone, did he?"

I thought back to the running high school dare to have sex on the witch's tomb.

"No! His energy just shifted, and he got cold and aloof."

"Ugh, boys!" she replied, but it didn't look like that was what she really wanted to say.

"I guess. I've never really been out with one before."

"I'm sorry to hear he acted that way, honey. I'll make sure to work him extra hard for treating my girl like that and ruining her first date," she said, a bit more relaxed and more like the Aunt Lindsey I was used to. She leaned back in her chair but still looked at me as though she were trying to figure out something.

My eyes wandered down to the disheveled table at all the repetitive pairings of cards.

Aunt Lindsey put her hand over mine and in a low, serious voice, whispered, "You know as long as you are under this roof, I will protect you?" She sounded more like she was trying to convince herself than me.

Her words and the gravity with which she spoke them caused the hairs on the back of my neck to stand on end. I flicked my gaze back to her, the pace of my heart jumping track in my chest. Protect me from what? What did she see that she wasn't telling me? There was a terror, a certain kind of nameless dread filling me up. It was old, something that I suspect my soul understood, even if my brain didn't. I stood up quickly, with the urge to get out of the room and breathe different air.

"Good night, Aunt Lindsey. I love you," I said, not giving her the chance to say anything else to me or have my questions answered about the witch that wouldn't stay buried. I suspected she knew far more than she led on, and hopefully, I'd get it out of her, but I needed the comfort of my bed—something level and not moving—so that maybe my organs could stop their rotation on the tilt-a-whirl that was going on inside me. And suddenly, I was totally drained. I held onto the sides of the wall as I made my way up the steps and to my bedroom. It was all I could do to flip the covers back and crawl in. I sat my phone on the bedside table and snuggled into my pillow, and while drifting in and out of sleep, I replayed the entirety of the night. Somewhere in the middle of reliving every blissful, romantic moment, I heard my phone ring, distantly. It was way too late for phone calls, and I somehow knew before even picking it up that Caius was on the other end.

Sighing, I answered the phone. I could hear him breathing on the other end, but he wouldn't speak. At the sound of his breath without a word of apology, all my previous anger came flooding back. Tears stung the corners of my eyes, and I snapped at him. Seconds went by between us with nothing said until Caius awkwardly told me he'd been dreaming about me.

Then he was gone.

I moved around in my bed repeating hellos in case I'd lost my cell signal, but there was nothing but silence to answer. I thought about calling him back. I wanted to. I wanted the unsettling feeling I had clawing its way around my stomach to stop, and hearing his voice, the change in tone, the warmth in it that felt familiar and safe, did make me feel better. And greedily, I wanted more. But, stubbornly, I waited for him to call back. And he didn't.

More than anything, I wanted the dread I felt when looking down at Aunt Lindsey's tarot card table to make sense. And somehow, I knew that Caius and I together had the map to get to the key to unlock that mystery. It was just one of those feelings I had. Something I knew to be true in the very core of my being.

The Emperor, the Empress, and Death. What message did they have for us?

****

My phone buzzed. Everything in me wanted it to be Caius, but it wasn't.

Jamal: **i miss my friend**

The few weeks in Bridgeport had felt like an eternity away from my life in Connecticut. Jamal's text reminded me so much of that previous life, and for a moment, as I swiped to open it, everything almost felt normal. Like deja vu all scrambled up and in reverse because it isn't, like, some grand, cosmic feeling of a past life—you actually know what you're missing out on. And I really was missing it.

The more I tried to figure out what to say back and the more I thought of him and the sound of his judgmental yet somehow soothing friend voice, the more I mourned for everything about Connecticut. Sitting up in bed after moping around for a week, I fired a text back.

Me: **when can we meet? ever?**

I watched eagerly as the three dots in the left corner of my messages waved up and down.

Jamal: **umm, school doesn't start until August 18th. i think my parents would let me come down for a week, but only because they love you so much**

My heart seized up in my chest. Jamal's parents had always been so kind to me. He and I had been friends for more of our lives than not. I'd spent so much time at his house, it was hard for me to think there would be no more days of me just getting up and walking over, or riding the bus to his house, or him randomly showing up to mine.

Me: **omg that would be amazing. really? you think so?**

Jamal: **totally...**

Me: **i'll ask the aunts. i'm sure they'll be fine with it**

Jamal: **hopefully, they'll be okay with me staying... what's there to do in Bridgeport?**

Me: **literally nothing.**

Jamal: **nothing? wow, that sounds great.**

Me: **Jamal...**

Jamal: **oh no. i can feel your texts. what's wrong?**

Me: **there's this guy**

Jamal: **guy?? deets!**

Me: **he took me on a date.**

Jamal: **Ooo... did he kiss you? Did Josie get her first real kiss?**

Me: **...but it didn't go all that great. Now, it's been, like, a week since we've spoken, and i am super bummed.**

Jamal: **ew. I don't like him already. Has this**

douche-canoe hurt my bestie? I'll bitchslap him so hard, he'll regret ever laying eyes on you

> Me: **no. i dunno.**
> Jamal: **i don't like the sound of your voice here.**
> Me: **we're texting.**
> Jamal: **shut up. You know what I mean.**
> Me: **his name is Caius.**
> Jamal: **what the hell kind of name is Caius?**
> Me: **a name, i guess?**

I smiled a little, imagining Jamal's ears perking up at this info dump. What I'd really die for was to have him here, comforting me. I would have loved to have my best friend holed-up in my room with me, eating ice cream, doing make-up, laughing and crying about boys, life … life without my mom. There had been so many major events within the last month. So much had happened to me. I needed my best friend's advice, the familiarity of something solid in what felt like a foreign land. And the longer I didn't hear from Caius, the more I felt like this strange, foreign land was going to swallow me.

> Jamal: **what are you not telling me?**

I didn't know that he'd quite understand all the other craziness, but Jamal had a way of picking up my vibe. He always joked that I was part of his "vibe tribe."

"Everything," I thought to myself, but instead, I texted something vague.

> Me: **i miss you. please make this visit happen. i'll tell you everything then.**
> Jamal: **tell me now!!!!!**
> Me: **it's hard to explain. He broke into my aunt's store, got caught, and now he's working off his debt…**

This was followed by a rap sheet of incoming texts.

Jamal: **are you crazy?**
Jamal: **have you lost your mind?**
Jamal: **wtf???**
Jamal: **a thief!?!?!?! A fucking thief?!?!?!?**
Jamal: **RED FLAG, JOSIE. RED FUCKING FLAG!**

I instantly regretted telling Jamal that part. I knew what I told him sounded bad, but I knew, regardless of how hurt I'd been at how our date ended, that somewhere deep down, Caius was not a bad person—that, in fact, he was good and kind. It was hard to explain something you just felt in your bones, but that was Caius ... a boy who was embedded in part of me somehow. That red electric moment of recognition triggered something dormant in both of us, but when telling someone else, that sounded completely crazy, and I knew it did. I knew how I'd react if Jamal were telling me the same thing about a boy, and it wasn't all that different from the way he was reacting. But what was between Caius and me was something more than a chemical reaction or a simple little crush. It was a matter of two souls speaking to each other. I could no more deny it than Caius could. Fight it, try as we may, we were coming for each other, and we had been coming for each other for a long time. We just hadn't known until a few weeks ago.

Three light knocks on my door drove me from my thoughts and took me away from Jamal's barrage of angry incoming texts that I couldn't answer. I knew I couldn't leave him on "delivered" forever, but now, I reasoned, I had a door to open—a different kind of call to answer, so it was sort of like call-waiting, and I was clicking over, putting Jamal on hold.

I slid off the bed and padded across the floor. The old knob fought with me for a moment before finally giving way and allowing me to open the door. As it swung open, I was glad I'd left my phone on the bed. Otherwise, I'm sure I would've dropped it and shattered the screen into a million pieces. It was another reminder of my mom being gone. Anytime I'd drop my phone, she'd yell at me, reminding me that she'd bought me a case protector that I always refused to put on because it felt too bulky. Leaning with one hand against the wall by my door frame like he owned the place was Caius, looking equal parts remorseful and smug. He straightened himself up, tucked his hair behind his ears, and parted his lips to say something, but I didn't give him the chance.

"What the hell are you doing here?" I was suddenly aware I hadn't really left my room for the better half of a week and that it was well into the afternoon. I'd had on the same pajamas for two days, and I couldn't remember when I'd last brushed my hair. "Better yet, how did you get up here?" I said, quickly moving my hands to my hair, trying to smooth down what frizz I felt.

"First, I work here, remember? Second, Linds is the one who sent me up after I'd mopped the floor and some other shit. Of course, she mentioned something about hurrying … I can't imagine why." He trailed off, a coy smile playing at his lips as he glanced up and down my pink elephant PJs.

I flushed but held my ground, letting several silent moments pass between us as I stared him dead in the eyes, and to his credit, he did not flinch. We were communicating without words.

He lifted his hand, hesitated, then continued with the motion of grabbing one of mine and cupping it in his. "I'm a dick, Josie. I'm sor—"

I crashed into his lips, hungry for a reunion. I'd waited a week to feel his lips on mine again, and we melted into each other. My arms draped around his neck, his curled around my waist. It lasted both forever and not long enough, but finally, I pulled away from him slowly, breathlessly.

"Wow," he said, as his breath rushed in and out with a quiet, happy resonance. "I can't say I expected to get off the hook that easily."

"Don't ruin it by being a smartass."

Pulling farther back from me, he ran his fingers across his lips like he was zipping a zipper, locking a lock, and flicking away a tiny key.

"You wanna go somewhere?" After all the moping I'd done, I was tired of the four walls of my bedroom and the confines of *Blair's Lair*.

"I absolutely do."

"Cool! Turn around and let me get changed."

"Oh, but I like the little pink elephants. I think it's a good look."

"Oh, you do?"

"I mean, I would prefer you out of them, but…"

"Shut up!" I laughed, feeling my face flush, then playfully tossed my pajama shirt over my head at him. "You can wear it if you want."

"Pink really isn't my color. It doesn't go with my eyes." Ugh, if he only knew that *everything* went with those eyes.

"Suit yourself, then." I popped back up beside him, fully dressed and with a coat of mascara on. We both laughed, locked fingers, and walked out of the room.

At the top of the stairs, before going down to the store, I curled my arm around Caius's waist and turned to kiss him again. Kissing, I'd realized, was absolutely amazing. I couldn't imagine anything more magical than the electricity of our lips moving together. I looped my thumbs in the belt loops of his pants and pulled him toward me, smiling. I tightened my grip on his belt loops in anticipation, and right before our lips touched, my finger brushed something cool and smooth.

I quickly moved my eyes downward and saw the tip of a card poking out of his pocket. It was a brightly colored yellow sun with the tops of two blood red wings. I didn't need to see the rest of the card to know what it was. I'd seen it a hundred times before. What I didn't know, didn't understand, like so many of the things that had been happening, was why Caius had The Lovers tarot card in his pocket?

But then his lips met mine, and nothing else mattered.

Chapter Twelve
Karma

Men are not punished for their sins, but by them.
—Elbert Hubbard

Caius

"Wait just a minute, you two." Lindsey stopped us as we were heading out the door of *Blair's Lair*. "Come in here. I need to talk to you." Her voice drifted through the beads of her witch hut.

I bent down and whispered into Josie's ear. "We can just act like we didn't hear her. C'mon."

She giggled quietly but grabbed my hand and dragged me through Lindsey's magic door.

I'd showed up to work on time, mopped the entire store, changed light bulbs, greased all the door hinges, scraped off all the gum, and picked up all the cigarette butts in the parking lot—eighty-six percent of which were Lindsey's—and I had replaced a toilet seat that didn't need replacing. Lindsey said she had added that last job just to adjust my shitty attitude, and I just smiled and nodded as she said it. Karma. You reap what you sow, and in this case, karma had gifted me a stinky, public toilet seat. I understood, but I was over it for the day. I was ready to spend the afternoon with this beautiful, amazing girl who'd found the grace to forgive me for my sins against her.

As soon as the last bead slinked off my back and we were in the room, Lindsey abruptly motioned to her table covered in a tapestry. "Sit down. The both of you. We need to have a talk, figure some things out." She was officious and firm, and those are two adjectives I'd never used to describe that woman.

We plopped down.

"Listen," she started. "I know you two are young, but there are some things you need to know. Sophie doesn't agree with my telling you—she thinks it will influence your decisions, but I think it's important you are both educated on the matter."

Josie's breath caught, and I knew what was coming.

"Lindsey, I know what a condom is, and I know how to not make a baby. It isn't 1950—everyone knows how to have safe sex."

Lindsey looked at me like I'd come from outer space, and I could see Josie's wide eyes in my peripheral vision.

"Look," I said, pulling the tarot card I'd swiped out of my pocket, "I didn't take this card because I wanted to have sex. It had fallen on the ground by the table."

Lindsey rolled her eyes toward me, skeptically.

"Honest. It was on the floor. The weird thing is, I swear to God, I heard the thing whispering, but when I picked it up, there was no sound anywhere. I even put the thing to my ear and said 'hello' like an idiot." I pulled the card out of my pocket and handed it to the local witch.

As she snatched it from my fingers, it slipped from her grasp and fell back to the floor.

"Well, this is interesting," she said. "Very, very interesting." She flipped another card off a deck on the table, looked at it, then put it in her own pocket. "Go on. Get out of here. Go have some fun, and come see me as soon as you get back. I need to meditate." Her eyes wandered, and her voice trailed off into thought. Then she said with a start, "Now!" With that, she was already up and digging through the drawers where she kept bundles of herbs.

"Aunt Lindsey, are you okay—"
"I said get out!" she snapped.

SASHA HIBBS & CHRISTINA HOOKER

Chapter Thirteen
Destiny, thy Double-Edged Sword

I defy you, stars.
—William Shakespeare, Romeo and Juliet

Josephine

I knew as soon as we got out of that room Caius was going to ask me what the hell was wrong with my aunt, and the truth was that I had no idea. Sometimes Aunt Lindsey was weird, and while I'd never seen her this strange before, I'd also never spent this much time with her nor under these circumstances.

As he sucked in a breath to start his questions, I cut him off. "I don't know. I don't know what she's talking about, and I don't know what is going on with her. Let's just get out of here and go have some fun." Smiling, I jokingly nudged him, but the truth was still there, perhaps silent and hanging between us, but ever present.

Caius looked at me from the corner of his eye, and then I watched his lips slowly turn up. "I like the sound of that. I want…" He hesitated, and I could see he was struggling for the right words. "Another chance." He paused again, turning toward me, raising his hand, gently motioning between the two of us. "A do-over."

"So, no witch's grave?"

He slid his hand in mine, and we started walking out of *Blair's Lair*.

"No," he said a little under his breath, and I could sense him turning somewhat serious, which was an interesting look on his face. I'd not seen his serious side yet. "But I know somewhere, in some fucked up cosmic way, that night, that place was important."

I knew he was referring to the toxic energy that occurred moments after arriving at the resting place of the witch who wouldn't stay buried.

We both slid through the door, and I clung to his hand, following wherever he was about to lead me. "I know what you mean," I offered up to him, to the fast-approaching dusk, wondering what secrets the universe, with its omnipotent power, clutched to its starry breast. There was so much left unsaid between us. I didn't want him to struggle alone. "Caius, I don't understand what this thing is between us. I don't know why you and I have this strange connection … all I know is that we do. It exists. And I like that it does." I glanced sideways at him, trying to gauge his mood, his feelings. "Whatever this is, I want it." I stopped, turning to face him. "I want *you*."

He tucked a loose strand of hair behind my ear, the gentle caress sending shocks of subtle heat down my earlobe, my neck, through my chest, and all the way into the pit of my stomach. He answered with a soft kiss, brushing my lips with the fullness of his. I knew those lips. Our lips were not strangers, and not just because we'd recently kissed. Through his sweet kisses, I wondered deep down if he and I would ever get to the bottom of our connection. He pulled away from me slowly, still keeping his arms around my waist, his face still inches from mine. "How does Dairy Queen sound to you?"

"I love ice cream," I whispered, my eyes still closed.

"Let me guess," he said playfully, as we resumed an even stride. "Chocolate is your favorite?"

"No." I smiled. "Straw–"

At the same time, I was cut off, him finishing my sentence as though in recognition, "Strawberry is your favorite."

Continuing down the sidewalk, I glanced at him and then back ahead. He seemed a little lost in thought, but whatever he was thinking, he kept to himself.

"You know, I kind of blew it with the local lore last date, but I do have one trick left up my sleeve."

"You mean other than getting ice cream?" I said, squeezing his hand in mine, trying to be playful.

"Yeah, I think it's better than ice cream … Josie," he said, and I loved the sound of my name on his lips, "how do you feel about carnivals?" He looked down at me with a hopeful, innocent smile, like he was asking me to accept him. It made me wonder if he'd ever been himself with anyone, had ever allowed himself to be vulnerable. I felt special that he trusted me.

"Carnivals, hmm..." I said, gently tapping my chin in playful thought.

"It's usually pretty cool. There are food trucks from all over—my favorite from last year was called Zombie Dawgz—they had one called Juan of the Dead that was great, and then they had vegetarian dogs called the Undead, and I'm a sucker for a pun. I hope they come back! And the city has perfected the fireworks show—it's famous across three counties. But, the best part about the whole thing is … the rides aren't janky. Bridgeport puts a lot of effort into summer going out with a bang."

"I think going to a carnival with you would be fun." And I truly did. Riding the Ferris wheel with Caius, sitting next to him as we climbed to the top of the sky, looking out at the city lights below us. It felt like it could be magical.

We stopped just short of the Dairy Queen counter. "I'll take a vanilla dipped in chocolate, and m'lady will have a strawberry cone," Caius said, pulling out a wadded up five-dollar bill from his pocket and slapping it down on the sticky counter.

"When is this carnival?"

"Right before school starts in August."

The wheels in my head started turning. I figured now was as good a time as any to tell him about one of my best friends, Jamal. "That's perfect."

"Oh yeah? Why's that?" he said, raising a skeptical brow at my playful tone.

The lady from the counter yelled back behind her to the kitchen. "Two cones! One strawberry, and one vanilla dipped in chocolate!"

We walked to the second window—the pick-up window—and Caius grabbed our cones, handing me my strawberry one. "Wanna keep walking?" he asked.

"Yes." I didn't want my time with him to ever end.

Chapter Fourteen
The Knowing

When you know, you know.

Caius

I knew I loved her. I could tell by the way her hand fit in mine, and the way her smile stretched across her face, quirking upward slightly higher in the right corner. I knew by the way the light caught the rose-colored gem at the corner of her brow and the hints of honey in her hair. I knew by the sound of her giggles, bubbles rising to the top of a glass. I knew by her anger, short waves of fierce intensity.

I couldn't stop thinking about the excitement of the carnival—the sweet cotton candy air, the neon lights … and the curve of her neck, and the arch of her back. The subtle way her fingertips traced the line of my jaw. The way I could infinitely let her lips move across mine. The way her hands felt in my hair.

I am a flower, full of need, and she is the sun after a long winter.

I think I have always loved her. All of my life, my soul has searched for something I could not define. When Josie's hand touched mine, I knew, without a doubt, our souls were made of the same thing—cherry bombs, waiting for *that* moment to burst into red smoke and become the only air we breathed. She is the feast of my soul that's been starved across lifetimes, waiting for nothing more than the taste of her.

Sweet and beautiful Josie.

In all the world, there will never be a love more perfect for me than hers, just as my love was made for her and her alone.

And then something bit through me—a feeling colder than cold, something so cold it burned, and somewhere in the far back of my mind, I heard that vicious laugh and shuddered.

Chapter Fifteen
Cosmic Stuff

*So we beat on, boats against the current, borne back
ceaselessly into the past.*
—F. Scott Fitzgerald

Josephine

He grunted and shivered. We walked on without
speaking for a few moments, eating our ice cream, but
Caius seemed like his mind was somewhere else.
Nervously, I interrupted the silence. "Ice cream
headache?"

"Um, yeah, so, as I was saying, a carnival at the
end of summer would be great." He looked at me as
though, for a moment, he forgot I was right beside him.
"Oh, yeah, sorry. Go on."

I smiled. "Where were you just then?"

Through a quick lick of his ice cream, he replied,
"Oh, nowhere. Just in my own head. So, why's the timing
of the carnival so perfect?"

"You'll get to meet my best friend, Jamal," I said,
taking a nice chunk out of my strawberry cone.

He scrunched his brows together, lines of worry
slightly visible around the edges of his eyes. I thought the
look was a cute one on him. "Does she live around here?"
he asked, turning more fully to me. "I think I'm confused.
You have friends here?"

I chuckled. "No. No friends but you here. Jamal is
from Connecticut and *she* is a *he*, and *he* will be flying
down here about the same time as this carnival—right
before school."

Caius nearly choked on his cone, a few flakes of
the chocolate hitting his black shirt, quickly melting to

invisibility. "Jamal's a dude?"

I laughed so hard I almost spit ice cream. "Yes, Jamal is a dude. We've been friends since first grade…" I trailed off, thinking, then got more serious. "I've actually been kind of lost without him. I told you about him a little bit on date one. I see how much you were paying attention," I said with an accusatory look. "He's always been there, and now, there's so much space between us that it's weird. Like, he used to come over every day before school and make sure my outfit didn't clash with his. Now, when I put on a t-shirt, there is no one to tell me, *'Oh, honey, we can't walk down the halls together with you in* that*'.*"

"I mean … I can, if you want … but Nirvana," he said, pointing to the big, yellow smiley face with X's for eyes on his t-shirt, "pretty much goes with anything." He threw his lopsided grin, put his arm around me, and kissed my head.

****

The shadows were growing longer as the sun began to set. Caius and I had long finished our ice cream, but we were still walking the streets of Bridgeport, for lack of wanting to go home. The fading light and the prospect of our date coming to an end made me overly sentimental. "You know," I began, "there are moments when I forget she's gone. It's like I wake up, and the world is just as it should be. My heart is full, and everything is peaceful. It's usually just as I am waking up. I'm coming out of some dream, my eyes are closed, and I'm expecting everything in the world to be what I am used to it being when they open, like, for everything to be the way it's *supposed* to be. The way it's always been. Then I open them. And I'm not in my bedroom. I am not in my apartment. I am not in Connecticut. And I don't have a mom. And it's like this fist with razor-knuckles punches through my stomach. And it's like she's just died all over again."

"I'm so sorry, Josie, truly and epically sorry that your mother was so special to you, and you've lost her. I'd break into Heaven and steal her back for you, if I could. I'd give you mine, but you wouldn't want her. I'd trade anything to take away this ache for you. I really would."

My gaze was fixed on Caius. The way his lips moved, the smallest of dimples that appeared, but you had to be up close to even notice them, the glimmer in his green eyes that shone for me, for us, and I knew those small flickers of light illuminated based on a belief in us together, and my heart, overfilled with emotion, felt as though it could burst from my chest.

My fingers found his, and as our hands locked, so did our eyes. There was so much spoken between us, communicated wordlessly between our souls. I had no doubt in this very moment Caius and I were speaking the language of love, an old love. We were not new to each other. My soul recognized his, and his, mine. As the sun sunk below the horizon, rays of fuchsia and orange reaching out into the beyond, I didn't question our connection. It felt right, and I accepted it. I rejoiced in it. I squeezed his hand, ignoring the apprehension I'd kept in the back of my mind since meeting him, the feeling I couldn't quite put a finger on, trying to keep it contained for fear that if I acknowledged it, I'd lose everything— the feeling of electric red we shared, that evil that showed itself at the witch's grave, something else would conquer our love and take him from me.

I thought about cards. I thought about the cards Aunt Lindsey had drawn over and over again. I thought about The Lovers in Caius's pocket. I hoped Aunt Lindsey had something, even an intuition, that would piece this all together, because as I held his hand in mine and our eyes spoke of lifetimes, I finally felt hope. I felt a purpose. And more importantly, I knew regardless of what the cards held, Caius and I were designed for each other. We were made of the same cosmic stuff. And I knew beyond anything in this world or the next, that I loved this emotional-wreckage-misunderstood-loner-longing-to-be-found man-child sitting beside me, looking at me as though I meant everything to him.

Because he did to me.

Chapter Sixteen
The Soul Connection

You and I, we are embers from the same fire, dust from the same star, echoes of the same love.
—Crieg Crippen

Caius

Lindsey was fluttering around her room with a braided hunk of grass and a giant feather, wafting the smoke into the four corners, and chanting. An unlit cigarette bounced at the side of her mouth as she repeatedly recited, "Into this smoke, I release all that does not serve this household. I rid all negative energies and only allow joy and love to fill this space."

Leaning down to Josie, I whispered in her ear, asking what in the actual hell her aunt was doing.

"Cleansing."

"That doesn't look like cleaning to me."

"Not cleaning. Cleansing. She's using white sage to purify this space."

"Looks like she gathered yard clippings to me." I couldn't begin to imagine the mask of utter confusion that was plastered on my face.

"You see," she continued, "negative energy has a way of accumulating, especially when you do what Aunt Lindsey does for a living, and bad vibes tend to stick around and affect everything. So, every now and then, you need to cleanse yourself and your surroundings. White sage … it just gets out all the gross."

Before I could react, Lindsey turned to us. "Good, you're back. Sit down." She motioned to her fancy table. It was cleared of all her crazy cards and colored rocks and had a shiny, colorful shell sitting like a dish on the edge of it. Josie and I sat, side by side, and Lindsey plopped down, tossing what was left of the hunk of grass—er, white sage—she was burning into that shell. Smoke curled upward and hung, creating a haze between us. Lindsey tossed her unlit cigarette on the table, took both hands and wafted the smoke farther into the air. Closing her eyes and taking a deep breath, she murmured, "So it is." Then she exhaled.

I grabbed Josie's hand, winding my fingers through hers and looked at her, mouthing, "So what is? What the f—"

Before I could finish, Lindsey opened her eyes, and Josie squeezed my hand, silently shutting me up. "What's up, Aunt Linds?"

She did not immediately respond with words, but hurriedly reached under the table and pulled out two bright red candles tied together with what appeared to be more dead grass, another shell, and a translucent pink rock that resembled the gem on Josie's brow. Grabbing a lighter out of her hippy skirt pocket, she focused intently and began burning the wrong end of the candles. I felt like I was in a strange reflection of the real world— nothing was wrong, but nothing was quite right, either. I had no clue what this woman was doing.

Finally, she spoke. "You two, I believe, are twin flames, and a twin flame is a very special bond. Do you know what that is?"

"Like a soulmate." I was proud I knew the term.

"Uh, no. Nothing like that."

"Well, shit. There went my credibility."

"Please," Lindsey said jokingly, "don't act like you ever had any."

I smirked. "You got me there."

"Your twin flame is very different from a soulmate because a twin flame isn't a simple mate or match—it is the other half of your soul. It is one soul residing in two separate bodies. For that reason, the relationship between twin flames is incredibly intense, special, and on an entirely different level to a normal relationship or even a soulmate relationship. Since your twin flame is a part of you, there's a deep sense of understanding, love, and connection going on. It is said to be the most important and valuable experience you can have on earth, and you need to treat it as such. It can be a lot for two young people."

"We're fine, Aunt Lindsey." Josie giggled.

"Don't be flippant. Josie." Lindsey looked at her very seriously. "Your mother and father were twin flames."

Josie froze, holding even her breath. From our conversations, I knew she'd never heard anything about her father, and she obviously had no idea how to process the mention of him.

Lindsey didn't pay mind to Josie's reaction. "This is serious because with the good also comes the bad. Your twin flame mirrors your flaws and insecurities and brings them out into the open. There is nowhere to hide from your twin flame. You're exposed, open, and vulnerable. And, in a more intense way than any other relationship, you'll have your issues brought to the surface—not only human issues, but also karmic issues. That's how problems can arise."

"M-my dad?" Josie stuttered.

Lindsey released the lighter flame and jammed the soft end of the candles down into the clean shell until they stuck and pushed them to the middle of the table.

"Yes. I know you've never heard about your father. Your mother, against our advice, wanted to pretend he didn't exist."

"But, why?"

"Things didn't work out—they couldn't work out—"

Josie interrupted. "But…"

Lindsey put her hand up in the air. "Let me finish. Your mother and father met when they were almost exactly the age of you and Caius. Your father was friends with Caius's uncle, Kurt. See, Kurt and I were madly in love at the time." She paused to smile. "Janet, being two years younger, had this crazy crush on him and wanted to be with us constantly. So, Kurt, wanting a little privacy, as nineteen-year-old boys do, had the idea to drag Joseph along. And, Josie, once your mother saw him, it was like no other boy had ever existed.

They had this intense and instantaneous connection. Janet and Joseph were inseparable, and you could tell they were meant to be. They adored each other, and they absolutely completed each other. The more that time went on, the more it was obvious they were true twin flames lucky enough to be born together in this lifetime."

I watched Josie process this information. "But if they were meant to be together, why didn't things work out?"

"Remember—with the good comes the bad. When you meet your twin flame, you find yourself staring at the mirror image of your soul—everything is the same, but it's different at the same time. Backwards, kind of. Do you two understand what I am saying?"

Josie nodded, but I didn't really have any clue what Lindsey was talking about. "Um, I guess."

"A soul will go through various stages in its journey toward ascension or enlightenment, and twin flames, while created together, often don't know each other through many lifetimes. That means each individual part of the soul, even though it is made of the same star stuff as the other, comes with the baggage of its own journeys. It's how we learn and grow. Some souls always journey together somehow, like family and friends. Some souls always search for each other. Some souls hide from each other. But you're meant to unite with your twin flame, eventually. You're meant to become one again. It's like going home, but that doesn't necessarily mean that house is sturdy. Because of what it's been through, you might have to rebuild it completely. So, it's like a reprieve, but it's also work. Does that make sense?"

That time, we both nodded.

"The relationship has to be one that is based on honesty, love, and purity. Because if it's not, the other person knows. It's not that they know the exact truth or can read each other's minds, it's just that they understand each other's energy, and they immediately know when something isn't right." Lindsey waved her finger between us. "Have one of you felt when the other isn't being quite honest with you?"

Out of the corner of my eye, I saw Josie agree with her aunt, but I couldn't dare bring myself to look at her. I was the one who hadn't been totally open with Josie.

Lindsey continued. "I know I am taking you the long way to your answer, Josie, but I want you to understand what you're both dealing with, as well as what your parents were. Not only do you know when your twin flame isn't on the right path, your twin flame knows that you know, which can cause some self-destruction. No one likes to see their own ugly truths. It would be like looking in the mirror after you get your teeth busted out. Your face hit concrete. You felt the pain of them cracking. You know your teeth are jacked and mangled, but you don't want to see the actuality of it in a mirror because it's easier to not see."

Lindsey turned to me. "I'm sure you don't know the stories, Caius, but your uncle had a bit of a wild streak back in the day. He came to a crossroads in life not long after you were born—he had a choice: the path of light or the path of dark. I kept seeing it in the cards, and I kept telling him, but he never believed in any of what he called my 'witchy woo-woo ways'." She shrugged. "He definitely does now, though. Anyway, he and Joseph got a little too involved in partying, and they made a lot of really bad decisions.

"It's why Kurt and I initially split up—he chose the path of darkness, and I warned your mother, Josie, I did. I told her that it wasn't the right time, that she and Joseph needed some space and that he had some things he needed to figure out before he was ready for them to be together, but you can't tell a seventeen-year-old who is desperately in love anything. Especially when you're a nineteen-year-old idiot yourself. That's when I tried to enlist the help of Sophie because you know how serious and scary Sophie can be." Lindsey giggled softly, without humor. "But nothing would get through to your mother."

She snatched up the cigarette she'd thrown on the table and poked it into her mouth before continuing. "Back then, with the cards, I kept pulling The Emperor, The Empress, and Death. Other cards would be smattered in the layout, depending on the questions asked of them, but always those three—it's how I knew you were coming before she did, Josie—the cards told me." Lindsey lit the cigarette, gave a long inhale, and exhaled slowly.

I could tell she was getting to the bones of the story. I waited for Josie to pitch a fit over the smoking, but she didn't. She just sat quietly, twisting and untwisting her hair, waiting for the rest of what her aunt had to say.

Lindsey continued, the cigarette visibly calming her. "Joseph got into the deep end of the whiskey, but we couldn't keep your mom away from him. No matter what he'd do, she'd just go on loving him, which is brave, but not smart, sweetheart." She reached across the table, and as she stroked the side of Josie's face, her eyes welled up with tears. "Then your mom got pregnant with you. Janet was so convinced that you'd save Joseph, Josie. That he'd look into your little eyes, and he'd come back to her. And he did, for a little while. For the first year of your life, things were as they should have been. Your mother had never been happier—she'd graduated high school, had you, and you all lived in this tiny little house in the middle of Bridgeport. Janet had her perfect little family."

"I didn't know we'd ever lived here."

Lindsey ignored Josie. "By that time, and to this day, I don't know how he did it, Caius's grandfather had laid down the law and forced Kurt into the police academy." She turned around, reaching for the counter, stubbing out her smoke in an overflowing ashtray. "But the only person there for Joseph was your mom. He'd been working for a while at Plaza Service Auto Repair, doing really well—he just had this knack for fixing anything with gears—and then he got in an argument with a customer who said he'd scratched his car door. One thing led to another, Joseph hit him and ended up losing his job. When he came home that evening, he downed a fifth of Jim Beam, and it was a short slide to the bottom from there. He didn't stop. And *didn't* stop turned into *couldn't* stop.

"Your mom stayed until you were two, trying so hard to love your father into sobriety, but the fact is, you can't slay someone else's dragon. Truth be told, I think she'd have even settled for a tame dragon, and Joseph knew that, but he couldn't help himself."

"Why didn't he love us enough to just stop?"

"That's the mystery of addiction, honey. I don't think it's about love, though. I think it's about what's inside you."

"What do you mean?"

"I think it's about genetics and brain chemistry. I think it's about trauma. I think it's about coping mechanisms. I think it's about a loss of self so complete, you have to redefine your entire life before you can move forward. But it's not about love, or lack of love. He tried to be better. He certainly didn't want to let her go, because he did love her, but the longer she stayed, the angrier he got at her."

"I don't understand. Why?" Josie asked, her voice a crack.

"Because every day he woke up and saw her, he knew how far he'd fallen, and I think he constantly felt like a disappointment. Without even trying, she was showing him how much he was failing—because looking at her was like looking in a mirror, smiling really big with a bunch of busted up teeth."

"Every day, he saw the ugly thing no one wants to see," I muttered under my breath.

Nodding, Lindsey made eye contact with me. "Exactly, Caius. Then one night, he passed out while he was supposed to be watching you, Josie. It took you being put in danger for your mom to finally realize she had to go. That night, she packed your things, came here, and we put her on a bus to Connecticut for a women's shelter."

"Why Connecticut?"

"It was the first bus leaving."

Damn, so Josie's whole life had been determined by a bus schedule. I let go of Josie's hand and scratched the back of my head, uncomfortably. This was some heavy shit.

"The hardest thing Soap and I have ever done is put our broken-hearted little sister and niece on that bus and say goodbye, but Janet knew that if she stayed close, she'd never have the strength to stay away from Joseph. When you walk away from a twin flame, it is always due to the fact that they are in some way not ready to heal themselves—be that past life or present life—and Joseph just wasn't. For whatever reason, he couldn't allow himself to let go of the anchor holding him down so he could have a life.

"It's like this—your twin flame will always love you, and they will never abandon you all the way … because they *are* you. If you tune into your heart center" —she pressed her hands together in prayer position and put them to her chest— "you know this—you can feel them. But love doesn't mean you can stay together.

"Your mother loved him, so, so much, Josie, but she loved you more. Your mom wanted a better life for you than what she could offer you in this place, because in the state he was in, Joseph was only going to drag you both down. That's why when she left, she never spoke of him again … unless she was coming to visit, and she'd ask if he'd been around. He never did come around, though. Partly because I think he understood, and partly, because I don't think he had the balls to ever see your mother again."

"Because he couldn't get better, and he couldn't bear to see the ugliness in himself again," I said, understanding.

"You're right, Caius."

"I think it's a cop out. If he'd really loved us, he would have wanted to stop. And if he wanted to stop, he would have stopped."

"Love and life are complicated things."

"So, what happened to him?" I asked.

"We don't know. I don't even think your uncle knows. He got into some trouble, breaking into a house not long after Janet left. Kurt covered it up, and Joseph took off. I've honestly never seen him around here again."

"Why wouldn't she tell me any of this?" Josie asked.

"She had her reasons, honey. They were mostly to protect you. We told her she should tell you, even Sophie told her, because it wasn't fair to act like he didn't exist. Despite the ending, they did have a beautiful love story, and Joseph did love your mother well, and then as well as he could, which, admittedly, was half-assed, compared to Jim Beam. My guess is that she didn't want to romanticize a half-assed love story. There was an incredible amount of love between the two of them. But sometimes love alone isn't enough, and I think Janet wanted to save you the disappointment of coming in second place to a bottle. She wanted the world for you, Josie."

I looked at Josie. Her face looked like a pastel painting of itself.

"This is a lot to take in, Aunt Lindsey."

"I know, honey, but I want you two to understand what you're dealing with when it comes to loving each other." With that, Lindsey took her lighter and lit the wicks of the candles that were tied together in the middle of the table. "I want to say a blessing over the two of you coming together and finding each other. Focus on the flame of the candle and repeat after me: My heart and soul are ready to love and accept love. I burn these candles to call in strength and courage as I walk my path with my twin flame. May I realize the blessings my twin flame offers me on my path to enlightenment. May our love be healthy and true, and our soul strong enough to withstand all obstacles thrown into our path."

Though I felt a little ridiculous, I did as I was told. Josie seemed into it, and I figured I needed all the blessings I could get.

"Now," Lindsey said, tossing leaves at us, "I want you each to write down on this bay leaf a wish you have for the other. Once it's written, place it over the flame and let it burn."

My leaf flaked a little as I wrote out: "PEACE" with a black sharpie. The burning bay leaf released a sweet scent into the air as it crackled and popped, blackening then turning to ash over the candles. I waited patiently as Josie held hers over the flames, stretching my eyes, trying, unsuccessfully, to see what she'd written before it burned.

"There," said Lindsey. "Now as these candles burn, and your blessings and wishes are released into the universe, I want you to ask me any questions you may have about what we just discussed."

I asked what I thought to be the most obvious question. "Are you and my uncle Kurt twin flames?"

She laughed. "No."

"Soulmates?"

"Not exactly. We're a karmic bond relationship, I think. We have a deep connection, but we're here to teach each other lessons. When we're together, and believe me, we've tried many times, we're a roller coaster of emotions and an airplane ride full of turbulence ... because no one wants to learn hard lessons about themselves. In a karmic bond relationship, while you might be together to overcome different unresolved issues, the purpose is the same for you both—channeling out the negative karma. You have a soul agreement to help each other grow—a contract made in the spiritual realm before your essences took shape on earth. And it is not necessary for the relationship to end badly—though often they do—but you will always appreciate this person and the important lessons they taught you in the long run of the relationship. I love your uncle dearly, and he loves me, but *together*, we aren't good."

Josie came in with a smarter, more meaningful question. "How do you know we're twin flames?"

Why hadn't I thought of that?

"Because, honey, I'm pulling the same cards with you two as I did your parents. Almost exactly. It has never happened before now—not with anyone. And I don't quite know what to make of it, other than what I've told you. There's something I know I'm missing, and I think I missed it with your parents, too. I can feel something lying underneath all this, just waiting, but the cards aren't revealing it yet, so it must not be time to know."

"Oh," she replied. I don't think she knew what to say.

"What other questions might you two have?"

The room fell into a silence so awkward I didn't know where to look, so I analyzed the cracks in the tile floor, then the sway of the candle flames, the dust I knew I would have to beat out of the drapes in this room. I watched Josie as she picked at her nails, twisted her hair. All the while, I could feel Lindsey just staring at us, waiting for questions neither of us seemed to have. The seconds were nearly audible as they ticked by. Finally, when I couldn't stand it any longer, I grabbed the gemstone off the table. "What's this pink rock?"

"Rose quartz is the ultimate stone of love. Its vibrational energies dissolve emotional wounds, promote self-love, and strengthen bonds in relationships. It isn't a rock." Lindsey replied, still staring at us as intently as she had stared at the wrong end of the candles earlier.

"Right," I replied. "Of course, it isn't." My words piled up, feeling pointless and light, doing nothing but filling space they didn't belong in.

More silent seconds ticked by.

I cleared saliva from my throat and swallowed hard. Josie was about to blow, and I knew it. I could feel the heat coming off her, her emotions boiling, but I didn't know what to do to stop it, and before I could decide on a plan of action, she stood up so quickly her chair flipped to the ground. "I don't understand why she would never tell me. And now she's dead, and she can never tell me. I'll never know. Never!"

She took off out of the room, leaving me with the witch who wouldn't stop staring. I looked at Lindsey, turning the corner of my mouth up in an uncomfortable smile, and shrugged one shoulder. "Maybe I should..." Letting my voice trail off and die, I motioned toward the door. I didn't know what I *should* do, but I didn't want to stay in that room with Lindsey any longer.

"Go," she said, dismissing me with a wave of her hand.

SASHA HIBBS & CHRISTINA HOOKER

Chapter Seventeen
Ashes, Ashes...

*There are all kinds of love in this world but never the
same love twice.*
— F. Scott Fitzgerald

Josephine

My world was spinning, a merry go round I had
been thrown onto, and now, it was out of control. How
could my life be whirling with such joy and sadness all at
once? The bitterness of losing my mother. Grief. A
strange thief-boy. Red dimensions. Supernatural chaos.
Anger. A connection with Caius so profound I thought
my chest would burst. The truth of a father I'd dreamed
about my entire life. The letdown in finding out a bottle
full of alcohol was somehow more powerful than the
entire divine universe? What kind of shit was that? What
was even the point? I was dizzy. And sick.

I ran out of Aunt Lindsey's parlor, not really
thinking of where I was going, keeping my eyes fixed as
though the answer to everything were just ahead and all I
had to do was get there faster, faster, faster. I sprinted up
the steps two at a time and, rounding the corner to the
hallway, I saw Aunt Sophie at the end, poised, a tightly
secured bun at the base of her neck, waiting as though she
were expecting me. I knew by the look in her eyes that,
though she'd been dreading this moment for years, she'd
always known it would come.

I stopped just short of her, not sure what to say or
how to say it. I felt like a fool, like I didn't know
anything at all, and that I'd never known anything at all. I
was angry. I was empty. I'd had enough, and it felt like I
was coming undone.

"Josephine, sweet Josephine." She sighed, her gaze toward me soft and filled with sympathy. "I know what's troubling you."

This was *not* the kind of relationship I had with my Aunt Sophie, Aunt Lindsey maybe, but not Aunt Sophie. I tried remaining composed. I did not want my emotions to spill onto Aunt Sophie.

"What do you mean?" I asked cautiously, feeling like Aunt Sophie should be more in the dark than what she seemed to be right now. I wasn't sure what she meant, and I made a real effort to keep my face from scrunching up in absolute confusion.

"Your Aunt Lindsey forgets two things," she said, motioning for me to follow her. "First, I'm more in tune with her than she gives me credit for. We *are* twins, and when you share a womb with someone, you share a connection almost as intrinsic as your own pulse." I trailed behind her down the hall, through the living room, and as she stopped in front of her bedroom, she relaxed a hand on her doorknob. Pointing one finger at the floor, she finished, "Second, she forgets about the vents in the ceilings downstairs, and that noise carries something fierce through these old store walls."

The pain and confusion of learning about my father overshadowed the extreme embarrassment I would've normally had about what my quiet, straight-laced Aunt Sophie might have heard between me and Caius or between me and Aunt Lindsey, really between any and all of us. But my cheeks still flushed shades of pink as I wondered about the extent of Aunt Sophie's knowledge, what she allowed to go on, while being a silent spectator. We crossed the threshold into her bedroom.

"Shut the door, please," Aunt Sophie said, turning her back on me and walking a few paces to her antique dresser. Her reflection in the faded mirror that sat atop was sad and stern. She gently pulled out a drawer, retrieving a folded envelope, notably old, yellowed around the edges, and then she slowly turned to face me. She squared her shoulders back as though a rigid posture would somehow give her the strength she was looking for, then circled around the bed and sat down on the edge. Patting beside her, she said, "Come here, Josie."

As I lowered myself to sit by Aunt Sophie, she began. "Lindsey and I have two different approaches to most things in life. But the one thing she and I can agree on is we both love you, and when you love someone, rules are bent. Sometimes, they are broken. Lindsey and I came into this world together, and we've shared our entire lives ever since. We shared the joy of your birth, the loss of our mother, and the great sorrow of your mother's death. Together. As different as we may be, I cannot imagine my life without her, and I wouldn't want to." I wasn't sure where she was going with this impassioned speech, but I listened intently.

She sat for a few moments, head down, rubbing the folded paper between her thumb and index finger before sighing. "I'm not naive about this business of you seeing Kurt's nephew."

"His name is Caius," I said, cutting her off. I didn't want her to be dismissive of my feelings for Caius.

"I am well aware of what his name is."

"You could use it."

I saw a flash of anger at my sass, but she stifled it. "What I am trying to tell you is that I understand the feeling of not being able to live without someone. But I am also trying to warn you. You're young, Josie. So very young." She finished, almost inaudibly, to herself, but I understood her intent. "Just as I know who Caius is, I was also completely aware of who Joseph was," she said, tilting her head toward me, eyes boring through me, reaching somewhere inside me, begging for me to understand what she was about to tell me.

I flinched inwardly at the mention of my father's name. Aunt Sophie reached over and grabbed one of my hands, the other still clutching the paper tightly.

"I loved my sister, and you remind me so much of her. Right now, you remind me of a young and in love Janet. Your father and Janet were much like fire and gasoline—hot, intense ... and beautiful, but caustic. They'd burn everything and anything for each other, and when there was nothing left, they'd start all over again. And it can be wonderful to feel that passion, but you need more than passion to thrive. The hotter the fire, the faster it burns, and you just can't keep throwing gasoline. It isn't practical." My practical Aunt Sophie, always looking at the sensible side of things.

"I don't feel like Caius and I are that way."

She bowed her head as though in contemplation, reflection, worry ... maybe all of it. "No?" she asked, looking at me again. "I hope you aren't. I hope you keep your head, Josie." Her face was full of sorrow, one that conveyed a longing for a different outcome, as though I were my mother and could somehow right all those past wrongs, have a happier ending.

"My dear girl, you've lost so much. I would never try to minimize the hurt of losing your mother. There isn't a day that goes by I don't think of mine. But don't fill your loss with fire, Josephine. Don't go looking to fill the hole of all the love you've lost with just any old love. Do you understand what I mean?"

"But, it isn't *just any old love*, Aunt Sophie. It's like nothing I have ever felt. He makes me feel like a whole person. And Lindsey said my mom felt that, too."

"I know you think that, but make sure your heart

listens to your head, too. That's where your mother went wrong. She was so stubborn and wouldn't listen to any reasoning. She waited until all that reasoning slapped her in the face, and she had to uproot her whole life. You, Josephine, have been uprooted enough times. Don't you go looking to be Janet. Please pay attention to what I'm telling you."

"I am listening. But, you aren't–"

She put her hand up to quiet me. "I don't expect you to understand what it means, how it feels, to lose a sibling. Losing a sibling and losing a mother are entirely different. Both hurt beyond measure because the love you feel for them is beyond measure. But I assure you, losing your sister, so young and full of life, is the most unnatural occurrence. The most wicked thing that I can imagine enduring." Tears welled up in Aunt Sophie's eyes. My heart hurt for her, for me, for everything. "And what keeps me going is the beautiful contribution she made to this world—you." She squeezed my hand. "And I do know that if she hadn't made all the choices Lindsey and I thought were so bad, we wouldn't have you. So, maybe they weren't so bad, but I'd like everything, both good and bad, to be on the table. You need balance. That way, maybe we can save you from the heartache your mother had to endure over her young love."

The anger I felt moments ago evaporated, and a deep feeling of despair filled its place. Tears fell freely down my face. Throwing my arms around Aunt Sophie, I nuzzled my face into the crook of her neck. She smelled of home, of security, of that maternal love I'd lost, and I sobbed against her as she patted my back and whispered in my ear about how much she loved me and how it would be okay, if I just listened to everything and kept my head. And I believed her. At least in that moment. She allowed me to sob until the tears between us dried up, and I finally relaxed and leaned back.

"Janet gave this to me for safekeeping when you two left. I had strict instructions for it to never see the light of day until she was ready." She handed over the letter. "She said this would help you to better understand your father. Of course, she'd planned to give it to you herself when she felt the time was right, but..." She paused. "But here we are. And this is just how we have to do things ... the rules have to be broken."

Unsure of what to expect, I opened the letter gently, like an ancient relic, wondering what additional information about my past was contained within. As I unfolded each side, circular patterns embossed on the paper came into view. I imagined opening this mysterious piece of the puzzle would be like opening the gateway to a past I knew so little about—the proverbial yellow brick road that I'd finally been led to, and everything in my life, everything I'd just heard about, would make sense. But like everything else in my life, I didn't get what I expected.

Instead of clarity, all I got was more confusion.
"Ring around the rosie,
A pocket full of posies,
Ashes! Ashes!
We all fall down."
And I loved him anyway.
~ Mom

My hands began to shake. The paper felt like it was on fire, and this feeling, this shadow that I'd always felt chasing me, felt thick and tangible, like it was growing and looming against me, forming a soul, an entity long suppressed finally being set free, now staring me down as the object of its loathing.

I felt like invisible hands were reaching out, each finger slowly wrapping around my neck, pressing, one by one, into the flesh of my throat, ready to cut off my air supply at any moment. With a quick gasp, I threw my own hand around my neck, scratching for release, but there was nothing there. Shadow hands weren't what was choking me. A flash of an image came to life, rolling past my eyes. It was me—yet not me—head limp and tilted, my lifeless body swaying with the wind. The noose from which I hung was red.

Dazed and terrified, I looked up from where I sat beside Aunt Sophie to her dresser, and there sat a framed picture of the Justice card staring back at me—a woman cloaked in a purple robe poised between two pillars, a sword in one hand, scales in her other. I knew, from Aunt Lindsey, she represented karmic balance, cause and effect, life lessons. It was the perfect card for Sophie. What I didn't know is why the woman seemed to be smiling at me, why the scales were tipping wildly, trying to right themselves, to find equilibrium.

"Josie, are you all right?"

I shook my head and moved my eyes away from the picture. "I'm fine, Aunt Sophie."

Like Pandora taking the lid off her box, as I opened the letter from my mother, out swarmed all kinds of trouble, a thick evil, something that should never have been.

I was not fine.

Chapter Eighteen
We All Fall Down

I want to know you moved and breathed in the same world with me.
—F. Scott Fitzgerald

Josephine

I left Aunt Sophie sitting on the edge of her bed as I rushed back into the hallway. Letter still in hand, I leaned against the wall, allowing everything to wash over me. There had been so many surreal moments, so many unexplainable things. I knew the universe was screaming at me and at Caius, and I knew it had brought us together for a reason, but what was it? Had I understood what Aunt Lindsey tried explaining about twin flames—and that Caius and I had bounced through lifetimes with each other. Who had we been before? If Aunt Lindsey was pulling the same cards for Caius and me as she had with my parents, were we destined and, therefore, doomed to follow in their footsteps? Is that why I kept having terrible, sinister visions? Is that why all this bad stuff was happening to us? Had it happened to my parents?

My thoughts and questions were an ocean in which I was drowning, and there were still no answers. Groaning, I pushed my fingers through my hair, rubbing my head, trying to make it all make sense. Then I felt him behind me and turned before he could speak.

"Um..." He faltered, gauging how best to approach the situation. "Hey, Josie."

"Um, hey."

"Yeah, listen, I don't know about everything that was said back there. I don't know what's true and what's not, but I do know" —he waved a hand back and forth between us— "*we* are real. This thing between us ... this twin flame..." He paused, searching my eyes. "It *has* to be real. Don't you feel it?"

I nodded.

He continued without paying mind to my response. "And if we are gonna have a better future than your parents, I think we better start listening to what Lindsey ... or the universe, or whatever the fuck, is trying to tell us. Because I believe in us. I love you. I *know* I do. I feel it here." He put his right hand to his chest, and with his left, he grabbed mine, placing it overtop of his heart, too.

I smiled up at him, my heart burning with this honest avowing.

"If we are mirrors of each other and shit, then I guess there's no point in hiding things. And I want you to know everything, anyway. So..." He let the sentence dangle, his expression deepening. "I, um, want you to know that I haven't been completely honest with you."

"What do you mean?" I asked, a bit guarded, scared of what he'd say. I'd had enough bombs dropped on me for one day.

"So, I'm downstairs in that room, listening to everything your Aunt Lindsey is saying and trying to match it up with everything that's gone down since I first met you. And, it's like, I'm trying to make sense of ... *things*," he said, and I could tell it was for lack of better words. "And, that night when I took you to the witch's grave—"

I nodded, silently encouraging him to say more, wondering what was on the verge of spilling over his lips.

"Well, it's like this," he started, taking a few steps back and gently allowing my hand to slide out of his. He looked past me, his gaze wandering to some distant land before coming back to me. He ran a hand through his hair, let out a sigh, and then he went on. "It is my belief in *us* that is keeping the shit I don't believe—the shit that's totally unbelievable—buried. If I don't think about it and leave it in my mind's, like, graveyard or whatever, I'm not as freaked out, and then I don't question and obsess over it. Because I didn't think any of this could logically be true. Even my feelings for you. But my feelings *are* true, and if they're true, so is the other *stuff*."

"I think I know what you mean," I said, thinking about the vision I'd had in my Aunt Sophie's bedroom. It wasn't explainable, and to any logical mind, it shouldn't have been real, but it happened. I know it did, even if no one else could see it.

"That night I took you to the witch's grave," he said, lowering his voice as though afraid someone would overhear him, "I turned into a complete dick."

"Yes, I remember," I added, a bit confused why he was treading ground we'd already covered. I had already forgiven him for acting like an ass.

"Here's the thing, Josie." His entire demeanor tensed with fear, and as if in response to him, the hair on my arms pricked up. "Something happened back there that I've never had happen before, not in all the times I've been to that grave. At first, I thought maybe I was crazy, or maybe my nerves were getting the better of me, but if I'm being honest with myself and honest with you, that's not what happened."

The floorboards creaked as I came closer to him and grabbed his hands. I gave them a slight squeeze. "It's okay. You can tell me. You say you believe in us. I believe in us too. You can tell me anything." I smiled at him, trying to promote a sense of safety. "I promise. I'm right here, and I'm not going anywhere."

"This sounds crazy, like batshit crazy. But, Josie,

I swear to you it's true. I know what I saw and what I felt. It was like I was being possessed by something evil. Not just some*thing* evil, some*one*. It was some ancient, evil fucker, and it was everything I could do to keep any part of myself in there. It wanted me to abandon you there, leave you alone in the dark. But I couldn't. Not after you were so scared.

"I don't know exactly what happened to you and what you saw because I didn't see anything, but I behaved how I did because it ... *it* was making me. It was trying to take over, and it didn't want me with you."

I knew he was exposing a vulnerability to me, something he'd likely never done for anyone, and it made me want to wrap him up in my arms and keep him safe forever, love him for trusting me with his feelings. Beads of sweat sprung up on his brow. I knew he was terrified, and I could tell he was trying hard to mask the true terror of whatever was lurking in his shadows. But, now, at least I knew we were both having the same kind of frightening things happening to us. None of this could be a coincidence—the red, what we felt at the grave, my parents, the cards, the evil. The shadow I saw in Aunt Sophie's bedroom, it had to be the same one coming for Caius.

A dreadful thought went through my mind and out my lips before I had time to truly process the idea. "I think we need to go back there," I said, searching his eyes with mine. "I think whatever happened back there is real and not confronting it together is only going to continue to make it, whatever *it* is, grow in strength against us."

"Josie—"

I cut him off. "I believe in us. And all this. Part of believing in something is to say it, that way you make it real and then you face it." I leaned into him, burying my face in his chest. "And we will face it together."

"But what if we can't? What if it's too much and I lose you?" He slowly wrapped his arms around me, his fingers gently digging into me, a grip that was terrified of losing what it held.

But I wasn't going to let that happen.

****

We waited until dusk to start our journey to the grave. There was so much that hung between us, so much left unspoken, yet as we walked down the railroad tracks toward the grave of the witch who wouldn't stay buried, we couldn't talk. The only sounds were our feet crunching over the rocks. Occasionally, we would look at each other, eyes making contact, our glances making the complete sentences of all the things we were unable to say.

There was fear. There was hope that, joined together, our connection, our identifying and accepting what we were to one another, would somehow rise up and win against whatever foul, evil thing we were up against. Caius kept my hand clasped tightly in his, while his free hand remained in his pocket.

I thought back to the first time he took me to the witch. What a disaster that night was. It hurt thinking about it, but after listening to Caius spill the truth of his sort of possession, I knew now it wasn't Caius being terrible to me, it was whatever was tied to this witch, or the witch herself.

Caius came to a screeching halt, stopping so suddenly I collided with him. Trees choked in ivy loomed along the path that lay before us. I sucked in breath and held it. Fear permeated the air, as palpable as flesh and blood. Caius started breathing heavily and deeply, but with each breath, the fear gained intensity. If I could have reached out and grabbed it, squeezed it, I could have strangled it, and I could have calmed him. I settled for squeezing his hand, not sure what else to do.

"Hey," I said, standing on tiptoes, whispering into his ear, "I'm here. We're *together*. It's going to be okay." I took my free hand and, gently turning his face toward mine, I looked into his eyes, pleading with him to understand that, together, we could conquer anything. At least, I felt like we could. I placed my lips against his, breathing his rough breaths with him, and as I planted a gentle kiss into them, said, "I won't let anything happen to you."

The trees groaned, and again, I recalled the night we first came to this place. I shuddered.

I expected him to reciprocate my tender feelings, but instead, he was harsh. "Come on, Josie. I'm not an injured kitten."

"I just—"

"Don't coddle me."

"I'm sorry—"

"No!" He shook his head as though he were trying to clear it. "Damn it. I'm sorry. It's happening again. I can already feel him … her … it. It's trying to make me angry … make me hate you." He broke away from me slowly, leaning his forehead against mine. "I could never hate you."

"Try hard to keep yourself. Focus on your heart and your soul. *Our* soul, right?" I smiled at him. "We're in this together, both right now and ever after. Through all things, even time, it's you, and it's me. Always."

"I hope you're right. Are you ready for this?"

"I'm as ready as I'm ever going to be."

He took in a deep breath and let it out, a sigh against the dimming light, a prayer into the wind, nervously given to the universe as a plea that some greater force would hear the call for help.

And answer.

Still clutching my hand in his, he kept his gaze focused ahead as we traveled up the worn-down path leading to the gravesite. We walked in foreboding silence, crows swooping and cawing out to us. With each step, the air around us grew thicker, an invisible spider web hoping to ensnare us. I kept thinking about the first time I met Caius, remembering the power, the sheer force of touching one another, that gentle brush of each other's skin turning into a burst of red electricity that transcended time and space, and I tried to draw courage from it. It was so powerful it had woken something beyond the grave, and what could be more powerful than that? Surely our connection would protect us. It had to.

His palm turned sweaty against mine, but I clasped his hand tighter, tethering him to me. We could figure this out. Together. Whatever force we were up against, I could feel that it wanted us apart. Divide and conquer, and I wasn't going to let that happen. Caius and I were going to stand united. Two souls back together as one.

The old burial vault came into sight, and we kept going, each of us giving the other courage to move forward. And then he stopped short of the grave, fishing his hand around in his pocket. I watched as he withdrew a rose quartz. He rolled the crystal around in his hand.

"Linds said something about this promoting love and healing," he said, his voice shaking. "I swiped it," he admitted, "but I figure that's a great place to start with whoever this witch chick was … and that's stealing for a good cause, right? Kinda negates the stealing." He smiled with the corner of his mouth. Releasing my hand, he took steady steps closer to the concrete tomb.

I stayed a few steps behind him.

He brought the rose quartz to his lips, whispered something against it, and placed it on the witch's grave.

We both held our breath in anticipation.

Nothing happened.

Several seconds went by with us staring at the rose quartz against the gray concrete. Caius finally took a few steps back and turned to me, wearing a defeated expression. "I really thought that would work. Maybe it's nothing but in our heads. Maybe we were dosed LSD, and we're having flashbacks. Maybe it's made us both fucking crazy. But this," he gestured slinging his thumb over his shoulder, "is fucking stupid, and I'm–"

And then it happened.

No warning.

No signal sent out by the universe.

No time to react.

One moment Caius was pointing behind himself, pissed his rose quartz offering to the witch who wouldn't stay buried had changed nothing, and in the next moment, the air around us turned to ice and cracked, and the ground beneath began emitting a low, resonate vibration, like a growl. The rose quartz rattled against the concrete then lifted off the tomb, shaking in mid-air, and began spinning. As it spun, it shattered into a million pieces, then those pieces shattered into a million more pieces, and those pieces did the same thing. Pink particles floated around us, star dust from another dimension, standing still against the evening's dimming light.

But as quickly as it had exploded, the pink dust began undulating, coiling in and out of itself, and in it, hundreds of tiny snakes took shape. As they formed, they coiled and hissed, then began rushing toward each other. They collided with a loud crack, echoing through the atmosphere, and together, they formed a single snake with a long, thin tail, who folded herself into a tight figure eight, writhing and turning against herself until she'd grabbed ahold of her own tail … and she was eating it. She was eating *herself*! When the snake got to the end, unable to take one more bite, the rose quartz reformed with a silent implosion and fell with a clatter back to the tomb.

The force of the supernatural explosion had knocked me backward, and Caius had fallen behind me, smacking his head against the ground with a dull thud.

"Caius! Caius!" I screamed, deafening, shrill, all the panic in my chest spilling into my lungs as I screamed his name over and over again. Finally, I managed to stand in enough time to see Caius lift himself up. I wanted to run to him, but it felt like my legs were filled with lead, and I had two anvils in place of feet. I was planted where I stood, absolutely unable to move.

There was a panic in Caius's eyes, but also something else, something deeper, something lying beneath the panic. I could see it seeping its way through his body, wrapping itself around his veins like a malignancy, and each breath of oxygen he struggled for seemed to fuel the growth. He moved one leg in front of the other in stiff, awkward, and unnatural movements, as though he had been turned into a puppet, the puppet master invisible, pulling his strings, making him walk over to the witch's crypt.

"Run," he croaked, and I knew in his frozen, mechanical state, Caius had worked with everything left in him to get that word out to me, that whatever had him under control was restricting him from speaking and moving freely. It was the same puppeteer holding me hostage, and I was terrified.

"I can't!" I screamed.

His arm jerked and shot out, snatching the rose quartz, and as he lifted it, the most sinister laugh I'd ever heard thundered through the air. It came not from Caius, but from behind him, out of eyesight.

He looked at me, horror in his eyes, unable to do anything other than be under the control of whatever force was working against us. I stood, frozen, nailed to the ground where I was, as he balled his fist up and launched the rose quartz at me. The stone hit my eyebrow piercing that covered my old scar and made a new split over top of the old one. I cried out as fresh, hot blood oozed into my eye, slid down my cheek, and dripped onto my shirt where it spread and feathered on the white fabric. I blinked my eyes, but it was only making my vision worse.

There was a ripple in the universe–a transparent wave rolling in the air, crashing, then cutting through us, releasing the evil hold. I collapsed. From my knees, I glanced at Caius, and he folded like a man with no bones. He hit the ground without breaking his fall, and, moving his face against the dirt, he looked at me.

I stared into his green eyes until they blurred, and nothing was in focus. With all the strength I had, I reached out my arm to him, and he did the same. Our pinkies looped together in the silent promise that we were in this together.

The last thing I heard before losing consciousness was my Aunt Lindsey's voice, bellowing through the night. "Enough!"

Chapter Nineteen
Fire & Flame

Never turn your back on fear. It should always be in front of you like a thing that might have to be killed.
—Hunter S. Thompson

Caius
Journal

Fate. Do we control it, or does it control us? Is it staring at us, stalking us, playing us like chess pieces from some other dimension, or is it the choices we make? Or is it all just happy or unhappy little accidents that prevent us from dying ... or kill us?

Demons. Stories of demons who seize control of humans are as old as mankind itself. Interdimensional journeys that end in possession. Millions of people believe in that shit, so what if those people aren't bat shit crazy, and it's actually true? Are there demons that follow us through lifetimes? Do those demons make the choices for us and shape our lives? And if we live many lives, do they shape each of them? But, if there are demons, there have got to be angels, right? And angels have got to play some part, too. Are we constantly walking a razor's edge just to see where we fall—good or evil? I'd imagine the only people who could tell you are those who've fallen, and if you fall, you die, don't you? Then comes the reckoning. Then what—the reprise? Because it's not like you can come back and tell the living what you've learned. You're just plain dead. You just have to hope you remember and take your lesson with you into your next cycle on this Earth ... where you come back to get played and do this stupid shit all over again? Which brings me to...

Death. Can you die all the way, or does your BODY die, and whatever stuff is inside you moves on? If I've always existed ... who have I been? Better yet, who am I now? I feel like I've been lost, a victim in my own vicious cycle. Until I found her. (Again? Always? Is finding her always my human mission? Do I make the choices I do JUST to find her again and again and again?) She's become my light ... she's the kind of good I want to be. I want us to stay in this life ... together, united, free from demons of the past. Because this doomed from the start stuff is total bullshit. Is there a living death—one where you're reborn as the same motherfucker you always have been? But different somehow... better. Better because you know. You know what's on the other side of this wicked door of life.

Josie and I didn't know how to talk about what had happened at the grave, and we were too tired to care. Lindsey had come, gathered us up, and drove me home. She'd told us we'd talk about it later, once she'd had time to meditate on it, whatever that meant. Josie and I had nearly been pulverized by … I don't know what, and all I got when I got out of the car was a tiny tin can of her homemade calendula ointment tossed to me with instructions to rub it into all my scrapes and to make sure I was on time for work in the morning.

I limped from the curb to our walkway and groaned when I saw a light on. My mother had moved her nightly party to the front porch.

"What the hell have you been doing," my mother laughed into her chardonnay as I walked past her sitting crossed-legged on the glider, "wrestling pigs in the mud?"

My body was covered in dirt and stinging scrapes, and my hair was dreadlocked with clumps of grass and earth. Every inch of my body burned and ached, and

Lindsey had shown me more compassion than my actual mother.

"Yeah. Keep drinking, Aleka." I called her by her name when I really wanted to piss her off, but tonight, she just turned away from me and finished her glass in a single gulp. "Whatever," I muttered as I headed down to my cave.

****

The sun was gentle and warm as I slid out of the glass doors from the basement. There was no way in hell I was trying to see if my mother had passed out outside and poke that bear awake. It was one of those July mornings that felt more like the end of summer than the middle, and though it wasn't cold, the closer I got to *Blair's Lair*, the more I shivered with the weight of the previous night filling me.

I tried to shake it off. The bell jingled as I opened the front door and crossed the threshold into the store, but no one acknowledged me. The entire store felt stiff and unnatural. The baking pepperoni rolls didn't even smell inviting.

Lindsey was in the aisle where she kept her herbal remedies, rearranging displays and scribbling on a clipboard, all the while keeping hawk eyes on Sophie, who was at the counter, lips flat, brows furrowed more than usual, ringing out a man.

He tried to speak. "Sophie, I just–"

"One forty-ounce Budweiser and two packs of Marlboro Reds. Nineteen dollars and seventy-six cents, please," she said stiffly, bagging the items.

The man, whose skin was the dark tan of a man who'd spent a lot of time outside, reached into his pocket and tossed a wadded up twenty-dollar bill onto the counter. Sophie cleared her throat and swallowed roughly before reaching out to take the bill.

"Could you just tell me what happened? Please." It sounded like the man was about to cry.

Sophie looked up, her face more rigid and cold than I'd ever seen it. "You lost the right to know that a long time ago. Now, I'll suggest you get your boozy ass out of my store before I—"

A loud clatter interrupted Sophie.

Lindsey had dropped her clipboard. Her eyes were wide, and, for a moment, she froze when both Sophie and the man looked at her. Clumsily, she ducked, hiding in the aisle, and the man turned back to Sophie, nervously putting his palm on his neck and scratching through his dark hair.

The back of his hand was covered in a brilliant tattoo. It was a red rose slowly fading in color to black and gray ash where vibrant orange and yellow flames were consuming the petals. "I've never loved anyone else, Soph."

Sophie boomed from behind the counter, "You have no right!"

Her voice made me jump.

The man crumpled like the twenty he'd thrown onto the counter, every ounce of his weight sliding into his feet, and he grabbed his brown paper bag. He didn't even look at me as he shouldered past to leave the store.

When the door shut, Sophie began to tremble, and Lindsey rushed to her. She leaned against the counter, shaking with sobs, as Lindsey rubbed her back, whispering things to her I couldn't hear.

Uncomfortable and unsure of what else to do, I pretend to cough.

"Caius, just go wake Josie up or something. Give us a minute."

****

I gently shook Josie's shoulder to wake her,

whispering into her ear, "Good morning. Time to get up."

She stirred and grunted, unwilling to be coaxed out of sleep.

I tried with more force. "Josie. Wake up!"

She moaned and rolled over, jerking her shoulder out of my reach.

"Josie, the house is on fire!

She didn't move.

I knew what would get her attention. "Hey, does Sophie have an estranged boyfriend?"

Her eyelids sprung open, and she flipped over to face me. "What? No. Why? I mean, I guess I don't know, but no one has ever talked about Sophie with a man."

Flopping down onto her bed, I told her what had happened downstairs, and she sat up, stretching and yawning. "Are you sure he told Sophie he loved her?"

"He said he'd never loved anyone else and just wanted to know what had happened. Like, she broke up with him or something. Then Sophie started to cry. I didn't think Sophie could cry."

She nudged into me playfully. "Stop. Sophie is a really great and loving person, once you get to know her."

I laughed and joked, "Which is just code for she's a bitch, unless she likes you."

She giggled, looking at me out of the corner of her eye.

My phone buzzed in my pocket. It was Lindsey telling me to keep Josie upstairs for a bit longer. I tossed my phone and smiled, planting a kiss on Josie's lips, first soft, then greedy. I had a few ideas.

The phone buzzed again, this time, pulling our lips apart. I reached for it, stretching my arm across Josie, and pulled it in close, in case there was another secret message from Lindsey, telling me what the hell had happened downstairs, but no such luck.

"Did she say anything about Sophie," Josie asked, eagerly.

"No," I said, sighing. "Duty calls."

I left Josie to her cozy sheets and made the trek downstairs, where Lindsey handed me a paintbrush, a roller, and a gallon of paint with a roll of lime green tape on top of it. "My room needs to be painted. First, take down all the drapes, wipe down the walls, and tape everything off. I'm sure there is a YouTube video, if you don't know how to do it."

"Are we even going to talk about what happened earlier?"

"Absolutely not. It is none of your business."

"*Okay*," I said, drawing the word into many syllables. "What about last night? Can we talk about that?"

"Not now, Caius!" She reached into her skirt's pocket and pulled out a cigarette, placing it in her mouth.

"Can I get one of those?"

She rolled her eyes as she dug in her other pocket for a lighter. It came out empty, and she ran it, frazzled, through her hair, flipping it from one side to the other. "Just go paint my damn room, okay?" She said, the unlit cigarette bouncing with each pissed off syllable.

Without a word in response, I parted the beads in the doorway and headed to Lindsey's witch's hut.

I had always hated painting. It was tedious, and the paint itself always seemed intent on being as fucked up as possible, no matter how hard you tried. And as I slapped on the first roller full of twilight purple, I knew it was going to be a pain in the ass. Each minute was an hour. There was paint in my hair and on my face, not to mention my favorite Metallica shirt.

I was fumbling through my pockets, searching for

my earbuds, when I heard Josie behind me.

"Knock, knock."

I could tell by the sound of her voice that she was smiling. I loved it when she smiled. I turned to her, grinning.

She was wearing an oversized pair of overalls, and her hair was twisted up and crazy like on the first day I'd met her. She held up her own paint roller. "I asked the aunts what happened, and, as punishment, I got sentenced to community service. But I don't mind so much. I heard a cute boy was working…"

"Oh, yeah?"

"Mmm-hmm," she said, gently kissing my lips.

"Well, I hope he's not here today. I'd like you all to myself."

She playfully pushed me. "What can I do to help?"

"I've got this side under control, but if you would start taping off the baseboards over there," I said, motioning to the far corner of the room, "that would be super helpful."

I showed her how to do it, and as she started, I plugged my headphones in and got back to work. I was three songs deep, bobbing my head along and singing softly to Led Zeppelin's greatest hits, when Josie tapped me on the shoulder. I jumped. "Woah! You can't do that to a guy who is haunted by the ghost of twin flames past!" Giving a light chuckle and turning, I continued. "Hey, laugh or cry. Am I right, or am I—" I stopped mid-joke when I saw her mouth was quivering, and her eyes were glassy with tears.

"Um…" she said.

I ripped out my earphones. "What's wrong?"

"I found this stuck behind the baseboard. It's my mother's writing." She handed me a small square of thick paper. Its edges were frayed, showing its age. In the center was a colored pencil sketch of a rose engulfed in flames. Overtop of the drawing was a poem, bubbly letters written thickly in black marker.

I yearn to be devoured
by your love.
I urge you to keep living
with the fire of fierce belief,
for I cannot live without you.
Through Hell's fire and love's embers.
Ashes to ashes.
Always.

On the back, there was a note.

You crank down the window to flick your cigarette ash onto the pavement rolling below. Some of the embers get carried off, melting with the wind. Some consume themselves. The ones that survive shatter, orange glitter over asphalt, tiny sparks screaming for survival against all odds. Those are us.

I, like your cigarette, am on fire. I envision my heart, as red as a rose, erupting in flames when I think of you. And then the flames engulf my entire body. And your body. Then the seats we're on. Then the car. Then the neighborhood you're driving through, each house, a hot whomp of fire. Each tree, the sharp strike and fwoosh of a match. Then the city. And the state. The country. The world. An entire universe of ash burned from our love.

And, together, we'll rise again and again and again.

I love you, Joe.
-J

I couldn't believe what I was seeing. "Josie," I said. "The man from the store today … he had that image tattooed on his hand."

Realization flooded her, the corners of her mouth

went slack, and her lips bobbed open. "You think that man was my dad?"

I nodded, reaching out to take the paper from Josie. As soon as I touched it, a shock of red bolted through me. My mind was sucked into a pit of fire. All I could hear was a roar, growing louder and louder until, just as my ears were about to bleed, I realized the noise was two different voices calling out words that were all jumbled up, fighting each other. "Ashes to ashes..." It echoed, a constant loop in a ridiculous sing-song, bellowing over whispers. *"(sacrifice)."* It was so hard to concentrate. "Ashes to ashes... *(alone)*. Ashes to ashes... *(save her)*. Ashes to as—"

For a split second, the chanting was sucked into a vacuum, and a female's voice spoke softly, distantly, *"Ouroboros. Mind the snake, Caius. The unity of two depends on the sacrifice of one."* An image of the same snake from the grave appeared, slithering in and out of a rose, its tail the fire setting each petal alight. I watched as the snake writhed and coiled herself back into a figure eight, then swallowed the flame, devouring herself ... again.

Then the other voice, a male voice, loud and lethal, gobbled up the female's voice, shouting, "Ashes to ashes, you're all gonna die! You're all gonna die! You're all gonna die!" The words came fast, crowding each other, audio on fast forward, speeding faster and faster until they became a single screech. But I understood. I felt it in my blood. It wasn't time to be afraid. It was time to take control.

And then the evil laughter I'd come to know so well squeezed through the channels of my brain, exploding every synapse, and it brought me to my knees.

SASHA HIBBS & CHRISTINA HOOKER

Chapter Twenty
The Past That Wouldn't Stay Buried

Ever has it been that love knows not its own depth until the hour of separation.
— Kahlil Gibran

Josephine

The Emperor was a striking man, but cold—ruthless, intimidating, selfish. He stood well over six feet, eyes as hard as stone, and a heart to match his gaze. His build was thick and imposing, as though he could crush all in his path. His gray stone stare swept across the crowd below his balcony. Disgust contorted his face and oozed out around him, permeating the air.

Behind him, beyond the veiled burgundy curtain was the Empress. She was petite with long hair falling over each shoulder and swathes of emerald silk draping over each breast, ending in a pool of gorgeous fabric at her feet. Where the Emperor was hard, she was soft, her gaze tender and searching. She stood dutifully behind her husband and to the side of the curtain that kept her hidden from the crowd below. She was unnoticed by the Emperor, but there was someone else whose gaze penetrated her.

A guard who loomed stood just behind and to the side of the Empress. Perhaps stationed to protect the royal couple? The man stood straight and still, a spear in his right hand, the other stationed behind his back. Had his eyes not given him away, one would think he was a statue—tall, unflinching, the epitome of masculinity with hard lines chiseled into his arms and legs–no doubt the result of years' worth of training. But his eyes held something, some kind of warmth when they fell upon the Empress.

But the symbol on his hand—of a snake, twisted, eating its own tail, like an infinity symbol—was the oddest of all.

Since what had gone down at the witch's grave the night before—being thrown backward, losing consciousness—I was having dreams, or visions, both ... I dunno. The line between those was a blurry one. It was like one minute I was in the here and now, and the next I would be sucked into this out-of-body experience where it felt like I was an aerial viewer, watching these glimpses of someone else's life.

It occurred without warning—sometimes as I closed my eyes, sometimes when I opened them—but always the same three figures: the Emperor, Empress, and guard who watched them both, especially her. I could never predict what would trigger these visions. In this moment, it was my hand crossing Caius's as we passed an old letter from my mom to my dad. I don't know what it was about the letter, our hands touching one moment without issue and then sending us both reeling the next, but for me, these strange things were occurring more frequently.

The crack of Caius's knees hitting the floor helped pull me back to the present. Even in a dream state, or whatever it was that was happening to us, I was so connected to Caius that love would help to pull me out of wherever I was and back to him.

I rushed to him, dropping down to my knees beside him. My only thought was him and me needing him to be okay. This torment had to stop. What was the universe trying to tell us?

"Are you okay?" I whispered gently into his ear, cupping his face in the palm of my hands. His eyes, wild and searching, looked to me for some sign of reality. I tried using my gaze to ground him, convey he was here, in the present, that he was okay, *we* were okay. "Just breathe," I said, taking deep breaths myself to encourage him, as though I could breathe for the both of us.

He finally placed his hands over mine, his eyes relaxed, and his breathing evened out. "Josie, I, we, I—"

"It's okay," I said, wanting him to take his time. "What happened? It was him again, wasn't it?"

He nodded his head.

I leaned back on my heels, still clasping Caius. I let my gut settle, willing it to do what my gut does … produce a much-needed instinct. I needed one right now more than ever, some kind of guidance. These visions, this malignant feeling was growing and I needed to find a way to keep us safe.

I thought back to the vision I had moments ago of the Emperor, the Empress, and the guard. I searched for clues, anything that would help put me on the right course of discovery. But all my gut kept screaming, kept going back to, was the letter we just discovered.

My mom. My dad.

"An entire universe of ash burned from our love."

"What?" I heard Caius say, completely bewildered.

"Ashes to Ashes."

"Josie?"

And it came to me, that gut instinct, that feeling of knowing what to do, what was right. I leaned back up and rested my forehead on Caius'.

"We need to spread my mom's ashes."

****

It didn't take Caius too long to recover from whatever possession had taken place. But it was horrible to watch. I felt so helpless. And just as I knew my love for Caius was an old one, I knew getting to the source was important. Sometimes I felt like our lives depended on it. I felt like I had to put the past behind me in order for us to have a future. Allowing my mother to finally rest—releasing her ashes—was part of looking forward.

Ashes to Ashes.

I'd kept my mother's urn beside me in my room since we picked it up from the crematorium. There was something, some part of me that cried inside at the thought of letting her go. But the other part of me, the part I channeled, told me it was something I had to do.

Caius was waiting for me outside the store. My heart was relieved to see him look more like himself than hours earlier, crumpled to the floor in some twisted, involuntary state. I placed my mother's urn in a soft backpack, slung gently over my shoulder. With my free hand, I slid my fingers into Caius's.

He squeezed my hand in his "The witch's grave?" he asked, looking straight ahead, already knowing what the answer was.

I first shook my head in silent resignation, and then answered, my voice barely above a whisper. "Yes."

He knew. I knew. The both of us knew we had unfinished business there. What drew us there? Why, after every seemingly horrible event that occurred, would we ever want to go back there? And yet here we were, holding hands, walking side by side down this path we were destined to walk, no matter how scary or wrong it might feel in the moment, until we got it right. Did we feel the need to go to the witch who wouldn't stay buried and survive the supernatural elements the universe was throwing at us?

As Caius and I walked in silence toward an uncertain future, I thought back to the first time he took me to see her. I'd felt complete sorrow for the possibility this woman had suffered in life and complete anger that, at the hands of stupid teenagers, she was being disrespected in death, too, like her entire life had meant nothing. And at the same time, Caius had been overtaken with an evil he could barely keep from consuming him. And then we went again. The second visit was more intense than the first.

Walking down the tracks, through the park, over the bank, closer and closer to the witch's tomb, it occurred to me.

My mother. She was with me. Protecting me. I glanced over to Caius, hoping to assess if there were storm clouds brewing. He must've felt my gaze. He glanced over at me, and his eyes were a reflection of myself. Just like Aunt Lindsey said—we were mirrors of each other. I felt calm, at ease, and I knew through me, he felt it too.

We will prevail, Caius. We will prevail.

I squeezed his hand. He returned the favor, a gentle caress of his thumb against my index finger.

As the tomb came into view, the earth hummed, a strange yet soothing vibration. I released Caius's hand. "It's going to be okay," I whispered.

"I know," he answered. "It has to be."

I gently lowered my backpack to the ground, loosening the straps holding my mother's urn within.

"Josie?" Caius said, in a low voice laced with a little panic. I looked up at him, while lifting my mother's urn out of the backpack. "I feel *it*."

"I'm right here, Caius," I said, walking back over and standing beside him. "I'm right here."

"Will you always be, though?" he asked, and while there was the faintest tone of sadness, I could still hear it. "Will *I*?"

I could tell the words he spoke were riddled with

doubt, but my gut told me it was the evil working its way to breach the bay of his soul.

"We are here, now. Together."

Caius gave a swift shake of his head as though trying to clear the lingering fog. I knew what he was trying to work through. Whatever *it* was, whatever *he* was, the two of us together were not going to let it win.

"It's time," I said, and as though my voice somehow commanded the wind, a breeze picked up, rustling the draping willows, an elegant dance of weeping branches caressing each other.

I felt the reassuring caress of Caius's hand drawing little circles in the middle of my back. My heart was tight in my chest, a tidal wave of emotions—each a crescendo of love, loss, heartache. I wanted my mother so badly right now. The woman, the single constant in my life, who always saw the best in me, who always encouraged me, who always loved me even when there were times I added unnecessary stress to her. The woman who witnessed the worst in me—the selfish, childish moments—but she loved me through it. She *loved* me. Always. She also believed in me, and she taught me the power of that belief. No matter what I ever chose to do— the stupid science fair, take art classes or snowboarding lessons, read Gone with the Wind in third grade—she always reiterated her unshakable belief in me. She always believed, not that I *could do*, but that I *would do* whatever I set my mind to do, and by her believing in me, she cultivated that belief within me. She taught me that belief was powerful, and the belief that you can do something was *everything*.

By running through all these thoughts, I was stalling. It was hard to find the courage to open the urn, and Caius seemed to sense that. "Maybe you should say something," he said, encouragingly.

I nodded. He was right. "I miss you every moment of every day, Mom. When I wake up, it's the first thing that hits me, then there are infinite reminders of you throughout the day, and the fact that you're gone is the last thing my mind marinates in before I finally close my eyes. I hope your love and your belief, and your compassion and your uniqueness, never fade within me. I hope I make you proud. I hope I am doing what is right. I love you, Mom. I'll miss you always."

As I said the last words, I slowly lifted the lid to the urn, and like the veil from this world into the next had been lifted, my mother's ashes drifted in a methodical dance from the urn into the breeze. My heart picked up. The idea I was somehow losing my mother all over again nearly overwhelmed me. As fresh tears sprung up in my eyes, each speck of her ash in the wind grew luminous, like a firefly coming to life, brighter and brighter.

I leaned into Caius for support. Maybe we both held each other up. It was difficult to fully assimilate in my mind what I was witnessing. I could still feel the vibration under my feet, the wind groaning in response, my mother's ashes growing brighter and brighter, slowly forming outlines, silhouettes that were taking on shapes.

"Josie," Caius said, low and cautious. "We don't know what that is."

"It's okay, Caius, I promise. Somehow, I know this is okay. Mom would never hurt me." I could no more explain how this was happening than I could the other times Caius became possessed, or I saw past visions, or how Caius and I shared this red line, this red thing, this red thread of ... fate, pulling us together, cinching us up tight like a corset, sewing together something time and space had ripped, but the wheel of fate was a mighty seamstress, she would always patch us back up. We would never break.

I would never understand how I could be standing here, at the witch's tomb, the witch who wouldn't stay buried, and watch my mother's ashes take on light, come to life, as though she were somehow resurrected and choosing to be part of the world in this particular way, but as I watched the firelit ashes swarm in and out of each other until settling into shape, I realized my mother was trying desperately to send me a message from beyond the grave.

"That's her, Caius," I whispered against him, the warmth of my tears trailing down my face.

"Your mother?"

"No," I whispered. My mother's ashes were a vessel, a tool she was using to send me a message. I just couldn't figure out what message. "The Empress—the one I always see."

I couldn't believe what I was seeing. My mother's ashes depicted The Empress perfectly. The only difference this time was she was visibly with child. The Empress looked at me and smiled. Caius's finger bit into me softly as though he were afraid something, or someone, would take me. We both supported each other, captivated and mesmerized, at this show.

The ashes thinned and split, taking the image of The Empress with it. The ashes, much like the Red Sea, parted, forming snakes, but these snakes thinned more and more, stretching outward toward me and Caius. And then they began wrapping around each other, braiding like ropes. Shadows grew in the distance, two small figures coming into view like fairies from a shadow world. Caius and I clung desperately onto each other and watched in frozen horror as the two thin ropes formed nooses around the necks of the shadow figures.

"They're going to die. *You're all going to die.* That's what *it* said to me," Caius whispered, as he threw his hand against his temple.

"No!" I screamed, breaking loose from Caius, running toward these shadow figures as though I could save them from the same terrible fate that took their lives years and years ago. But just as I headed for them, my mother's ashes dissipated like dying embers, and I realized I couldn't outrun fate. Fate had been chasing me like a bloodhound my entire life and would eventually catch me. But could I change it?

Falling to my knees, I captured a small dusting of my mother's ashes, like fading fireflies, stars whose light, much like my mother's, was growing dimmer, going out. I gently stood up, cupping my hands together, careful not to lose the last of my mother's ashes, and I replaced them in the urn. I thought I was ready, and maybe I was as ready as the universe would allow, but my mother deserved to be more than a message. I knew wherever her soul was, however it was that she was working beyond the grave, she was looking out for me. But I wanted this for her, I wanted her departure to be special, to be private, to mean something more than a past riddle.

And nothing could draw me more back to the present than the ghostly white face of Caius staring at me. I walked back to him and I could see him struggling. My heart swelled with gratitude that he fought his way through the presence that always seemed to linger nearby, in order to support me. But to what end?

Caius leaned into me, wrapping his arms around my waist. I glanced over at him momentarily to see a look of horror come across his face. While the ashes were gone, *ashes to ashes*, he looked off in the distance as though they were still there, dancing, playing a scene from some past life. He whispered, a low tremble in his voice, "I recognize this."

"What?"

He didn't answer with words, but a kiss, and all our past and future poured between us.

"It's all going to be okay, Caius. In the end, it will all be okay."

But he didn't seem convinced.

Chapter Twenty-One
The Wicked Witch

It is by no means an irrational fancy that, in a future existence, we shall look upon what we think our present existence, as a dream.
—Edgar Allan Poe

Aunt Lindsey

Life is a strange series of events, the past even more so. Sometimes your current path is strung together by past lives intersecting like highways, one life like a bridge, crossing over another, and another, and another. I'd say since Caius broke into our store, our world has been turned upside down. But the truth is, this feeling, this growing cloud, stretching and reaching, so close, had been hovering since Janet died.

The stars, my cards, my stones, every damn thing I have at my disposal has been like a broken compass, spinning in circles like some twisted wheel of fate. And I keep waiting for the head of the needle to land on Josie, land on Caius, but it feels like fate is always one step ahead of me, keeping me on my toes. And when fate was a fickle bitch, you had to be a wicked witch if you were going to keep up.

I was convinced Caius and Josie would both be dead had I not planted black obsidian on them before they went to the witch's grave. While the tea leaves had been elusive, they did tell me shit was about to hit the proverbial fan when those two left my den. They weren't bait. They were children. But I had to allow them to navigate their life path to see where it was taking them, hoping it would reveal what they were up against so I could prepare some kind of battle strategy.

"She took Janet's ashes," Sophie said matter-of-factly.

"I know." And I did. While Janet was dead, her ashes still had some kind of strange energy to them, and once that energy left the house, I was acutely aware.

"They're going to that damned witch's grave, aren't they?"

I ran my fingers across the leather of my cigarette case, itching to pull one out, and feeling the need to quit at the same time. High levels of stress were nearly impossible conditions in which to quit under, but I kept hearing my sweet Josie chastising me for my poor habits, and I wasn't too old to listen to her.

I picked up my tea cup and held it out for Sophie to see the pattern of leaves left at the bottom. "It would seem so."

"Should we let her?" Sophie asked, her brows knit tightly together, a severe look shadowing her face.

"I think we must," I answered hesitantly. "We can't interfere with fate too much. Fate is stronger than me."

"Well, we can follow them," Sophie said. I knew my twin, knew her like the back of my hand. I knew she was a bundle of nerves and apprehension. Aside from each other, Josie was all we had left. Sophie didn't have a knack for the otherworldly element of the universe. She had something else entirely.

****

Sophie and I stayed several feet behind. Caius and Josie had no idea we were following them. It was heartbreaking on so many levels watching my niece carry what was left of her mother, knowing through one release, another prison of sorts would be created.

My gut was raging, instincts flying like red flags at a race. The closer and closer we got to the witch's grave, the more aware I became of a presence—not necessarily an evil one like the last time, but something lingering just on the outskirts of the shadows, something waiting, watching…

The branches of the willows parted, giving way to the grave—one I hadn't been to in years until recently. I glanced over to Sophie, her gaze fixed straight ahead on our niece and Caius. Neither of us spoke a word. We stayed back far enough so they couldn't see us, but close enough we could see them. There was so much energy swirling about, it was hard to distinguish the source of each.

I watched in silence as Josie removed the lid from the urn, and was awestruck by the scene unfurling before me and my twin. The ashes of our beautiful Janet danced up in the air like carefree fireflies, soaring, weaving in and out of each other, but then they formed images. Strange images. As terrifying as this was for me to watch and try to decipher, and as gut wrenching as it was to see my niece's reaction, there was a presence just beyond the grave, and it distracted me. Focusing, I honed in on it and felt the pain of a broken heart. It radiated through my entire body and deep into my soul, which felt torn apart.

Twin flames.

Of course.

I scanned the field and tree line until I found him. His posture was slumped in sadness, his head slightly bowed as he took a long swallow from a brown paper bag then ruffled agitated fingers through his hair. Joseph would always find Janet, in every life. And as strange as him knowing Janet's ashes were being scattered, it wasn't as unsettling as the holographic image going in and out of focus in between him and his daughter.

Joseph didn't appear to be phased by anything other than watching Janet's ashes soar, an invisible hand weaving together an old story. He didn't even budge when Josie ran toward him, unaware he was there to begin with. He remained hidden, but I could see him. I could also see the apparition of a man in front of him, as though Joseph's body was casting a ghostly shadow, a man from long, long ago.

Tall and muscular from whatever hard labor he'd been subjected to, poised as though alert at all times, but just as Joseph had a look of longing and despair watching his twin flame's ashes being dispersed in the air, the apparition of the man in front of him had a simultaneous look of love while gazing at my sister's ashes—rather the image of a woman, a noble woman.

Joseph poured the contents of the bag onto the ground, tossed it, and turned to leave.

Chapter Twenty-Two
Ouroboros

No matter how powerful, all curses can be broken.
—Rumpelstiltskin

Caius

   Journal—

   Ouroboros. The Ouroboros expresses the unity of all things which never disappears but perpetually changes form in an eternal cycle of destruction and re-creation. It was fate. It was fate constantly devouring itself and being reborn—different but still the same—but the ending couldn't change because it was constantly being chomped by the head. There wasn't a way to change it ... unless you chopped the fucking snake in half. And that was my job.

****

   In the dark, a beetle skittered across uneven cobblestone, pausing to sense the air, twitching antennae this way and that, before moving on quickly. An old man with a yellowed beard sat at a desk of stone in front of a fire, vehemently cursing as he vigorously smeared a tacky red substance in circles around a large parcel of parchment. The man himself paused, glancing into the fire where three figures—one female and one male took shape. The Empress and the guard. They were clutching each other in clear distress.

   The evil entity laughed, a deep and evil sound. "Your love will never be free from my curse."

   And it echoed as a ripple through time.

   In the dark, I woke from the dream, gasping for breath and clutching my sheets—the fabric, damp from sweat, woven between my fingers. After the releasing of ashes, Josie and I had tried our best to get to a normal place, to just be teenagers, but both of us felt the evil undercurrent. We were both having these episodes of some kind of awakening to the past. I had a history teacher who always said if we didn't understand the past, we were doomed to repeat it, so I was a trying to accept what was happening as lessons, but damn, sometimes it was just fucking scary.

I reached for the cigarettes on my bedside table and rummaged through my pack, but they were all broken, courtesy of Josie. She was adamant I stop smoking the "cancer sticks". She'd poured out my beer, too, saying I used it as a crutch. She wasn't wrong, but all my vices were gone at once.

I threw back the sheets, letting the cold air from the ceiling fan wash over me. Sighing, I got up and sat down at my desk to write, reflecting on all our experiences, but nothing would come. I wrote the date, scratched it out, scribbled my name, then Josie's. I doodled like a little kid in the corners, letting my mind wander—sometimes that helped my process—and before I knew it, my hand, as if by its own volition, was drawing a Ferris wheel. I glanced at the Lover's card and the Death card I'd swiped from Lindsey's room while I was working. I couldn't help it—I'd wanted them close so I could really study them.

The carnival was coming up soon, and Josie's friend was coming in. Jamal was all she'd talked about for two weeks. *"When it comes to friends, Jamal and I are real. We can just be ourselves. There are no secrets between us."* The more she told stories about their friendship, the more I wasn't sure how the meeting would go. Jamal liked things to be perfect—from matching outfits, to obsessing over winged eyeliner, whatever that meant—and "perfect" freaked me out… because what lay beneath the surface of all that "perfect"? It had to be chaos. There was nothing else. And that was me. I was chaos; a hurricane in the suburbs. I wasn't so sure Jamal would take to hurricane Caius.

Jamal also seemed pretty protective of Josie, and well, I was too, so I just couldn't be sure we'd get on well. I was anxious, but I was still looking forward to the carnival. I'd win my girl a giant teddy bear. I could see the smile on her face as she carried a bear as big as she was through the crowd, and her setting him up and waving to him as we rode the rides. And if Jamal won her a bear too, well, I'd just have to get a bigger one.

I shook my head, trying to not set any preconceived notions about Jamal. "Her best friend is coming to visit, dude," I whispered to myself. "Snap out of this shit. You're acting like it's the end of the fucking world."

It was then the Death card fell over onto my sketch of the Ferris wheel.

Chapter Twenty-Three
The Hanged Man

Love never dies a natural death. It dies because we don't know how to replenish its source. It dies of blindness and errors and betrayals. It dies of illness and wounds; it dies of weariness, of witherings, of tarnishings.
—Anais Nin

Josephine

The Emperor was a cruel man. Perhaps the responsibility of ruling an empire made one cruel. He never showed sympathy. Mercy was foreign to him. As Emperor, it was required of him to take a wife. He'd never settle for the woman who actually loved him despite his wicked ways. Instead, he sent for the fairest princess from a noble line, one that stretched back to the dawn of time itself.

The Empress was not his equal in cruelty. On the contrary, she was boundlessly kind. Her spirit would be crushed under his tyranny because love was also not something the Emperor was capable of. To the Emperor, the Empress was just another possession, one made of flesh and bone, one that had a soul he cared nothing for. Because the Emperor liked his possessions guarded, the universe offered the Empress a boon in the shape of a guard, the strongest gladiator in the empire.

Their love was forbidden, and once the Emperor was apprised of the Empress's deception, his rage and anger was inconsolable. He couldn't kill the Empress because she was beloved by their people. But he couldn't bear the treachery, the absolute insult of her turning from him—the Emperor who was mighty, powerful, and rich— to a mere gladiator, a peasant. There had to be punishment. The Emperor turned to dark powers, the powers of the witch who loved him, who had always loved him. The witch had always done anything and everything he'd asked of her without question. But this time, she had terms and conditions for her services, for which he wasn't prepared.

She confessed her love for him and told him she would no longer do his bidding unless he would surrender his heart to her, or her dark magic would be withheld. The Emperor agreed, but little did the witch know, he had no heart to give.

The witch was blinded by her love of the Emperor, and her heart was broken tenfold when he betrayed her. They would all pay—the Emperor, the Empress, the guard. She was the Fool.

****

"So let me get this straight," Jamal said, squinting one eye at me as though trying to crunch facts that were not facts in his brain. "You believe lover boy is possessed by some evil dude who's been chasing different versions of you two throughout time, and you both are cursed?"

"It's a bit more complicated than that." I sighed. "But, well, yes."

I watched Jamal try to digest this information dump while sipping on some kombucha we'd snagged from the store.

"Honey, has he been giving you drugs?"

I laughed under my breath. "No. Jamal, this is serious. Try to understand. I know how it sounds. Everything, all of it, sounds like a bad dream."

"Girl, that does *not* sound like a dream, bad or good. It sounds like you ate some mushrooms or took acid and don't realize you are straight tripping," Jamal said, one perfectly manicured eyebrow arched high in obvious doubt of my account.

"I'm sure," I added, sitting down beside him on our porch swing, tucking my knees up to my chin. "Jamal…" I looked over at him with eyes that said *we've been friends since we were little kids. I'm serious. I'm scared.* But what came out of my mouth instead was, "I feel like I'm going to die." The last thing I heard before drifting back, my brain like particles floating away in the wind to another time, was Jamal screaming for my Aunt Lindsey.

****

The Empress was repulsed at the sight of blood, of anguish, of death. The Emperor, on the other hand, made sport of it. He decreed a single son from each peasant family be given to the empire when they reached the age of sixteen. Once donated to the Empire, each boy was given crude lessons in fighting, readied to be junior gladiators. Human devastation and sacrifice were the Emperor's new entertainment for himself and his land. This sick, twisted sport made it so friend killed friend, cousin killed cousin, and so on. To say this practice was cruel was an understatement, but despite the sacrifice of their children, crowds gathered at the events, cheering and jeering the young men in the arena.

The Empress knew if she openly opposed the death matches, the Emperor would only require more fights each night, meaning death would come earlier for some, and she didn't want that responsibility on her soul. But when the Emperor wasn't watching her, she would look away as much as possible and pray to the universe to somehow put a stop to this misery. It's odd how the universe answers you.

"Tonight is an auspicious night! Tonight, we celebrate my Empress, your Empress!" the Emperor roared from his pulpit to the crowd below. Already knowing how twisted he was, the Empress dreaded

whatever scheme the Emperor had come up with. "The man who emerges as victor tonight will retire from the ring and serve as personal bodyguard to my Empress."

The crowd erupted in cheers, but her heart descended into despair. Just when the Empress thought it impossible for the Emperor to devise a plot any more sinister than the last, he always managed to top the last sick game. How many men were in the ring tonight? Ten? Twenty? All with the thought she was their ticket to freedom? If she could offer herself up as sacrifice to atone for the sins of her wicked husband, she would.

****

"Josie! Josie!" I heard Aunt Lindsey say firmly while the smell of lavender and rosemary drifted up, helping me to come out of the other realm, the one ruled by an evil Emperor. I felt my eyes flutter open. I was met on my right by Aunt Lindsey, and on my left was Jamal, wearing the most concerned look I think I'd ever seen on his beautiful face, despite his eyeliner swirling in black pools at the corners of his eyes.

"Jamal, you messed up your makeup," I said, teasingly.

Immediately, his hands went to his face. "Oh, shut up. It's acceptable to cry when your best friend tells you she's going to die and faints right in front of you."

"Oh, I think I fell asleep," I said, giving them both a reassuring smile. "Really, this heat, the swing, reconnecting with my best friend … I just got comfy and voila! Did I snore?" The kombucha I'd had in my hand was spilled out all over the ground.

"No ma'am. Don't you even try that," Jamal said, shaking his head vigorously. "*Not* true."

"Come in where it's cool, and I'll fix you some cold sweet tea," Aunt Lindsey said, grabbing my hand, pulling me up gently.

"Really, I'm fine. I promise," I said, standing with limbs that felt shaky, but I dug deep to show my aunt I was steady as a statue.

"Jamal, if you don't mind, please walk beside her just in case she's pulling my leg. We are going to the parlor. I'll know if you're lying then," she said, regarding me skeptically.

"Josie, I don't believe you," Jamal said under his breath as I leaned into him for support to appease my aunt.

"I promise it really was just the heat and the swaying of the swing. I guess I'm not too old to be rocked to sleep like a baby."

"Puh-lease," Jamal said, and as I gazed up at him, I could see he totally wasn't being fooled. "That looked like that one kid, oh, what was her name?" Jamal asked, face scrunched up, trying to remember. "You know the girl that had seizures?"

"Annie," I said, shaking my head. "And I don't have seizures."

"Bingo! Annie! You had an Annie-style seizure." Jamal had a momentary look of relief flash across his face before the worry set back in. "Josie, we've been friends since before we were fully potty trained. What happened back there wasn't the heat getting to you. Now, you stop lying about it."

I lowered myself down at Aunt Lindsey's table while Jamal sat across from me and she rushed into the kitchen.

"Jamal, I really do feel fine now. I'm sorry I worried you."

"Yeah, well, that part where you said you felt like you were going to die, that'll work every time."

"My aunt knows some of what is going on, but honestly, Jamal," I said with a soft sigh, "I don't even know if I understand what is going on."

He picked up a loose deck of tarot cards, and normally, I would've told him they were off limits because everything in this room was sacred to Aunt Lindsey, but something in my gut told me to let him shuffle and see where they took him.

"Have you ever had your cards read before?" I asked.

Tucking a dark curl from his pristinely fluffy hair behind his ear, Jamal laid the deck down and answered nonchalantly. "No."

"Spread them out and pick five cards but don't look."

Jamal gently fanned out the deck of freshly shuffled cards and began thoughtfully selecting five. After, he laid them in a stack in front of himself.

"Well, allow me," I said, sitting up and leaning into the table, hoping the playful animation would take his mind off what happened outside.

I flipped the first card over.

Before me lay a card with a man in a blue cloak and red tights, hanging upside down by one foot from a t-shaped tree. Lindsey had told me that tree represented the tree of life, a tree which is rooted in hell and stretches to heaven. Both the man's arms were behind him, and one leg folded behind the hanging leg, giving the man's limbs the shape of an inverted triangle. The man's head was illuminated by a halo, which Lindsey had instructed me represented the soul.

"The Hanged Man. This card implies that there is a difficult situation coming up in your life. You look to The Hanged Man for perspective—can't see a situation the right way? Try looking at it upside down. Use your new perspective to accept things and learn something because you're stuck, whether you do or don't."

"Interesting," Jamal said. "I wouldn't mind being in a difficult, upside position," he continued, snickering.

I flipped the next one. "The Hanged Man. Reversed." The same card, situated the opposite direction. Oftentimes, reversed cards had a different meaning than upright cards, but Lindsey had never really explained it to me. She'd told me to get a good grasp of the upright cards before adding the complexity of reversed cards, that some people don't read into reversed cards at all because tarot is all about interpretation and doing what works for you. Still, confusion set in across my face. There weren't two of The Hanged Man in one deck. There are no double cards in any deck, and Aunt Lindsey was meticulous in her care of her decks. She always kept them separate.

I hurried and flipped the third card.

The Hanged Man. Upright.

The fourth card.

The Hanged Man. Reversed. Goosebumps erupted across my arms.

The fifth and final card.

The Hanged Man, right once more.

Jamal looked at the cards in confusion for a split second, and then all the muscles in his face relaxed, and a strange calm seemed to come over him. He looked from the table up to me. "It would seem this little man in tights is attracted to me." With a half smile, he shrugged and said, "I've had worse."

"Here we go, kids." Aunt Lindsey entered the room with two glasses of tea and two of Sophie's famous pepperoni rolls on a tray. I could see the steam rising from the bread. Lindsey had been smiling, but suddenly stopped dead in her tracks, staring at Jamal. I looked to see what had her so transfixed, and for the faintest of moments, I could've sworn I saw the yellow glow of a halo around his entire head.

"Is something wrong with my hair," Jamal asked. "Is there a bug in it?" His voice went a pitch higher, as he patted his curls.

His words made Aunt Lindsey come to. Snapping out of whatever had her hypnotized, she delivered the snacks and tea to us. "Oh, no, dear. I was just admiring how perfect it was." A smile stretched back across her lips, but I could tell she was still slightly shaken, or spooked, or both.

"Aunt Lindsey, what is the meaning of the reversed Hangman?" I asked, trying not to sound too interested, lest I pique her concern in why I was asking. I swiped my hand over Jamal's card spread, stacking them, getting them out of the path of Lindsey's gaze.

"Depends on the reading. It can mean that your old ways aren't working for you anymore. To quit seeking shallow gratification, and to look instead for a deeper meaning. It can mean you're too impulsive, or you're dragging your feet against changes that need to happen. You must always remember that you are never powerless in life—you have the control."

I tried to ease my concern at the oddity of the straight five card reading by making a joke. "Well, Jamal, looks like you're going to have to stop searching for shallow hook ups and look for something deeper like I have with Caius."

"As if," he replied, laughing and swiping his hand dismissively in front of my face. He bit into his pepperoni roll. "Oh my God. These are heavenly. Just as delicious as I remember them being the one time of year you'd bring them back home," he said, switching gears. "Good enough for me to forget my carb strike, anyway. Now, forget this silly little hanged man, and let's get down to business. Tell me all about this carnival. I wouldn't mind meeting a wholesome West Virginia boy while I'm in. I could go for a lumberjack type. You know… because I'm so shallow."

I laughed.

"I think you both will enjoy it," Aunt Lindsey said while fluttering about the room absentmindedly picking up books, rearranging them, moving crystals around. "I'll have a booth for reading cards. Even Aunt Soap will be there. I think it's the one time of year every person in the tri-county area crawls out from underneath their rock to come."

Aunt Lindsey walked up behind me. Resting a hand on my shoulder, she said, "I think you should get some rest. I'm keeping an eye on you. Another episode like that, and there will be no carnival for anyone."

"The carnival needs to happen for everyone," Jamal said absentmindedly while chomping down on the last of his pepperoni roll.

"I beg your pardon?" Aunt Lindsey said, still behind me. I could hear the confusion riddled throughout her voice.

"The carnival," Jamal said, not missing a beat, "is a stage in which we all must perform." What a strange thing for him to say, but even stranger it was like he didn't seem to know he was saying it. His voice had none of his usual Jamal inflection and flair.

I craned my neck around to observe Aunt Lindsey's reaction. Her face was an unwavering mask of stoicism. "Indeed," she said under her breath, but I heard her.

"So, can I get the recipe for this? I *cannot* go back to Connecticut without these little bad boys in my life," Jamal said through bites of my pepperoni roll that he'd snatched from my plate, as though some other person possessed him minutes ago and just vacated, leaving my best friend in his place.

Chapter Twenty-Four
The Open Arms of Death

The Death card is probably the most feared of all the cards in the Tarot deck. It's completely misunderstood, though.
—Josephine

Joe

The young gladiator had a family once. He'd had a father, a mother, a sister—a sweet baby sister who was tenderhearted and kind. Each had died indirectly by the hand of the Emperor.

His father, a farmer, had fought to keep his only son hidden away from the emperor's knights when they came to collect him for the junior gladiators—he couldn't bear to lose his only son to the horrors of the gladiator ring. For that, the farmer was brutally beaten over a period of several days while the young boy, his mother and sister, were forced to watch.

When his father had finally given up and taken his last breath, the knights celebrated with wine and feast from the family's provisions, clinking glass after glass and congratulating themselves on a job well done. Once the men were sufficiently drunk, they turned to the boy's mother and sister.

One knight held the boy's eyes open as the others committed unspeakable acts against the women. The boy squirmed and spat and bucked against the man holding him, but he was too weak to do anything but suffer against the knight as increasingly brutal atrocities happened to his mother and sister until they begged for death.

After the savage murders of his family, he swore

to breathe in and out, put one foot in front of the other, and kill anyone standing in the way of his vengeance. His heart had blackened when his father passed and had been ground to ash when his mother and sister took their last breaths. All that remained in him, all that flowed through his veins, was a cold, hard resolve to avenge his family.

It took him more than four years of killing in the ring, killing old mates, killing his own blood. Even killing the brother of the girl he'd been supposed to marry before revenge was the only thing that kept him breathing, as ash coursed through his veins as blood, sparking and fueling the fire that had become his soul. A scrawny sixteen-year-old boy, now a twenty-year-old man, muscles chiseled by countless victories, to finally have the opportunity he'd prayed to the universe for. Funny, how the universe answers you.

The evening was just like any other. The crowds were a mix of people filled with horror or excitement at the fighting. The stadium enclosed the gladiators—some ready to die, some believing they wouldn't—and then there was the Emperor and the Empress. Every time before fighting, all it took was one steely glance of the Emperor to add fuel to an inferno of hate housed within the wall of the gladiator's chest, and the gladiator always emerged the victor. Not because he wanted to kill—he'd gladly die, wanted to die—but not before taking away everything the Emperor loved and the slow torture of the Emperor himself. It was only then the gladiator would close his own eyes forever and rest at last.

When the Emperor announced whoever emerged the victor would be personal bodyguard to the Empress, the gladiator could hardly believe what he was hearing. It had been what he'd prayed for, for so long—the chance to get close enough to the ruling family to degrade and butcher them—and now, victory would be his.

The gladiator sliced and stabbed his way through the meat and bone of men, wasting no time disposing of those whose time he knew had come too early. But with his final endgame so close to his grasp, he wouldn't allow himself to care, or even see those men as men. The gladiator was death, the living embodiment of death. Death was all he knew, and soon, at his hands, it would be the only language the imperial family spoke.

After being cleansed from the human debris, the gladiator was told he'd be introduced to the Empress the next night, and he was briefed on the etiquette: he wasn't to speak, and he was to keep his head lowered at all times. To this, he rebutted with absolute authority. "Do you think I kept my head lowered in the ring? My swords are only as good as my eyes. How am I to defend a woman whose eyes I cannot meet?" He received no argument.

After a celebratory feast, the gladiator slept that night in the palace on a cold, hard cot, dreaming of victory and vengeance. His revenge was so close to him now he could smell it in the air. He'd seize the first opportunity he had. Maybe snap her neck, crush her windpipe, or slit her throat, and then quickly seek out the Emperor. After all, the Emperor would surely keep the Empress close to him, and the Emperor couldn't be too far away when he disposed of the Empress.

For the first time in nearly four years, he thought about his parents and sister when they were all alive and happy. After the massacre, he'd refused to allow himself to remember them any other way than that of his father's beaten and bloody corpse swinging off a tree in the middle of their village for all to see what would happen should you refuse to offer up your sons, and the frozen looks of horror on the swollen faces of his dead mother and sister. Those images were seared into his brain that night, and they kept him going. But tonight, with relief from this life soon on its way, he allowed himself the simple joy of happier times, for the gladiator would see them again, soon.

The next day he was briefed on matters of security, toured through the palace, drilled on protocol. And then, at last, after four grueling years of existing, of waiting and wanting, the moment to avenge his family was at hand. He was led to the Empress's chambers. Two large doors made of finer material than he'd ever seen in his life were opened to reveal the Empress standing with her back to him. He glanced back and forth, astonished to find the Empress alone, not even a chambermaid to be found, but the sound of closing doors snapped him back to the task at hand.

He now stood at the foot of all he'd ever wanted. And better yet, this was too simple. He rested his hand on the hilt of his sword, seconds passing as he digested what death blow he'd deliver to the Empress. He'd seen enough blood and guts, felt enough flesh severe from bone... He'd keep this a clean kill; he'd snap her neck in a split second.

He stepped forward ever so quietly, stretching his fingers out in anticipation of wrapping them around her pale neck only to twist and crush the life from her, and make haste to the Emperor.

He'd prepared himself for every scenario the Gods could throw at him. The possibility of dying before living to see his family avenged and having to beg forgiveness from them in the afterlife. He'd considered years and more years of fighting in the gladiator's ring, an old man by the age of forty, ready to fall under the next champion's sword. He'd imagined so many possibilities, but always with the hunger to deliver justice, death always at the end of it.

But never, never in a million years did he ever consider the love of a living, breathing woman. He'd been ambushed by the Empress as she turned, stunning him with her mirror-like eyes, long hair draped around her, the sadness etched on her beautiful features somehow making her all that much more beautiful. And then as she threw her arms around him and buried her tear-stained face into his neck, he felt something he'd not felt in four years—a heart that beat differently, a soul that stirred in recognition, the birth of two flames that would chase each other life after life.

He didn't snap her neck. Instead, all the bitterness of ages melted away as he embraced her in return. In that embrace all the pain of yesterday, every death, every agonizing breath, every shred of guilt at being responsible for the death of his family, every bit of sorrow turned to sand, and like particles slipping through an hourglass, it all dissipated and soon his hate turned to something else. Something he hadn't been prepared for the universe to send him. Love.

But while their love was an eternal one, it wasn't meant to last. Curses were.

*****

My heart beat was nothing more than an ache, drumming against the hollow of my chest. Loss ran through my veins as blood. Janet's face burned behind my eyelids, and each time I blinked, I dreamed—Janet laughing beside me; Janet humming lullabies to our daughter. The dreams started as hopes, but they became nothing more than memories, reminders of what I allowed to slip through my fingertips. As time stretched between us, the dreams grew less and less clear, like looking through a busted windshield—the visuals were still there but distorted, colors muted, figures blurred just out of recognition.

The tragic sense of fundamental loss remained, however. The longer I drowned them in booze, the more parts of myself I lost, expecting to one day wake up not even recognizing myself in the mirror, and it was then the past would be erased—there would be no more Janet because there had never been a Janet. We had never made Josie—my sweet baby girl, Josie, dragging blankets as she toddled through the house. But in fifteen years, that hadn't happened. Every day, I woke up to the same disappointing motherfucker as I had the day before. Because I couldn't forget. Janet was as much a part of me as my heart, broken as it was, and I'd learned the hard way that even a broken heart keeps the beat, sustains a life, keeps you existing.

But existing isn't the same as living.

Not at all.

It's being the living dead.

I am Death.

In each life, I chased my twin flame, fanning her fire like oxygen feeds the inferno. Happiness, sheer bliss, was ours but for a moment—such was our curse. As I watched our daughter release her mother's ashes, I closed my eyes and felt each life burst like aneurysms in my brain, the remembrance of an eternal love waking up my soul. And always, always right before I fulfilled my duty as Death, I would remember how it all began, how each life played out, a horror and fate worse than death. Suffering—that was my role.

In this life, I'd had Janet for a brief few years. Such agony to have lost her in this life to my alcoholism which quickly dissipated in my awakening, like a puddle drying under the sun and was no more. Along with my mind and soul waking up, my body began taking on its former attributes, like aging in reverse in time to complete my task. Over and over again.

But the worst part of the curse wasn't losing the love of my many lives, because I knew—no matter how brief—I'd see her again, but something more dark and more sinister than even loving and losing was being the one cursed to take your daughter's life. My mind was awake for each and every time her death occurred, but my body was not my own. Its movements were controlled by an evil puppeteer.

I'd been the hangman, the executioner operating the guillotine, the marksman, countless men delivering death. Always to my little girl.

And when I put on the blaze orange and yellow vest embroidered with *Gamble Amusement*, I was going to operate the Ferris wheel at Bridgeport's annual carnival.

Chapter Twenty-Five
The Hanging Night

You must forgive me, for I struggled only for you.
—Emily Brontë, Wuthering Heights

The Fool

The girl grew up in poverty, moving from one hovel to another, living in filth and knowing nothing more than the pangs of hunger and cold, sleepless nights, until her mother secured a position within the palace walls, cleaning. The girl watched her mother work herself to death, slaving day in and day out, the epitome of morals and hard work. Her mother never complained. If anything, her mother was grateful because she considered their situation in this wretched life to be fortunate, for her daughter no longer had to starve. The girl couldn't understand it, couldn't grasp why her mother chose this hard life when the Gods had blessed them with magic.

Her mother refused to use magic, saying that while it ran through generations of their female bloodline, and that blood ran through the girl as well, evil could spawn from the slightest misuse of it. "Every gift comes with a price," her mother would say, and she'd rather work her fingers to the bone than wager death with the flick of her wrist.

The girl didn't mind the price.

When she wasn't helping her mother scrub floors and empty chamber pots, she was busy hiding, honing her extraordinary skills in secret for fear her mother would discover her dishonesty. While she wholeheartedly disagreed with her mother's outlook on magic, she loved her mother completely and did not want to disappoint *her-her mother was much too kind and good a creature for that. But as the girl grew into a young woman, she watched her mother grow in sickness, her health steadily declining over the years.*

Her mother was all she had, and she meant everything to her. She took on half her mother's chores to compensate for her mother's diminishing strength, limiting her ability to work. She also sacrificed half her sleep, slipping off after her mother was fast asleep, staying up most of the night to practice the dark art.

As her mother's skin grew greyer and her breaths more ragged, the urgency to preserve life was paramount. The girl started out by reviving flowers, their wilting petals springing back like they'd freshly sprouted from the earth, and then next a frog—legs kicked and soon the rest of its body followed, and then, the final test—a deer. She went deep into the woods, collecting ingredients as she went, chanting words foreign to all but a witch's tongue, a language that lived and thrived within her.

She followed the stench of death, knowing it belonged to the carcass of a deer. At last, she'd found her final test to prove she had the true strength of a witch powerful enough to bear the title, powerful enough to defy death.

But the cost of life was death. And the cost of death is a life.

Her heart rose higher and higher as she chanted, watching the torn flesh knit itself back together until the fallen deer was whole again. And the thrill of her being, her soul singing in victory as she watched the deer perk up, looking around strangely as though it had been in a deep sleep. When its dull, black eyes met the witch's, they conveyed she'd disturbed a rest that should've been left alone. A fly crawled from its nostril, froze for a moment, then ascended to the sky. The deer rose, unsteady at first, then took off through the trees.

It was then the girl's heart sank, falling to depths from which it would never rise again. For in giving life, she stole the life out of another.

She ran and ran. The palace had never been so far away as it was now. She chanted, sang, screamed into the night, her power boiling to a dangerous tipping point. And as her shrill screams pierced the night, two streaks of white hair framed a face that was once crowned with raven black hair—a reminder of what she'd done.

She burst through the modest room she and her mother shared, dropping beside her mother whose breathing was shallow. Her mother's face withered as death began to harvest her, rip her from the arms of a daughter who loved her more than anything in this universe. How could this be? What had she worked for all these months but to conquer death all in the name of saving her mother from the very hand snuffing her out?

"Mama! Mama!"

Her mother turned her pale blue eyes toward her daughter. For an instant, she saw the deer's black eyes reflected in them before all the light began draining from behind them. Why? How? It would be the last time she was ever looked upon by any human being with flesh and blood and a beating heart with love in their eyes for her.

"Don't leave me!" The girl sobbed and sobbed, clinging onto her mother where her magic failed to. "I tried, Mama. I tried..."

"Giselle," Mama said, brushing one of a thousand tears away from her daughter's wet face. "My darling daughter, your magic came with a price." She could do no more but smile weakly at her daughter and breathe her last breath as her pale blue eyes closed forever. The young witch's heart turned to stone and

cracked.

She would never be called Giselle again. Only the Fool.

****

In the end, Giselle was given enough time off from her duties to bury her mother. She could've used magic to do it, but in honoring her mother, she dug the grave by hand, and with her mother, she buried every shred of honor she'd had.

After that, she had turned her attention to the young Emperor in the palace. She wanted power, the kind of power only he could give her. She had magic and had perfected the dark art, but she craved position within the palace. She wouldn't believe she was destined to be poor, to live the hard-working life her mother had. A woman born with the magic she possessed was meant to rule an empire.

The witch wove her magic so that the two of them were constantly crossing paths. She grew into a beautiful woman, thick raven black hair along with a shock of white on either side, framing her smooth and pale oval face, obsidian eyes, matching her thick, wavy hair that fell down to her narrow waist, just brushing the tops of full hips. And soon, the Emperor took notice of the beauty cleaning his chambers.

What started out as the witch planting herself on a chess board full of pawns, turned into a match far greater than her magic was equipped to deal with. What she expected was power. What she didn't expect was love.

What started as a dream for power became a dream of being his Empress for love. She found herself gently encouraging the Emperor with her magic, just the slightest bit of influence because, deep down, she wanted him to love her naturally, not because she forced it through dark means. She began daydreaming about being his bride. Lust for an empire became love for an Emperor.

The first time he took her into his bed, she'd bought into the idea he felt the same way about her, forgetting, or rather turning a blind eye, to the fact that while the doses were small, her magic was all consuming. In time, she even revealed to him her hidden talents, the sacred power within. And so blinding was her love that the witch couldn't see that while the Emperor may have lusted for her in bed, out of it, he only wanted her for what her magic could do for him and for his empire. She desperately wanted to be the queen on the chess board, but in the end, she was nothing more than a pawn.

Giselle, witch of the empire, scorned lover of the Emperor, had her heart broken for the second time with the announcement the empire was to receive an Empress. Who had she been fooling? Nobility didn't course through her veins, just magic. She was born into poverty and no amount of magic would ever change the peasant she was born as. She hadn't cried since her mother's death, but on that night, she sat at her windowsill looking out into the night, the light of the moon beckoning her as though telling her she had a home there. She felt the wetness on her face and the pain in her heart.

She began talking to the moon, as though that ball of glowing energy could hear her, had power stronger than hers, and she heard herself bargaining into the night, asking for the Emperor to love her. But she was only answered with the soft chirp of the katydids' song being carried away with the passing breeze. For who could ever love a witch? For who could ever love a fool?

She began her journey wanting to save her mother, but in the end was responsible for hastening her death. All these years later, she began another journey wanting more power in the empire, and it had backfired on her again. By believing she was worthy of being loved, she'd gambled with her heart and lost.

She thought back to her mother's warning and reflected on everything her magic had cost her. She swore to never use it again. Vowed to the moon and stars she'd be good and virtuous like her mother. She'd offered her services as a chambermaid to the Empress in order to remove herself from the path of the Emperor.

When she met the Empress, she was not prepared to see the great beauty before her. The Empress was indeed regal. She carried herself with an air of grace and elegance one would expect of only the most refined nobility. She was as kind as she was beautiful. She was everything the witch wished she herself was. Envy began to grow in her heart. And soon the witch realized she would never be what she desired above all else—to be the object of the Emperor's love. She fought with herself daily, and the envy in her took on a life of its own, whispering encouraging words into her ear, daring her to use her magic to take what she wanted. But the image of her dying mother would somehow come into view and provide a grave reminder of the consequences abusing magic had bestowed upon her.

But time took care of all things, if you waited long enough.

A gladiator was removed from the ring, appointed personal bodyguard to the Empress. And the Empire's little darling turned out to be an adulteress! As her chambermaid, the witch saw everything. The Empress thought she'd had the witch's loyalty, had confided in her, begged her not to tell. But the witch couldn't bear for the Emperor—her Emperor—to be made a cuckold! And when she told him of his Empress's betrayal, he was furious indeed, boiling over with red hot anger. The witch expected heartbreak from the Emperor, not anger. Perhaps he didn't love the Empress after all, had never loved her, because his heart harbored love for the witch...

The Emperor came to the witch. He asked her to curse the gladiator and his Empress for this betrayal, but the witch swore never to use magic again; it had cost her too much. The Emperor was shocked at the witch's refusal. So he offered her something he knew she couldn't refuse.

Curse the Empress and her gladiator, and he would forfeit everything to be with her, the lowly peasant girl who loved him above all else. He offered himself, all of him, all of his heart and soul.

Giselle agreed without hesitation. She'd won her Emperor at last! Goodness was repaid with more goodness, and like her mother, morals and virtue could bring you reward, if you had faith. She'd refrained from using her magic. She was finally being accepted for who she was—a poor girl who loved the Emperor more than he deserved.

That night, she waited silently in the shadows for the Empress and her gladiator who was always near. She tapped into her magic, opening herself up as a vessel to receive the energy from the universe. She'd shut down that part of her for so long it took a minute to realize there weren't just two souls tethered to this curse, but she could pick up on the faintest beating of another heart. The Empress was with child. This changed things.

She went back to the Emperor with reports the Empress was expecting a child and she couldn't complete a curse involving a child. She just simply wouldn't.

"I understand," he said, his voice low and impassioned.

"You'll still honor your end? You will still leave

with me?" the witch asked, hope rising in a fragile heart.

What she didn't realize was that the Emperor had made a promise he never intended to keep. He'd allow her to believe they'd meet at the border of the realm, but what he intended was to have his men waiting on her, ready to dispose of her. She was too powerful, and he was done with her. Without her magic, she was of no use to him now.

"Go, my love. Meet me under the cover of the giant willow once the moon is high. I'll be there."

Her heart rose higher from the depths than she ever thought it could. Could love truly be at the border waiting for her? Would the fool get her happy ending?

The third and final time her heart broke would be the downfall of them all.

****

Giselle had struggled her entire life with doing what she wanted versus what was right. She knew love. Her mother had shown her in the way she looked at her like the sun was in her eyes and she wore the moon for a crown. Her mama would sing her to sleep while brushing her hair away from her eyes, a sleepy caress that always worked. But Mama died, and Giselle's hand had been what delivered the death blow.

It didn't seem to matter to the Gods how hard Giselle tried, they constantly set traps along the way of her life, as though she were destined to fail. Giving her magic and not giving her guidance on how to hone and use it. Allowing her to fall in love with the Emperor and being too beneath him to be truly considered as anything more than a toy to play with and a pawn to be used. The Empress—the other woman—cleaning after her, day in and day out. Things that don't bend break, and just when she thought she'd be the latter, the Gods finally took mercy on her—love would finally be hers.

She made her way to the willow, a massive tree with a trunk stretching to the sky and limbs draping wide. It was the largest willow in the empire. Giselle's heart hammered in her chest, trying to beat its way out of a home where no heart belonged. She looked around. Her Emperor nowhere in sight, but men, the Emperor's men, guards from the palace, were placed strategically around the willow, spears and shields in hand.

"Have you come to take the Emperor back to the palace?" Giselle asked, stopping abruptly as she approached the hand-picked army. She shouted the Emperor's name. "Come out, love. I can handle this army! I can keep you safe!" Her magic could keep them both safe from the men. She hoped, but deep down knew better, that the Emperor's plan to run away with her had been discovered and these men were here to drag him back to the palace. She combed the landscape again for her love, but the Emperor was nowhere to be found. "Come out! Let us go! Let us be together!"

Nothing happened.

As Giselle's heart crumbled inside, she felt the warmth of love being steadily replaced with the iciness of hate, her blood running cold in her veins.

The men closed in on her. One shouted with perfunctory rudeness. "By order of the Emperor, you have been sentenced to death, witch."

Giselle cursed the Gods. The little girl witch who failed at saving her mother was no longer young and weak. She was fully grown, and in that moment realized her heart was what had held her back from her full potential all these years, but now her heart was dead and she felt the deepest well of dark magic within her, screaming to be released. She felt the hum in her body, her blood a network of an ancient language, words uttered that would kill, kill, kill.

And she uttered them.

Every single syllable.

Every word that came to her was released in a whirlwind as bodies dropped and littered the ground under the willow tree. It was a battlefield of her own making, and she bathed in their blood, smiled and relished in it like it were sweet perfume.

As the last man fell, she turned her attention back to the palace. She wasn't finished yet. This night would end one era and begin another.

She burst through the palace, brick and mortar flying in an explosion. Those who attempted to stop her were disposed of with the chanting of her lips, poisonous words finding their way to the ears of those who stood in between her and the Emperor. Blood dripped from her as she ascended the large, ornate stairway as though she were finally a queen, each step staining the white marble with red.

With a flick of her wrist, the doors to the Emperor's chambers flew open, revealing the wicked man himself. He was a devil—a handsome, sweet talking liar whose forked tongue had uttered its last untruth.

"You always were so beautiful to me, so godly," Giselle said, approaching him slowly.

"I–" the Emperor began, but Giselle clenched her fist and with it sealed the Emperor's mouth shut.

"Oh, no, my love. Now, you will listen to me," Giselle said, closing in on him. While clenching one fist, with the other, she held her palm up, freezing the Emperor in place. The panicked look in his eyes did nothing to garner sympathy from her. Sympathy could only be felt by one who had a heart.

She stopped just behind him so they could both look into the floor length mirror. She looked wild, her raven black hair turned wiry, crusted with blood, crimson spatters on what should've been her bridal dress—a mere peasant's cloth with embroidered flowers. Evil permeated the air around her. She began chanting in words foreign to the Emperor.

"You've always loved yourself, only yourself. Your vanity," Giselle laughed, a throaty roar that echoed throughout his chambers, "is wicked." They both watched in the mirror as the once beautiful, Adonis of an Emperor, turned old. His marble-like, sun-kissed skin faded from a golden brown to parched and cracked, his hair yellowing as though stained, his posture sinking in on itself until an old ragged man withered by the hand of time stood in the place where the Emperor used to be.

"How handsome you are!" Giselle said, her lips curling up in satisfaction, two streams of blood running down from her eyes in place of tears. "But I'm not through with you." She leaned in closer, a whisper in his ear. "You'll never be rid of me." She wiped the smallest bit of her bloody tears with a single finger. With a smile, she grasped his face and reached into his mouth. Grasping his tongue, she pulled it out as far as it would stretch. She wiped the blood of her tear into his tongue, a scarlet dot searing a witch's mark into the wet flesh.

He writhed in pain, muttering muted, unintelligible words.

The witch laughed, and she left him in a frozen state to admire himself in the golden mirror while she strolled down the expansive hall toward the Empress.

Snapping her fingers, she threw the doors open to the Empress's massive chambers. The gladiator, ever quick to protect his Empress, had his sword drawn in an instant. But metal was no match for her. As she narrowed her eyes, the metal crumpled in his hand until it was no more than a useless ball.

"Gladiator." Giselle closed in on him, a slow

descent with precise movement. "Since it is death you love to deliver, it is Death you shall be."

He was in the same suspended state as the Emperor, frozen, unable to move, all except his eyes. The line of his gaze followed the witch, his eyes growing bigger and bigger, bulging as though the harder he strained the more likelihood he had of escaping this witchcraft and protecting the Empress.

But the witch was too powerful.

"Do you know my name?" Giselle asked, black hair swirling around her like a cloud of doom.

Silence was all that passed between them, and Giselle had to give the Empress credit, the only movement she made was to gently fold her arms across her rounded belly.

"I do not," the Empress said in a low, soothing voice, calm and graceful.

Giselle narrowed obsidian eyes at the Empress. She despised the Emperor, loathed him for his betrayal, but she hated the Empress, hated her with every molecule that made up her being. She hated her because the Empress represented everything she wasn't, possessed everything she had wanted. The Empress was beautiful, kind, loved by the empire, married to the Emperor—the only man Giselle had ever loved. The Empress was to be a mother, the child growing in her belly would be loved. Love. Love. Love. It was permeating the air, making Giselle sick with it, making her blood boil.

"You wouldn't," Giselle began. "For I am poor and beneath your notice. But if you were the insides of a chamber pot, you'd know me."

"I am sorry if I have wronged you in some way—"

Giselle snapped her fingers, an invisible hand clamping the Empress's lips shut. "Uh-uh-uh," Giselle said, shaking her head no. "The time for apologies is over. Time for you ... is over. My mother," Giselle said, glancing down at the Empress's rounded belly and then back up, "only had thirty-four winters before she was taken from me."

Giselle proceeded to walk closer yet to the Empress. She circled her like a predator circles its prey. The longer she took the Empress in—her beauty, her presence, the more unhinged Giselle became. She wanted them all to hurt, to break under her curse. She wanted them to die, and live again and again and again, so she could crush them over and over and over again.

And so it would be. They'd know suffering. They'd know heartache.

Like the judge, jury, and executioner, Giselle stepped down so the gladiator and the Empress both could see her as she sentenced them to an eternity of hell.

"By the Gods, you two shall have each other— twin flames that you are—each life will end for you, Empress, at thirty-four winters, never seeing your child grown, and never there to comfort Death when he takes her life over and over again."

And just as with the Emperor, Giselle marked the Empress and Death both with her blood, the smallest speck of red on their foreheads, hardly visible to the eye, but it unfurled like wildfire through them all—a root system that spread like an invasive disease connecting them all across space and time.

And with the snap of her fingers, she was back at the willow tree. Her hope was born there, a hope for a future with a man the Gods cursed her to love. And it was here at the willow tree all her hope would die. She'd marked them all, a blood curse, one that required the sacrifice of life to ensure it would never break.

Her mind was nearly gone, replaced with hatred

and loathing. But there was a grain, the smallest shred of her former self that still remained as she walked calmly to her demise. With each step she took, stepping over the corpses of men whose lives she snuffed out, she thought back to her mother. She thought about the briefest of moments when the universe afforded her a glimpse of happiness. She wondered what her mother ever saw in her. Why did her mother love her so much when she clearly wasn't worth loving? And her mother's ultimate punishment for loving her was death.

Giselle wasn't meant to love or be loved. She was cursed with darkness. Her mother's warning ran through her head as she climbed up the thick branches of the willow tree—her warning not to use magic. But magic was all she had, and she would use her life force, every last drop of the witch's blood coursing through her, sacrificing herself to ensure they all—the Emperor, the Empress, and Death—paid a heavy price. With branches roped together using blood and magic, she lowered the noose down to her and stepped into it, securing it around her neck.

With the flick of her wrist, her noose of willow branches tightened and vaulted her upward. One final thought flickered through her shattered mind, as the edges of the world went black.

None of them would escape her wrath now.

****

There was an old willow tree, an ancient looking one by the size of it, that provided a natural roof over an old tomb. There were so many stories that circulated about the witch who wouldn't stay buried. Some said it was a lover scorned. Some locals claim the tomb belonged to an actual witch burned at the stake. Some say the tomb had to be repaired every hundred years because mother nature would create erosion and damage to the tomb.

Regardless of the stories, the local lore, on one very humid night late into the summer, the tomb shattered, what lay within refusing to stay buried.

No one was there to see the obsidian eyes open once more.

SASHA HIBBS & CHRISTINA HOOKER

Chapter Twenty-Six
Carnival Part I

At the start of Creation
There was a dark without origin,
At the breaking of Creation
There is fire without end...
—Rabindranath Tagore

Josephine
The Empress had one friend in all the world, one confidant she was allotted to bring with her from her homeland—Jasmine—a sorceress by some accounts, a soothsayer by others, but to the Empress, Jasmine was her dearest friend in all the world. She was careful to keep their friendship a secret, fearing the Emperor in all his cruelty would somehow take Jasmine from her.

In a rare moment alone, Jasmine with her beautiful dark curly hair and soft eyes to match, rested a palm against the Empress's stomach. "You'll have a girl," she said, smiling up at the Empress.

A tear slid down the Empress's cheek, leaving a silver trail behind.

Jasmine knew of the Empress's troubles—an Empress all alone in an empire ruled by an evil Emperor. An Empress in love with the man selected to protect her. The two forbidden to ever be together. And fear, dreadful fear, of the Emperor discovering the love between them that had been written in the stars, a love she could no more outrun than she could prevent time from continuing on.

"When all else fails, hope must remain," Jasmine said, knowing dark days were ahead of them all.

****

The week passed fast enough. The days were spent at *Blair's Lair* working, and evenings with Jamal and Caius sizing each other up, figuring out how to both fit into my life. It was easy for me. Jamal was my best friend, always had been, always would be. Caius in a sense, was me, and I loved Jamal, therefore in time, he would too.

It was strange, the more time I spent with Jamal, the less the sense of impending doom hung over my head. I hadn't had any visions or flashbacks, or whatever they were since the one on the porch with Jamal, and thank God, Caius hadn't any possessions either. I still didn't know what any of it meant, but I wasn't questioning the break and therefore relief from it. Instead, I was simply enjoying being a girl in love with a boy, the summer coming to a close, and waiting with my best friend for the event of the season—the carnival. It was tonight, and the forecast was for perfect weather. Happiness buzzed through me.

"So, how's Maeve doing? I haven't heard much from her since I had to move." I asked about our other best friend from Connecticut. Maeve was never as close to us as Jamal and I were to each other, but we'd all grown up together until Maeve had discovered boys. The friendship had been mostly fair weather since then, her hanging out with us between boyfriends, crying to us over breakups, or asking for advice she'd never take.

"Oh, that one has been a total necktie this summer, hanging on every boy that looks her way. She's been super ghosty lately, so that means she's snagged herself some dark and mysterious man of some sort."

I chuckled. "Same old Maeve. No wonder I haven't heard from her."

"Girl, you know how she is—she'll call when he dumps her ass. Anyway, when's lover boy coming over to escort us to the ball?" Jamal said, smoothing out the wrinkles on the button-down shirt he'd no doubt spent an unreasonable amount of time choosing for tonight's festivities.

"His name is Caius, Jamal. Please call him that," I said through a half smile, while I paused applying mascara to look back at Jamal. "You'll grow to love him, too."

"Mmm-hmm," Jamal said, rolling his eyes.

"You know you're adorable when you do that," I said, a calm and happy ease settling through me. I was excited. I had my best friend with me—a reminder of home and the happy life I had led there—and my boyfriend was coming to take us to Bridgeport's event of the year, the big carnival. And maybe it seemed a bit childish, but I was excited to be under the canopy of night surrounded by all the bright lights, the smell of cotton candy and popcorn in the air, the popping of balloons as children won prizes, rides that made my stomach drop so I could squeal while holding onto Caius.

My heart was happier than it had been in several weeks. I couldn't explain it–the feeling of excitement and euphoria all at once as though my emotions were on a roller coaster ride themselves. The previous weeks had been riddled with things I couldn't understand—visions, hauntings, fragments of past lives, and I should've been guarded, but on a night where magic danced in the air, I decided to let my guard down, basking in the opportunity to have a normal night, like an ordinary teenager, like someone who was going to live forever because being this young and this content, the thought of death reaching me was too foreign a concept to grasp.

As the evening closed in, Jamal and I both added the finishing touches to our outfits. Aunt Lindsey was already set up to read tarot cards at the carnival, so it was

Aunt Sophie who waited on us before leaving herself.

She knocked on my door gently. "Caius is here," she said, peeking her head through the door.

I was glad she took the trouble to forgive him a little for his earlier offenses and at least use his first name.

"Well, let's not keep lover boy waiting," Jamal said, warm laughter in his voice.

"Jamal—"

"I'm just kidding! I'll be the perfect gentleman and bestest friend ever. I pinky promise," he said, cupping my chin, squinting one eye at me, inspecting if I used the right makeup pallet. "And dang, girl, those YouTube tutorials have paid off, not that you ever needed any make-up with such a perfect face."

"Oh please, Jamal," I said, smiling up at my best friend. He knew I was self-conscious of the scar on my eyebrow and took pains to conceal it. The eyebrow ring usually did the trick.

"One last finishing touch," Jamal said, dangling a small necklace in front of me. "Let me put this on you."

"What's this?"

"Do you remember telling me you couldn't bear to spread all your mother's ashes?"

"Yes," I answered, as I turned, lifting my hair out of the way for him.

"Well, you don't have to. The rest of them are in this necklace, and you can keep them close or put them away."

I let my hair fall, reaching my hand up to cup the small white pendant that contained all I had left of my mother.

"Now don't cry, dammit, you'll mess up your perfect makeup," Jamal said.

The tears set still in my eyes, unfallen. I was

overcome with sadness thinking about my mother, but I also felt a sense of calm having Jamal so near. And just when I thought I couldn't love Jamal any more, his entire demeanor softened, a very serious side coming out that had only ever occurred one other time in my life—when my mother died. "Josie," he said, brushing a loose strand of hair away from my scarred eyebrow, "you are beautiful. I hope I've taken every opportunity to tell you that. And Caius, well…" He gave me a lopsided smile. "He's all right. I *suppose*."

"Are you okay?" I asked, looking up at him suspiciously.

"You know," he said, as though deep in consideration, "I actually am. I have a good feeling about tonight."

I couldn't explain it, but I did too.

Jamal and I walked down the hall and then downstairs where Caius was waiting. It never got old, seeing him was always like the very first time, over and over again. He made my heart happy, my soul at ease. And I could see him light up in his own Caius-way. There were subtle things, like his lips twitching upward into a barely perceivable grin, and his green eyes somehow became greener, more animated when he looked at me. He bent to kiss my cheek. "You look really pretty, Josie."

I blushed and thanked him.

"You all go ahead. I'll lock the store, and then I'll walk over," Aunt Sophie said from behind us.

I didn't miss a beat. I walked over and slid my hand into Caius's. Jamal walked on the other side of me, gripped my other hand in his, and the three of us walked down Main Street.

"It looks like you didn't give two seconds worth of consideration to that outfit," Jamal said, glancing around me, looking up and down at Caius.

Caius looked down the length of his faded Zeppelin shirt, to his tattered converse shoes and then glanced over at Jamal with a look of mischief sparking in his eye. "Jokes on you, Jamie," Caius said, laughing under his breath. "I planned on wearing exactly what I'm wearing so I could win prizes for my gal and ride rides without worrying about ruining my fancy pants with kids' vomit."

Jamal looked down momentarily, and I could see the regret in his expression as he took in the tailored white pants he chose to wear, but he didn't miss a beat with his comeback. "It's Jamal, not Jamie," he said, rolling his eyes. "And the joke will be on you when I pick myself up a tall, dark, and handsome Appalachian hottie," he said under his breath.

"I'm not looking to impress anyone else. Just *my* girl. And I happen to know she loves Led Zeppelin."

"Who doesn't—" Jamal started, his tone starting to get extra sassy, but I cut him off.

"Okay, you two. That's enough," I said with a smile.

"Fine," Jamal said. "But don't you ruin her makeup tonight, lover boy. We worked way too hard on it. In fact, I better never hear of you making her mascara run. For that, I *will* get my outfit dirty, kicking your ass."

Caius smiled at that. "Noted."

I laughed. I enjoyed being between the banter of the two most important guys in my life.

Caius squeezed my hand, sending fire up my arm, sparks of red tying us together always on the outskirts, a reminder of what we were to each other. I couldn't be any more content. The sun was fading in the distance, and as the light of the carnival became more prominent against the approaching night, the sweet scent of cotton candy hit my nose, sending endorphins rushing out to talk my head into wanting some.

Chapter Twenty-Seven
The Fun Begins

Light is to darkness what love is to fear; in the presence of one, the other disappears.
—Marianne Williamson

Caius

The closer we got to the carnival gates, the clearer music got—retro eighties metal. There was always a theme, and at least this was better than last year's 1950s soda pop songs. It was kinda hard to feel badass riding the Ring of Fire with Doo Whop bands crooning in the background.

I laughed to myself at the thought of old metal heads with their chain bracelets and Iron Maiden t-shirts thinking, "Hell yeah! Fear of the Dark is the *perfect* carnival song!" Though, I had to admit, the song lyrics did echo my life as of late which was kind of weird, but the synchronicity was also kind of cool. It's like they knew (whoever *they* may be) I was about to walk in and played my personal theme song.

As the three of us crossed in, a clown sitting behind glass at the ticket booth smiled. Behind the makeup was one of the popular guys from school. He'd been in and out of trouble for being a dick to the less popular kids, and this had to be his community service. Fitting.

He glanced to Josie holding hands and chattering excitedly with Jamal, then to me. "Two tickets for the *friends.*" The word oozed out, lingering on his mouth. Then, he said, "And one for the third wheel?" He looked me square in the eyes, smiling like an asshole, and shoved three tickets under the glass.

I handed him the money. "Thanks, Bozo. I hope you choke on your funny bone."

That comment caught a side eye from Jamal, but I wouldn't make eye contact with him as I handed him his ticket and walked into the crowd. Despite him threatening to kick my ass, I knew I had to keep the peace for Josie's sake.

The scents of fair foods wafted through the air, pouring over us. I couldn't help but to be excited—the entire city looked forward to this to mark the end of summer. "Anyway, you guys hungry?"

"Yes!" Josie shouted so eagerly I laughed. "I need cotton candy!"

"Ditto, girl," Jamal echoed, a wide, almost child-like grin spreading across his face.

We navigated through the crowds, games, and vendors to find the cotton candy truck, aptly named Fluff n' Stuff. I forked over the money to get the treats for, what was quickly becoming apparent, both my dates. "I'm gonna go to Zombie Dawgz. I need a Juan of the Dead dog like nobody's business," I said.

Jamal grunted, a mouthful of light pink cotton candy, dissolving to magenta on his tongue. "Count me in for a zombie dog, too!"

Neon lights and excited screams came at us from all directions, as we headed to my favorite food truck. And when I put my arm around Josie, I gritted my teeth a little because as Jamal saw me, he threaded his fingers through hers.

As a unit, we all passed Lindsey's booth. Colorful, ornate tapestries draped around her tent, and flags with a single eye waved with the breeze. Smoke poured out, not from cigarettes, but from various bundles of herbs puffing in the corners, and the soft glow of fairy lights lit the inside. The top of the tent had a red vintage sign with light bulbs flashing TAROT. A hand painted, upcycled street sign sat at the entrance to her tent that said, "Witchy Woo Way." She'd posted that sign at the front of her tent for as long as I could remember, and it used to scare me when I was little for no reason other than it said "witch", but this time as I read it, I chuckled to myself. I had never known before that she had been giving a nod to my Uncle Kurt and his disbelief in her magic.

Lindsey was too focused on reading tarot cards to engaged listeners to notice us, and I left well enough alone, but Jamal shouted, "*Hey*, Aunt Linds!" She glanced up, flashing the briefest of smiles, as I rolled my eyes. Jamal was such an attention whore.

At Zombie Dawgz, we sat at the only picnic table, while I chowed down on two Juans of the Dead, Josie on a Frankenweenie, and Jamal on a Hunka Hunka burning flesh dog. A paper plate of Sliced n' Diced fries covered in ketchup sat between us. "Oh. My. God," he said, sauce dripping from his chin. "The food in this town already has my love handles growing. I can't even with all these delicious carbs!"

"That sauce on your face is about to hit those fancy white pants, dude," I said.

He slapped his fingers to his chin and grabbed a napkin. "Thanks. I can't have my chances of meeting Mr. Right ruined with messed up pants."

"They're just pants."

Jamal sighed and pulled a mirror out his back pocket, checking himself from all angles as he spoke. "These aren't the blue light Walmart special. They aren't *just* pants. These are vintage Tommy's. You have no idea what I paid a Japanese thrifter for these on eBay. Oh, lover boy, you'll just never understand."

"Nope. I guess I won't. My shorts double as

napkins," I said, wiping the grease from dinner on them. Jamal gasped in mock horror at my fashion faux pas, and we all laughed. Since he'd eaten, he seemed to have a little less sass, or maybe we really were warming to each other.

"So what ride's first, ladies," I asked, shoving the last bloody french fry into my mouth.

Handing me a napkin, Jamal said, "Please, spare your pants the atrocity. Even blue light specials have their limits."

Chapter Twenty-Eight
The Wheel of Fortune

The wheel of fortune tells us we all want victory. We all want triumph.
But we all have to learn to endure what comes. We have to learn to treat misfortune and great fortune the same.
—Phillips Gregory

Jamal

I insisted on riding the Ferris wheel first. I knew Josie would have to ride it twice—once with me and once with lover boy—who was growing on me ... like mold. I was pretty sure I could learn to coexist with him, but I wasn't sure I could like him. I could see his love for my bestie in his beautiful green eyes, and while he was poorly dressed, he did have a certain je ne sais quoi that lended toward charming, I guess. I just wasn't quite sure about him on the whole—the love for stealing, taking my best friend to graves, the Devil may care attitude (which was, admittedly, kinda appealing), but, oh, the dime store napkin-shorts.

"I knew you'd pick your Wheel of Fortune," Josie said to me, reminding me of our childhood. I was so happy to be by her side again. The last several months without her had been tough on me, and then I'd arrived in Bridgeport and found out she'd become super serious about a boy and had all these tall tales of souls, magic, and good versus evil. It totally didn't sound like the friend I'd known my entire life, and I couldn't help but throw blame to Caius for that. It wasn't that I didn't believe in magic, but could it really be happening to my friend, who just a few months ago was totally ordinary? I mean, like, extraordinary to me, but, a general straight up

Muggle, you know? Sure, she'd talked about her aunt being all witchy and said that sometimes she herself would know things before they'd happen—like when Maeve or I needed to pursue a certain boy, or what we should study for a test—but, she had never talked about this level of wizard shit. Did that mean what she was talking about was actually real, or was she losing her mind with Caius's help?

"Psh! Girl, you know your boy. Now put some gloss on those lips, and let's get rolling to my wheel."

I'd always loved the Ferris wheel. When I was little, I called it the Wheel of Fortune. Somehow, I guess I got it confused with the TV game show. But I liked to call it that because the ride always seemed like a metaphor for life to me, even before I understood what a metaphor was. Like, life looms, you know, just like a Ferris wheel. And you just have to go for it. You've got to find your wheel and ride it to the top. You've got to do the work to get there—hand over your ticket, overcome your fears, buckle in, and trust the operator, but then, you enjoy the damn ride with the people you've got in the bucket beside you. Because what else is there, and who else would you want to share the view with?

Chapter Twenty-Nine
A Tale of Two Witches

I think you are wrong to want a heart. It makes most people unhappy. If you only knew it, you are in luck not to have a heart.
—L. Frank Baum, The Wonderful Wizard of Oz

Aunt Lindsey

I'd been reading tarot intently since a young age. It was always the thing that brought me peace and clarity. From birth, I'd always had a wild spirit—the exact opposite of my twin Sophie. I was always scattered, busy, and riddled with anxiety because I always felt so much energy coming from everything. Once, after a particularly bad day, Sophie encouraged me to go to the library and find some kind of book that could help me with my issues. Sophie always subscribed to the notion that an answer is always somewhere if you look hard enough. And, she'd not been wrong.

That day, as I was wandering the library, I heard whispering, a low commotion of a noise, almost frantic, and I could faintly make out my name amongst the chatter. It led me down a hall, and on a shelf with board games, there was a deck of tarot cards in a bright yellow box. As I touched the box of cards, the whispers abruptly stopped, and I felt an incredible energy coming through them into me. And young me, with a chaos not much different than Caius, pocketed those cards and left the library. Those actions that day led me down a path of self-study, education, and inquisition. The more I studied and meditated with the cards, the more they led me toward self-awareness, and the calmer and more in tune I got with the world. And the more in tune I got, the more I accepted what I was—a white witch. White witches practice benevolence in all they do. They do not cast spells to harm others or practice their craft for selfish reasons. White witches believe in karma.

****

I'd been participating in Bridgeport's end of summer carnival for twenty years, and it was hard to believe I was the same age my niece is now when people started coming to me for deep advice and the life insights my cards provided. Each year at the carnival, though there were slight variations in the crowd, each was similar to the one before. Sometimes, I'd come across someone open and intriguing when I read them, eager to learn about their past, present, and future. Sometimes, people sat across from me, disbelieving, only in my tarot tent on a dare, and I'd have to lean to my flair for drama to appease them, playing the best witch I could play. Other times, people were black voids, and I wouldn't have much to go on but my intuitive understanding of the cards.

Tonight was different from every other carnival I'd participated in, though. Tonight, the night air buzzed with electricity, a strange energy that had me unsettled, had my guard up. I'd told Sophie about this and most times she brushed off what she called "nonsense", but tonight in yet another unsettling way, she simply said, "The cards will fall where they may. Everything will balance out." I didn't like her answer. I'd paced and paced all morning, trying to identify this knot in my gut, this ball of worry, and it didn't matter how much I walked, I was chasing a phantom.

Or rather the phantom was chasing me.

As I read cards for a couple debating marriage, Jamal caught my attention as he passed by with Josie and Caius, and a quick bolt of fear ran through me. Why was

I so worried about them? We were at a carnival, literally the grounds for nothing but fun. So, what was it?

The couple exited my tent, talking about their wedding plans, and as I was left alone, I trembled. Every hair on my body stood on end for several minutes until a woman parted the crowd like the red sea, fast approaching me. But this was no woman. She was something else entirely. She was otherworldly, because while I was far weaker, one witch recognized another.

And I had never been more terrified in all my life.

Not for me. No. For what was left of my sister's legacy. For Josie.

Each cell in my body screamed in a different pitch, revolting at the being who approached me in the shape of a petite woman. Her long hair was raven black with two shocks of white framing a slender face, and her eyes were voids, the color of onyx, leaving no room for where the whites should be. My mind raced, sorting through my scattered brain how I could get to the other side of this encounter alive.

She glanced up, reading my sign for the briefest of moments and registering my magic.

My fingers tingled, power being channeled or triggered, I couldn't tell which.

The woman entered, stopping just short of my table, resting a hand on the back of the chair facing me. She wore a tattered white gown and had the look of a Victorian pirate, which would go unnoticed at the carnival. She'd fit right in. But I recognized that lingering below her youthful appearance was an old, very ancient soul … a disturbed soul. A black soul. A black witch. My counterpart in every way.

She lowered her hand, allowing it to fall to her side as, simultaneously, the chair in front of my table pulled itself back to seat her. She lowered herself into it with all the grace of a trained assassin.

I didn't have to read cards to know that should this otherworldly witch have wanted to kill me, I would have been as good as gone. But something told me she wasn't here for me, and that terrified me even more.

"*Witch*," she said, as audible as though her lips moved, but they were shut tight, "*it's been many winters since I've encountered one of my kind.*"

As I heard her words resound in my head, my flesh crawled. Her beady black eyes bore into mine with a stare so piercing it could slice the soul straight from my body.

"*Tell me a story*," she said, her words thundering through my skull. "*A story with your cards.*"

My hands were shaky as I shuffled my deck of cards. I sent a silent prayer out into the universe to give me strength to deal with the power sitting in front of me. I gently laid the shuffled deck down.

"Cut the deck," I said with all the courage I could manage.

The cards raised on their own and began splitting into piles.

"No," I said. "You have to touch the cards."

The cards lowered back to the table, and she obliged me by parting the deck into three stacks.

I gathered her piles back into a single stack. "Ok. Select five cards," I told her, my voice low and calm.

The witch glanced down to the deck of cards, then back up to me. She held my gaze while never moving. Five cards wiggled out of the deck.

"*Go on.*" The witch's words echoed through my head.

I felt she was mildly humored by me, who had to look like an infant witch to her, but that smallest of details might have been what stayed her hand, because I had no doubt she'd kill me effortlessly if she chose to do so.

I played along, gingerly pulling each card she'd chosen and laying the face down in the shape of a V.

Crossing my legs, I sat up straight in my chair, trying to summon every ounce of confidence I could.

I flipped over the first card, gently laying it out for her to see.

"The Emperor," I said, cautiously. "Interesting this is the first card you drew. The Emperor is power and obstruction. The Emperor is about control, a strategic force who sees plans through." She didn't move. "Or is he literal? Are you having trouble with a man in your life who refuses to express his feelings for you?" Her body twitched, and I could tell I'd struck a nerve, but she remained silent, her gaze boring through me.

I flicked the second card up to reveal a beautiful woman sitting on a throne, holding a scepter in one hand, wearing a crown with twelve stars.

"The Empress," I said. "She sends the message that real love and romance is on the way. This card means all that you've dreamed of is coming to fruition." The black witch sneered, and with that, I knew I'd hit the nail on the head. But what was it that was coming to fruition? I touched the Emperor and Empress cards together and got the intuition to place them on top of each other. As I did, I glanced up to see a prominent vein raise on her forehead, branching out like roots, spreading slowly like spilled ink, a supernatural tattoo of sorts. I'd struck another nerve. I had to keep my wits and composure. I had to feel this witch out for her weakness.

I flipped the next card. "Death. The Death card is seldom about actual physical death. It's more about transformation and change. Seems to me that you need to let go of unhealthy attachments in your life." I gestured to the coupled Empress and Emperor. "Maybe it's time to break bad habits or unhealthy patterns."

The witch's eyes narrowed, the viney vein spreading blackness around the sides of her face and trailing down her neck.

I didn't let it show on my face, but sickness crawled through my stomach. These were the cards I'd pulled over and over again for years—first with Janet and Joe, then Josie and Caius, but I'd never had clear direction or a basis for meaning. I'd just known all along they'd meant something huge. And here was this black witch, pulling the story together.

"The Fool." My deck was unlike most in that the Fool was generally a man, but in my deck, the Fool was a woman, one that had a white rose in one hand, a bundle of possessions in the other, and a deer laying at her side, as she was unknowingly walking off the edge of a cliff. Not a care in the world, straight forward into the unknown. "Power. The Fool, a most powerful card. This encourages you to learn lessons, to take in your surroundings and focus on what you need to learn, but I also feel that its direct message is for you to lighten up." I tried to poke at her, verbally, joke. "Obviously, you have had some relationship struggles. But, girl, let it go! There will be better things for you, if you would open your heart to them."

The witch across from me laughed. A heartless and deep sound that morphed into a wretched wail. It turned me cold. Veins continued spreading under her skin, black turning into a crimson red. She reached across from me and flipped over the last card on her own.

"The Lovers," I said through a shaky voice, looking down at the card, trying to regain some courage and my slowly crumbling composure. "Love. Balance.

You need to think about your moral code, and the value you give it in your life. You have major choices to make. You need to make the right choice."

Smiling, she balled her right hand so tightly, her nails tore into her skin. As blood poured out of her clenched fist, she dripped it across the cards, then grabbed my hand and ran it across them, smearing it into the spread. It hit me then like lightning—I was witnessing a blood curse. An ancient one.

The sound of her voice bellowing through my head made me come to an abrupt halt.

"Now, witch, let me tell you a story."

I sat frozen, unable to move, watching as the cards—the Emperor, Empress, Death, the Fool, and the Lovers—took on a life of their own. I watched in shock as the Emperor went from an old man to a young handsome one. My gaze darted over to the Empress, a beautiful woman with mirror-like eyes, long hair draping over either shoulder. She wore an expression of sadness as her shape morphed, coming alive off the card, slowly emerging into my sister, Janet.

It couldn't be. My eyes were the only part of my body I could move, and as though stuck in cement, I painfully flicked my gaze up to the witch's. I could feel my eyes widen in horror as the veins continued growing down her arms, now lacing out around her fingertips like living organisms.

"There's more," her voice said, like a bolt through my mind.

I glanced back down, the Death card taking on shape. I watched the horseman slide off his stead, the horse vanishing altogether, a gladiator's pit in its place. The skeleton of Death grew flesh, knitting tissue back together to reveal a young man, muscular from what was likely long days of labor, fighting, perhaps both. His appearance changed. His long hair cropping itself short, his body aging to more of a middle-aged man. When the transformation was complete, Josie's father, Joseph, emerged momentarily before the Death card reverted back into the gladiator.

My heart was racing, pounding blood up to my ears.

Think! Think! Think!

Next, the Fool. The woman became animated, the deer at her heels springing to life, but there was something grossly wrong with this deer. The closer the deer came into view, the more obvious the rotting flesh became. The Fool, a woman, turned to look at me, growing in size as she came off the card, a tree springing up behind her. Large willow branches grew and grew, looming over this miniature sized production going on right before my eyes. Branches began weaving in and out of each other, forming a noose that fell over the woman's neck. She didn't walk off an edge like the card portrayed, but rather, she jumped from the tree, her neck snapping, her body swinging in sync with the swaying of the willow branches. I watched as red vine-like veins shot from her forehead and trailed down the length of her body.

I was sick. Frozen. Paralyzed and crippled by fear for how this story was soon to come to an end.

The Lover's emerged. The final card in her hand.

I watched as the card swirled, taking on the familiar shape of a girl on the left of the card and a boy on the right. They were reaching toward each other, slowly emerging from the card, two small figures before me.

They were reaching, stretching, desperate to make contact. And just as they did, I saw a flash of comfort and relief on the faces of my niece, Josie, and Caius right before the witch's red vines shot out from her palms, looping circles around their necks, synching them up tighter, tighter, tighter...

"*Why?*" I communicated with her through our minds. I knew she could read mine.

"*Because I am the witch who cannot stay buried. That old willow has been my constant companion for a millennia. Every lifetime I return to ensure justice is meted out. I can sense they are near. Do not interfere and I'll allow you to live. Interfere, witch, and I'll kill you.*"

And just as she'd sauntered up to my booth out of thin air, the cards fell one by one, releasing me from her invisible hold, and then she was simply gone, vanishing into thin air.

Chapter Thirty
Carnival Part II

I seem to have loved you in numberless forms,
numberless times...
In life after life, in age after age, forever.
—Rabindranath Tagore

Caius

The universe would always remain a mystery to me. Time, if nothing else, was a train that moved you forward whether or not you were prepared. It was just that why couldn't it take you where you *wanted* to go instead of along some predetermined track? Life was just like: All aboard! Next stop? Shit Town! Enjoy the scenery ... or don't because we don't care anyway!

Our literal next stop was the Ferris wheel.

As Josie, Jamal, and I navigated the general chaos of the carnival, making our way toward the wheel, time seemed to slow for me. I noticed everything. Every sound, sight, and smell was amplified. I watched Josie, hand to her chest, throwing her head back in laughter. I watched Jamal radiate with happiness as he placed his head on her shoulder. I watched the Ferris wheel come to a stop as the carnie pulled the lever. It was as we approached the wheel that I had a realization, and I knew as it hit me it was the most important realization I'd had in this lifetime. And as the universe decided to christen me in truth, all the noise, all the smells, and all the disorder sucked itself into a vacuum sealed portal, and all that remained was clarity.

"You ready for the fun, kids?" the carnie said to Josie and Jamal.

They nodded and loaded up into a seat that had

once been brightly colored but was now faded and chipped with rust.

I watched as they rose above everything. They were happy, oblivious, and it hurt my heart.

When the ride was over, Jamal came giggling off the Ferris wheel that he insisted on calling The Wheel of Fortune with my girl matching his laughter.

I had only minutes to relive lifetimes and decide what to do with that truth.

"Well, lover boy, you ready for seconds on The Wheel of Fortune?" Jamal asked dryly.

When Josie's eyes connected with mine, time stopped. The carnival lights glinted in the pink jewel at the end of her eyebrow, and her smile glowed across her whole face. She was so beautiful. Like a movie screen, I could see each lifetime we'd spent together play before me across her irises. She was the girl whose face I'd scarred hundreds of years ago who grew up to love me anyway. She was the girl who sat dirty and afraid in my lap, clutching onto me like if she held me tight enough, we'd somehow save each other from a curse neither of us had any-fucking-thing to do with. She was the beautiful girl with tracks of tears cutting through the grime on her face who had been hanged beside me. We were literally the proverbial children paying for the sins of their parents.

"Are you ready, Cai?" Josie asked, grabbing my hand in hers. Our hands locked together, fingers woven, one over top of the other.

When she spoke, there was this implosion of everything and nothing. All the words ever said and the ones left unspoken. I gave her hand a squeeze. "Are you kidding? I was born ready," I said, smiling at her, swallowing all the shit that threatened my courage.

A million things ran through my head, circling

and fighting each other as desperation lingered on the edge of my mind. I knew the same fate that always caught us was just around the corner, but I couldn't help but hope. I wanted to keep my composure for Josie's sake. And just like that dirty thief from another lifetime, I would be calm for the both of us now.

I put one foot in front of the other, and as I did, I thought about those who'd had a hand in my life—this life—and I wasn't one for sentimental shit, but staring up at the looming carnival ride was like staring down the barrel of a gun. I thought about my grandparents and my mom, who couldn't find herself on the right side of a bottle even if her life depended on it. I thought about my piece-of-shit sperm donor and how he'd broken my mother's heart so thoroughly he'd taken her from me. I thought about Uncle Kurt and felt regret because he'd always tried to fill the holes in my life I acted like I didn't want filled, and in that moment, I couldn't have loved him more for trying. And I hated myself for not being a better human, something Josie led me to discover, that I actually wanted to be better, that I *could* be better. But, I also knew that the whole path of my life had led me right where I needed to be, which was at the base of this stupid fucking wheel.

I knew this night would be the night. I knew it because like what happened in every lifetime, right before death, my entire being was sponge soaked in memory.

There were a few couples in front of us slowly lumbering up to their seats. A couple would secure themselves, and the carnie would pull the lever so the couple seated would go up and the next seat available would present itself to the couple eagerly waiting.

"The city is so pretty from up there," Josie said. All the happiness, all the life, all the goodness lit up her eyes. Her hair smelled like the first time I'd kissed her, and as I leaned in to do it again, I wondered how it all worked—the remembrance. We were the same soul, but there was no doubt she didn't remember. But why wasn't she remembering like I did? It was said that ignorance is bliss, and in this case, I couldn't agree more, and I envied her bliss a little.

"Is it?"

"I can't wait for you to see!"

I was so caught up in looking at her—every curve of her face, pure comfort to my eyes—that had she not nudged into the side of me, I wouldn't have realized it was our turn.

As I walked past the carnie, the hair on the back of my neck stood on end, and goosebumps erupted over my body. He was almost familiar. As he lowered the safety bar over us, I scooted up against Josie. I wanted to keep her safe, hold her, protect her. She nuzzled into me, and our seat gave a slight jerk as we ascended into the night sky.

Josie laughed. Dammit. That laugh. It made me smile, made my heart smile. Hers was a laugh that shouldn't be silenced. It should be heard around the world. But, suddenly, the beautiful music of her laughter faded and a familiar evil one returned, overpowering it. I closed my eyes as it all turned to the static of white noise and waited as darkness descended like a shadow on everything all at once.

I knew our time was at hand.

Somewhere through the gravity of what was getting ready to occur, I felt Josie tense up beside me. She would know, she would be able to sense through me soon enough, that something was wrong, but I couldn't let that happen.

I couldn't. In each life I accepted our demise.

Ours.

I took the chance to do what I'd done again and again. I lowered my lips to hers and remembered the red electricity that sizzled through us the first time in this life, back at *Blair's Lair*. I caressed her lips with mine while we both sat on top of the world. I would find a way to remember this, to remember sooner the next time.

I broke away from her, my forehead resting against hers, my eyes level with the scar I'd put on her years ago when she was visiting from Connecticut. My mind flickered back briefly to that day when she was skateboarding. Just like that grimy thief from hundreds of years ago when I threw that damned rock at her, I was a punk kid roaming around the streets of Bridgeport, destined to collide again and again with the love of my many lives. My beautiful, sweet Josephine.

"Are you okay?" Josie asked, and it broke my heart because I could hear the worry in her voice, the worry that was teetering somewhere between the edge of scared and the brink of awareness.

"I will be," I said, brushing a fingertip against the eyebrow ring covering the scar I'd made years ago. "*We* will be."

I held onto Josie tight while scanning the shifting dots below that were somehow people, until my gaze landed on what my cursed soul knew was there the entire time.

She was a frightening sight to behold—each lifetime never lessened that. The witch who started it all was standing like the evil puppeteer she was, red poisonous vines shooting from her palms that were invisible to the eyes … all but mine, it would seem. I watched the strings shoot out, spreading to her targets which, of course, were all of us.

All this time I'd thought there was an evil old man

who was trying to possess me and was the real evil mastermind behind this fucked up game of past lives. I watched as he was connected to her red strings too, bound by them, and frozen by her side. He was just another pawn in her game of torture. She was the puppeteer who'd been wronged one too many times. She was the creator of so much pain.

She was the witch who wouldn't stay buried.

Over and over and over again, this happened.

I watched as another red rope laced its way into the back of the carnie operating the Ferris wheel. And it hit me. He was no carnie. He was tied to us all—a failsafe to ensure her plan was always carried out.

He was our executioner. He was Death.

His eyes flashed to mine, wide eyes that were filled with panic, despair, and the agony of the ages. The thick red cords attached themselves onto his shoulders, his arms, his ribs—like an actual puppet, an automaton, and chills raced up and down my spine as I watched his backbone snap to the movement of her wrists. As she clenched her fists, tracks of red tears trailed from her black eyes. As they traced the length of her cheeks, they spread outward, forming a root system trailing down her body, connecting her to the ground. Her tears erupted the earth as those red vines rolled out from her, wrapping themselves around the Ferris wheel like poison ivy wraps around a tree, twisting and choking its way up.

Josie was shaking beside me. I looked at her with all the calm my body could hold. And in that very moment, as the devil herself was coming to punish the souls she believed to have wronged her, I could see in Josie's eyes that she knew. I could see all the sorrows of lifetimes at this very juncture catching up to her as suddenly as it had me earlier.

God. Damn. Damn this hell. Damn this witch.

Damn! Damn! Damn!

"Caius–"

"Shh. Don't cry. I'm going to tell you a story," I began, and Josie erupted in tears. I grabbed her by the shoulders, brought her to my chest, and with my lips up against her ear, I traced small circles on the back of her neck, soothing her. "Be calm, Josie. This story has a happy ending." She continued sobbing in defeat, already knowing our story—the one we lived out together life after life. "Once upon a time, there was a young boy who came across an old man. The old man stopped the young boy and explained that he was attached to his destined wife by a red thread and showed him a young girl across the way. Being young and stupid, the boy picked up a rock and threw it at the girl."

With her face pressed into the crook of my neck, from the corner of my eye I could see Lindsey, Sophie, and Jamal. The three of them were holding hands, a holy trinity, as blood trickled down their arms that joined them together. But these were not the Lindsey, Sophie, and Jamal I knew. These three were … something else.

I continued, as I did in every lifetime. "Many years later when the boy grew into a man, he found the woman he was destined to be with. She wore a veil covering her face, and once he lifted it, he saw she wore an adornment on her eyebrow." Josie sobbed harder, her body shaking against mine. "When he asked her why, she told him when she was younger a little boy had thrown a rock at her, scarring her."

I cupped her head in my hands and tilted her face so she was looking at me. I kissed her eyebrow, just where her scar was. "To this boy who grew into a man, scar or no scar, there could never be a more beautiful woman in all the land. The boy thanked the universe for forgiving him his earlier sin against his soulmate."

"I forgive you." Josie's sobs died down.

"Promise?" I said, strongly. Because it wasn't going to be *our* demise. Not this time.

"Always."

I looked to see the executioner climbing up, up, up. He was coming for us, being manipulated up by the red strings attaching him to the witch cursing us all. I followed the trail of red cords, tracing them back to the puppeteer. I could barely make out Sophie, Lindsey, and Jamal. They were fanned out now, forming a circle around the witch, and whatever they were doing was creating a struggle for the witch. I could see her one arm was tied by some invisible, binding force behind her back, while the other was still free and being used to walk her executioner up to dole out her punishment.

The world around us was going on as though nothing was happening. Their eyes were blind.

But mine had been opened.

There was one glaring problem I had with this whole fucked up song and dance with fate. I never asked to waltz with her ass to begin with. But, in all fairness, I was a thief. I was in every lifetime. I was selfish. I never went out of my way to hurt people, but hey, if they were walking on the same road as me and we crossed paths … Well, that was their tough shit, I guess.

But Josie, what was she? She was everything that was good, and kind, and giving. I deserved to hang like the thief I was. But dammit, not Josie. Never Josie. She didn't deserve it in any life. The only thing she was guilty of was loving me.

This time I wasn't going to accept it.

Fuck fate.

Fuck the universe.

And fuck that witch.

"Thank you for loving me, Josie," I said just as

our executioner perched at the side of the bucket seat like a raven coming to collect souls.

I quickly slid out from the safety bar, leaving Josie secured and staring in confusion. I leapt at Death, throwing him off guard, and just as I made contact, hugging him like a long-lost friend, I looped one of the thick red cords tethering him to the witch around my neck, and together we went over the edge.

I could hear my beautiful girl screaming. But as I fell through the air, the screams grew faint. And when I ran out of cord and my neck jerked, I was glad to feel the labor of my breath getting more and more intense because that meant I was getting closer to death and Josie was not. The curse meant for both of us to die together, not one of us to die alone. I'd broken the rules. I kept my eyes shut and could almost touch the vast emptiness encompassing me and taking me to wherever one half of one soul goes, and to whatever wicked door was next. I welcomed the relief.

And before the blackness of death swallowed me whole, I thought back to the beginning of summer. The beginning of an old love coming back into my life. I thought back to Josie and her aunt, and at the time what I thought was a bit of an idiotic witchy ritual, the one where she had us scribble a wish on a bay leaf before burning it. And as lights flashed behind my eyelids, bursting flames that threatened to take me away from this life and send me into the next, I remembered what I wished for.

Peace.

I didn't know it at the time, but as I felt myself slipping into the abyss, I knew it now even more than the certainty of my death. I had wished for peace, peace for Josie. And the universe was finally granting it. Finally showing me how to end this vicious cycle of love and death and death and love, the both of us hanging. Now, there was only me. I was paying the price with every pound of my flesh. The reward? Peace. Peace for my dearest, sweetest, Josephine.

The End

Evernight Teen ®

www.evernightteen.com